GRIT

The Tale of a Hunting Terrier

by Adam Howard

GRIT
Copyright © 2016 by Adam Howard
Cover art by Haley Howard

House of Howard Publishing
Oregon, USA
info@adamhowardbooks.com

adamhowardbooks.com

ISBN-10: 1-945130-00-8
ISBN-13: 978-1-945130-00-7

First Edition: March 2016
Printed in the United States of America

10 9 8 7 6 5 4 3 2 1

Contents

Coallie

The cold pipe did not interest Coallie, but rather the warm stink that came from it. She squeezed with pent frustration to enter the cramped space. She had done it dozens of times; her ancestors had done it millions more. This is what she was meant to do. This is what she lived and breathed for. She was full of a fire that could not be extinguished. Only action could satisfy, only action could calm her rage.

The fire burnt her insides up. She pushed and pulled her way into the irrigation pipe. She could see movement down the tube and knew. . . Her adversary was lying in wait there. Too confident in it's safety within the pipe to run and thus face the man outside, it opted to lay, mouth open, waiting for Coallie, the little hairy dog, to meet it in mouth to mouth combat.

That time soon came. Coallie met the initial strike with the side of her face, yowling her anger loudly for all to hear. The unseen enemy jabbed and reversed, jabbed and reversed. Coallie knew the routine. She pushed with the side of her face, pushed, pushed. She was stronger than the sharp toothed foe, both in spirit and in mouth. She could take the pain. She loved the pain. Working is what kept her life force burning. This is what she needed to do. One final jab and Coallie felt her opportunity. The lamb worrying fox had lunged too far. Coallie grabbed it by the side of the neck and shook with all her might.

The two combatants twirled and turned like tight woven wire in a small space. Each trying for an advantage; Coallie, being the only one finding true footing. Using her weight, she punished the animal into understanding it's position. It could not win. It could understand that. At first feeling of Coallie's mouth slipping, it pulled away with all the force it could muster. Backing away swiftly and out of reach, it made sure that Coallie's desires were frustrated. Coallie let out bark after bark letting the man outside know the game was out of reach.

Light shone into the tunnel. Red fur flashed from the tube, bolting into the open. BOOM! BOOM!

Two shots rang out and hummed through the pipe. Coallie exited to sniff out the carcass of the pheasant killer. In the open, she triumphantly ragged the wooly carcass in her mouth. That warm fox stink she so loved filled her mouth. Another morning, another wound, another dead foe. And it's all chalked up to. . .

Grit

1. Fire Crackers

Oregon, 1960s

Coallie was just one of several terriers owned by Joseph, a goatherd as tough as his dogs were gritty. He was a husky voiced old war veteran who lived on the Oregon-Idaho border in a small house surrounded by kennels, chicken pens and alfalfa fields as far as the eye could see. Herding dogs he had in plenty and pigeons too.

He watched his goats peacefully grazing by day. In the evening before sundown he sat outside and watched his pigeons fly in great circles overhead. Now and then, one would drop from great heights, tumbling artfully toward the ground, then be caught up again by its wings to the rest of the pigeons. This was an enjoyment shared by many a dogman across the world.

This man realized the deep bonds we share with animals. He knew his dogs and his birds were extensions of himself, the peaceful and the warring man. Neither was more esteemed in his mind. The people of the city had not yet beaten the true warrior out of him, the warrior that was full of purpose and dignity.

To the old goatherd, his little terriers reminded him of the bravery required to protect what is valuable. His little dogs were small but full of a righteous rage. Each dog had its task on the farm of protecting what could not protect itself. Each dog would die to fulfill its duty. The old man loved them all and they all loved him.

His little bitch Coallie was no exception. She was a scruffy little black dog covered in wiry hair. She was a perfectly average terrier. Honorable to the long lineage of workers behind her, Coallie fulfilled her duties. Not only that, she was as docile as a lamb when not working. She could be left to wander the farm and she would harm nothing, no bird nor lamb nor kid. She was shy to a fault. Only the goatherd could get much use from her. Others would borrow her to protect their poultry or to get rid of fox that were killing pheasants and quail on their properties, but she never liked people much, other than Joseph. She would work for others but with the goatherd she was as happy as a puppy.

Coallie was kept in a pen with a gruff old black and tan dog named Franz. Franz was a dog that didn't have a care in the world. He did his job but was not fearless. He was as nondescript as was Coallie but the both of them did their jobs and therefore had a place on the old man's farm.

As is known, keep a dog with a bitch and you'll get puppies. So it was here. Nine pups were born to Coallie; some blacks, some black and tans and two that were a sandy red color. The goatherd had little need for more dogs but kept a few for himself. One of which was the smallest sandy colored pup. He called this little sandy dog Grit and the big sandy dog he named Sandy.

The old goatherd happened to be known for having terriers that were good at their job. One hot, dusty day, a boy named Robert was passing through with his father. He had heard of the old man and his dogs and wanted to see what he had around at the time. When they arrived at the old goatherd's home, the old man walked out to greet them. Coallie ran ahead and put her paws up onto Robert's legs. She got a good head scratching.

"Coallie usually doesn't like anybody. But here she is, taking to you like a duck to water," said the goatherd.

The boy was a bashful but he liked the dog as much as she liked him.

"She seems like a fine dog sir. Does she happen to be the daughter of the Goldie dog I've heard about?"

"That she is," replied the old man. "She's not quite the dog her father is but she does take after him in a way, I suppose."

The boy was full of admiration and the farmer could see it. Never had Coallie shown so much joy and interest for a person other than himself. With little thought to the matter, he knew that the boy would care more for her than he ever would.

"How would you like her?"

Wide eyed, the boy couldn't believe his ears. "Like her? I'd love her! This is a dream dog!"

Joseph chuckled, "Well then, she's yours. Keep her well. She won't range like those hounds of your dad's, but she'll catch you a coon or two, now and again."

"Wow! Thank you! I don't know how to thank you enough."

"Well, these pups ain't quite weaned yet but I can feed mine with goat's milk. How about you just take this extra pup off my hands, so as to keep the mother from getting mastitis?"

Handing the boy Grit, the goatherd looked at the father of the boy to see if that was alright. Having seen the boy's excitement, the farmer had forgotten proper manners. The father shrugged his shoulders, "What the hell, might as well." Then he looked at his son intently, "I like that little bitch but don't go trying to breed that little mongrel pup of hers to my terriers. You hear?"

"I hear. I hear. This'll be a hunting dog, plain and simple."

"That's right. And if he doesn't earn his keep, he isn't sticking around."

"I know dad."

"Your dad is right," the goatherd spoke up. "I'm sure your father has taught you, it is just as easy to feed a good dog as a bad dog. No sense keeping second rate."

The boy didn't care much to hear all that. He looked at those dogs and had grand schemes. *No way*, he thought, *No way can these dogs not be good ones. I know how to make a coon dog and this'll be the best dog my dad's ever seen.* But the old man wasn't done teaching his lesson,

"The pup does not always determine the dog and the looks never do."

The father turned aside. "Now, my son may not know how to thank you but, I do believe, I do. Come on over to my truck and I'll show you something you'll like."

They walked together to the truck the folks came in. There were sheep in the back and two crates; one holding a couple hairy brown terriers, named Lee and Jackson, and one holding a kit of pigeons. The farmer laughed a husky laugh. "I'll be damned. You do know what a man likes. Let's see them birds."

The father pulled the crate out to reveal some homers, well-bred for performance.

"I take these birds with us wherever we go," explained the father, "and release them upon arrival at our destination and they return home. This trains them for the races. There's some good money made betting on a good bird."

"Well, I ain't much for gambling myself, but I love a bird that can perform."

"I'm not into gambling either but from time to time I'll pay the cost to put an exceptional bird in a race and let it do what it's born to do."

"Oh yeah, I hear ya," said the old man.

"How about I give you a pair in return for your gift to us. Take your pick."

"Oh I couldn't hardly take the liberty of that. Those birds are a man's pride and joy. I can't begin to presume to choose one off of ya."

"Then I'll choose for you," chimed in the boy. He reached in and grabbed two fine, deep chested birds, sleek but full of power, small as they were, great flyers.

"Whoooey! I suppose a man'd be a fool to turn down a gift like these. Though, I think I'm makin' out like a bandit here," said Joseph.

"Never you mind friend. The birds are yours and truthfully, my son's picked out my finest birds. They'll do well for you and I assure you, my boy'll love the dogs as much as you love the birds."

"Well, that's dandy then," said the old man.

"Now shake on it boy," the father told his son.

So the boy reached out to the goatherd and shook his hand.

"You'll love these dogs," the old man told the boy. "They're firecrackers!"

○ ○ ○

When the boy and his father began their journey home, the boy held Grit on his lap. He liked the long faced little booger. The old man with his gift had made an impression on the boy. That sense of gift-giving stuck with the boy well into manhood. The idea that a fine working animal was something to be treasured but not coveted, and the gift of such an animal was worth more to the soul than an exchange of money ever could be.

Robert could not fail to notice the similarities between his father and the man. Though possessed of very different demeanor, they both had the same passions.

"Dad, what is the deal with all these terriermen? They all seem to love birds as well. They've all got pigeons."

"It would seem so. There is a trio that is unexplainable; man, dog and bird. It seems almost every terrierman, at heart, does love birds. Perhaps, the doves of peace soothe the warrior inside of him just long enough that he can remember he is human after-all."

"Maybe so," replied the boy, while he pondered it a while. *An old man like the goatherd must have a lot of time to reflect on the battles he has seen.*

The father spoke again,"Yes, That man comes from another age, an age when good men respected every aspect of their nature. The peaceful and the violent, they embraced it all. Men knew what real life was then. They knew it was a damned hard life sometimes, but good and also at times, cruel. A man like that doesn't shun the cruel, anymore than he shuns the beauty. The lives of men then were enriched. Not like those whose thoughts neither turn inward nor truly outward. Nor like those who deny the ugliness of life and thus do not understand the beauties either. You'd be wise to remember men like that and emulate them."

"I will," promised the boy. How could he forget his friend, who so freshly knowing him, gave him a pearl of great price. But little did he know that the dog was merely a token; a token in memory of the great men come and gone, the group of which the boy would be a member, if not one of the last. Terriermen.

2. The Swim

Grit whined wherever he went. To Robert's father, Willam, he was the most annoying puppy on the planet. Which he pointed out time and again to his son. Whenever Grit would get to yipping in the kennel, Robert would hear his father griping in his head, "*That noise is normal for any pup for a time, but let Grit out of the kennel and he would make more noise than when he was in. That dog never shuts up!*"

Everywhere he went he yipped. He yipped if he fell behind. He yipped if he was excited to run ahead. And he yipped when he came to greet people or other dogs. He was full of constant noise. The boy took this as a good sign. *I'll know where this dog is. Not like my dog Jackson, who can never be found.*

Grit's first summer he spent everyday with Robert. Day and night Grit was with his new master.

They were learning together what makes the team of man and dog work. Grit got constant attention and infinite time being exposed to every situation the boy could provide. The boy took the harder path, so Grit would learn to climb logs, go around rock faces, squeeze through or under fences. To get him used to pressing forward where he could not see, Grit was taken through tall grass and weeds, which abounded in the western Oregon valleys and foothills. He was sent after mice and rats into dark spaces and piles of sticks. Grit followed Robert everywhere and Robert made sure that Grit was constantly learning in order to prepare for the life of work ahead of him. If Grit did not learn and succeed at his tasks later in life, he could not remain among the pack. The boy knew this well. He loved his dog but knew that no matter how much training, Grit may not make the grade.

Grit was fearless. Or if he had fear, he would overcome it. He had an independence of nature that even Robert's best dog, Lee, did not possess. While Lee was completely absorbed in his master's wishes, Grit had a mind of his own. Not unlike Jackson, another of Robert's terriers, he'd leave Robert in the dust. Unlike Jackson, there was always purpose in Grit's wanderings. Grit needed a scent to lure him out of control, or a sight to draw him away. Grit was independent and would go as far as the track would take him but unlike Jackson, he knew his name. He knew it well and was strictly obedient to Robert. The boy could stop him in whatever act he was in and Grit would respond and return.

But fearlessness sometimes brought Grit to grief, grief that the boy did not expect Grit to get himself into.

Many terriers hate water. For a terrier to be a great dog where Robert lived, not mediocre, it had to learn to love water or be born loving it. Grit was born loving the water. Robert made it a point to bring Grit to the water as much as possible. Robert loved the river. He spent everyday there, whether it be summer, swimming, fishing and cooling off or be it winter, hunting, canoeing, or simply walking the shores.

It was summer while Grit was a puppy. The heat could be seen, like a curtain, rising off the river rocks. Grit followed Robert to the river each day and romped in the shallow pools where the water was still. At times the boy would lure him into the deep and calm pools where Grit felt the limits of his confidence. He'd paddle halfway into these pools then return to the shallows, where he'd yip.

One particular part of the river where the boy and his friends loved to fish was covered in large stones and boulders. The stones offered smooth places to sit and even lay, though they were hard and not the most comfortable of places to be in the heat of the day. There were no trees over that particular expanse of rocks. Across the river there were sand shores and trees with shade. Also near the further shore was a rock set in the middle of the rapids. The boys could jump from the rock into swift water. It was an exhilarating experience, hard to resist.

A hot summer day was at it's hottest when Robert and his friend Jon were fishing and swimming from the rocky shore. Robert was lean, of average size and light brown hair, bleached blond by the sun. Jon was a tall, lanky blonde boy. He kept his hair wavy and unkempt. The others always teased that his wings, meaning his wispy hair that stuck straight out to the sides, would carry him away on a wind one day. Grit was there and enjoying bits of bass the boys would throw him from the small fire they kept going for cooking their day's catches. The ground was rocky and sandy enough the boys did not worry about fire, there was no brush near by. They caught about 30 fish that afternoon, most of which they released. It was good fun, but the rock across the river was beckoning them. They were enticed beyond their will to resist.

"Should we leave Grit here? You don't think he'll run away do you?" Robert asked his friend.

Jon stared at Grit for a second, thinking. "Yeah, he'll be fine. Coallie is definitely going to swim with us, but your dog Lee is here too, he'll keep him safe."

"I guess so. It's getting boring here. I want to explore across the way and we haven't been able to, 'cause a this pup. It's time he mans up, anyway."

Robert commanded Lee to stay, then dove from a rock into the water. Jon was already on his way. Coallie swam with the boys. She was a strong swimmer and loved the water more than any dog Robert had ever seen. Grit ran across the rocks barking for the gang to come back. But that was not enough to worry them. Grit jumped into the water, but the water there had a current and moved him where he didn't want to go, so he returned to shore to continue his whining there. Lee had a rock overhang to keep him shaded. He laid calmly waiting for his master's return.

"Good. I can see he won't follow us," Robert said. "He's scared to enter the moving water."

With confidence that Grit would stay put, the boys made it to the rock in the rapids. They each took their turns jumping into the frothy water and popping back up a ways downstream. They'd swim into a slower moving part of the river and go back upstream to get back to the rock. When they had finished jumping and swimming, they went to rest on the cool sands of the unexplored river bank. Coallie was already waiting for them there.

They laid there and talked about girls, the mystery neither of them could figure out, and things they understood better; shotguns, rifles, hounds, who caught the biggest fish of the summer, what actually qualifies size. A little while passed when they heard yipping closer than it should be.

"What the. . ." Jon lifted himself off the sand onto his elbows and looked at Robert quizzicaly.

"That sounds just like Grit. But he couldn't be over here. The river is super wide and fast."

"That's Grit!" they yelled simultaneously.

Grit had swam the river but only made it to the jumping rock. He was clamoring for his life upon the stone. He had swam right into the waves of the rapids. Had he not been saved by the rock he would have gone into rougher waters at a wider spot in the river. The rock was barely saving him. He could barely dig his small puppy claws into the stone and his legs were slipping for grip.

The boys were hollering in their angst to get to him. Jumping over rocks and flotsom, they ran to the riverside and dove in. Swimming with their might, they made it to the rock. Robert reached down to Grit and pulled him out of the water, drenched and exhausted.

"You little leach! You'll stick to me no matter what, won't you?"

They swam Grit to the sandy shore where Grit ran around in circles of jubilation.

"What a dog," Jon said. "I bet he'll be one hell of a coon dog! Look how he'll swim the rapids at only a couple months old. I don't think he's afraid of anything."

"I reckon you're right. Other than he's afraid to be without me."

"That's no problem. He'll swim through hell and back for you. So, if you want a coon, he'll swim to hell and back to get it for you!"

○ ○ ○

When the sun was setting, Curt arrived to meet Robert and Jon. His black hair and tanned skin indicated his Cherokee ancestry. That night the boys fed heavily on bass and blackberries. Summer camping trips for them were not known for preparation. What food they could catch or find they would eat. Depending on the season this could be any number of fruits or crops. They most often camped out on local farms or ranches and thus never went hungry. Though one particular day all they could scrounge up were a few blue jays they shot and roasted.

Grit quickly learned that getting fed did not always mean kibble or even meat. Lee taught him to eat whatever was tossed him by Robert. Blackberries and cherries were among his favorite foods but corn and apples also would find their way into his stomach. Produce grew all through the valley. Fruit and berries sprouted up wild all along waterways and ponds. Blackberries were more a nuisance than a blessing, despite their tasty fruit. They grew in patches miles long down the river banks, forming a hedge anywhere from five to 15 feet tall.

That night, fish would do Grit and Lee just fine. Grit scarfed his fish, while Coallie eyed it more suspiciously. Coallie had not been raised on such a varied diet. She was going to have to grow accustomed or grow hungry, one or the other.

The boys hadn't packed a tent that night but pitched camp high above the river on a hill. They enjoyed the open air, though the dew would have them drenched by morning, even during the hottest part of the year. They huddled their sleeping bags together then draped their sleeping area with a tarp to act as a water repellent sheet. The ground was dry and grassy and the trees acted as a green canopy. Oaks mingled with maples on the savannah groves.

The fire was put out long ago down by the river. It was built on the rocks, so as to have nowhere to grow. The boys huddled into the sleeping bags to catch some shuteye before waking in the middle of the night to harass more wildlife. The dogs were free to roam. Robert knew they'd stay close. Grit, Lee and Coallie, worn out by the exhausting day of swimming and with bellies full of bass, burrowed into their master's bag. The boy began the night holding Lee and Grit near his chest but when the time came to wake, the dogs were at the foot of the sleeping bag warming Robert's feet. A few hours sleep was all they needed.

Around midnight, the boys and dogs awoke. The boys had brought spotlights and had more living to do than sleep would allow. Jon was the first of them to awake. He pushed and shoved the others awake.

"Come on. There's some good gigging to be done."

They each whittled sticks into forked spears. Having grabbed and examined these implements of death, they hiked back down to the river. They had a spotlight to lure fish to the surface of the water and a backpack with a large battery to keep the light going late into the night. When they reached the shore of the river, little chirps could be heard, followed by small splashes. These were their prey, bull frogs.

"The french eat bullfrog legs, I've heard," said Jon.

"You know my motto," said Robert. "If it doesn't hurt me, I'll eat it."

"Y'all'll get a chance tonight," Curt assured the other two.

Curtis was always the most prepared of the bunch. He had extra lights and carried the spotlight. He owned the most powerful he could buy at the local store. He started the night out shining the light for the other two.

The boys got a few frogs with their spears but nothing worthy of eating. The big frogs were rare. There were hundreds of the little ones that had just grown legs.

"Not a frog big enough to eat in this place," Jon complained.

"Would seem so," Robert agreed.

Curtis was still intently searching for the big frogs. "Hey. Come over here."

The others came as beckoned and peered into the pool Curtis was shining into. There were several creatures of interest in this pool. Two large bass were swimming calmly in the water. And at the very bottom of the pool rested a turtle. The water was four to five feet deep there. Spearing the fish would be very difficult at that depth. The boys needed them at about two feet of water.

"I've had my fill of enough fish that I can wait on those bass. But I'd like to catch that turtle," Robert told the others. "Shine that light on 'm, Curt."

Robert didn't intend to eat the turtle. He just wanted a look at it and to let it go again, none the worse for being caught. It was into the colder hours of the night, so Robert didn't want his clothes drenched. He stripped down naked to dive after the turtle.

"You crazy hillbilly," Jon joked.

"Hurry up and catch that turtle. Your tan lines are blinding." said Curtis, holding his hands up to his eyes, as if he were looking straight into the spotlight.

The mud was still warm and mushed between Robert's toes as he approached the pool. He planned to dive straight for the turtle and grab it in one smooth motion. He knew it would be blurry under the water.

"Keep that light on the turtle," he told Curtis. Then he dove into the still warm water. The light under water was blinding. It was like a pool of sunlight. Nothing could be seen. It was as if he were staring into the spotlight in every direction. Robert still swam along the bottom, groping for the turtle but all he could come up with were hands full of leaves. After feeling around in the muck with his eyes closed, he surfaced.

"Man, you were way off," Curtis told Robert.

Jon grinned. "One look at his wiener and the turtle got frightened. . . Aaaah!!! A turtle with no shell!"

Robert laughed as he came out of the water. "I couldn't see a thing. The light reflected through every particle of the water."

Curtis turned off the spot light to save battery while he talked to Robert. "All well. You gave it a go. It's too muddy in there now to see anything. Luckily, the fish swam out into a smaller pool."

The boys gathered rocks and dammed the entrances and exits of the pool that the bass entered. They had them trapped for easy spearing. While fishing during the day, the boys released all but the largest bass, which they ate. They had grown hungry again, and knew they'd need breakfast as well. Spearing these fish would give them a meal.

Curtis wanted to spear these. So Robert handled the light while the others tried their skill at gigging the bass. They rammed their spears with as much speed as they could, but they always missed. They had to figure out how to aim with the water, which made the fish appear to be where they were not. In a short time, the spears were too blunted to be useful. Even if they did hit the fish, the points would slide along the scales, not puncturing.

Curtis got tired of the nonsense. "Ugh. This is a waste of time. I'm going to get my pole."

"Get mine too," Jon spoke at Curt's back, as Curt leaped along the river rocks.

"Do I look like yer momma? Getcher own pole, ya pansy."

Jon ran after Curt. Robert sat on the bank watching the fish in the trap. *Fish in a barrel*, He thought. The dogs snuggled into Robert. He was air-drying before getting back into his clothes and he was cold. The dogs helped warm him up, though they got him sandy and covered in hair.

Shortly, Jon and Curt came running back along the rocks. They carried their bass poles. When they arrived, they hurried to tie big treble hooks onto their lines. Curt was the first to finish. He bit the split lead bb's onto the line to help it stay taut, then ran over to where the fish were in the pool. Curt got the prime spot, so Jon had to hop water and get to the other side of the puddle.

They lowered their hooks in without bait. Robert held the lamp for them. The fish moved fast whenever they felt the line tickle their sides. The boys would carefully lower their lines, trying to get the hooks right under the fish' bellies, then they'd jerk up to set the hook. They failed many times before Jon finally set his hook with a yank and reeled his snagged fish in.

"Who says cheaters never prosper?" Jon asked, triumphantly holding his 3 pound bass for the others to see.

Curt soon set his hook as well. They got their fire going and fried up the fish on makeshift racks of willow wands. The fish weren't fully cooked when the boys ate them, but had a nice smoky flavor along with the river water taste all bass have.

The dogs curled up near the fire and dozed off. The boys laughed and teased, while they ate their fill of fish. Jon began to sing a popular upbeat country song of the day. He took it to the crescendo, then jumped up off the ground. He danced around the fire clapping his hands and slapping his legs.

"Come on guys! Jump right in!"

Robert jumped up and started in with Jon. They grabbed hands and jumped around like a couple of jolly hill folk.

"Get off your butt, Curtis. Join us," Jon said.

Curt shook his head. "No thanks. I'm fine watching you two be fools. No need to take part."

The other two grabbed his hands but he resisted and about pulled them both to the ground. Jon and Robert left him to sit. The dogs woke to the noise. Tails tucked, they moved in around Curtis to seek shelter from the craze. The dancers sang through every fun song they knew by heart, each trying to match the other in loudness and jumping. Curtis, meanwhile, laughed and hit at them with a stick whenever they got too close or tried to grab him off the ground.

Eventually, Robert and Jon could dance and sing no more. They crashed down onto the sand around the fire. Resting their heads on logs, they planned to catch their breath before heading back up to their camp on the hill. Jon fell to sleep almost as soon as he hit the ground. But Robert was slow to come down from the excitement. He laid quietly, looking up at the stars. Across the fire, a low voice started singing a slow sad song. Curtis was pushing the embers with his stick, thinking the dogs were his only audience. Robert soon fell to sleep.

3. Blood Lust

Grit grew from strength to strength. From pup to young dog. His muscles hardened. His bones lengthened and his hair thickened for the Autumn that laid ahead. He was not yet as strong as he would be, nor was his mind prepared for the burden of injuries incurred from true terrier work but he was growing none the less. His maturity was that of a teenage boy, strengthening, full of a belief that he could defeat the world. This stage in his life was the perfect time for developing his talents.

He spent the beginning of Autumn in the valley's cow pastures. Forests bordered the fields, giving a feeling of walking on the edge of civilization. On one side, the river and thousands of acres of grassland. On the other side, bears, cougars and wild bush. The weather was cooling. The boys swam less and hunted more; digger squirrels being the hunted quarry during the early Autumn days. The grass was not yet green, though the mornings grew more damp and the days waned shorter.

On such a day as begged for hunting, the boys, Robert, Jon, and Curt could hear the squirrels barking at the dogs from their underground burrows. This only intensified the dogs' lust for blood. The day was dedicated to watching and helping the dogs dig squirrels out of their burrows. The dogs would redouble their efforts each time a squirrel barked deep down in the earth.

Grit could hear the chirping of a squirrel six feet deep down its burrow. It drove him mad. He dug and bit at the earth. He whined and squealed. Robert ran to assist Grit with a shovel. The boys found that by helping the dogs dig, they could account for more squirrels. Robert dug to a fork in the squirrels' tunnels. Grit smelled, determining which way they must continue digging in order to catch the chirping rodent. The dogs tore and bit at roots and stones alike. Screaming to vent frustration. Grit's long face gave him that tiny bit of reach over the other terriers.

"Hold the other dogs back, guys," Robert told the others. "Let Grit use that long probe on his face for once!"

The others held back the team of terriers.

The squirrel's chirpy bark was getting more clear. Grit's angst deepened with the hole. He bit at the ground. Excited yips were coming forth with every mouthful of dirt. Impatient as his young dog, Robert shoveled as quick as he could.

Silently, out came the little squirrel in a gray flash.

The dogs that saw the squirrel were going ape but Grit was out of his mind frenzied. Focused on the hole, he didn't see the squirrel.

"Let 'em loose!"

Three dogs pumped their legs as fast as they could. Jaws snapped all around the squirrel, but not fast enough. The little fella chirped and spat, flying under, around, over and through dogs. Ten feet to his hole. . . Five. . . A dog blocks his way. . . Detour. . . Back on track. . . Six feet now, the squirrel's in the home stretch, teeth still snapping at his tail.

"OH! OH! She's got 'im! Coallie's got 'im!"

That she did, but not in the vitals. Coallie had the little pesk by the tail. He balled up around Coallie's nose and took a good hard bite. Shocked and needing a better hold, Coallie shook her puny punisher. He was slick as greased lightning. His tail slid right out from

31

between Coallie's teeth. The brown dogs, Lee and Jackson were there to grab the fumbled squirrel. It hardly had time to make a peep before the three dogs tore it apart and devoured its pieces.

By then, Grit had noticed the other dogs' focus on where the squirrel actually went. He tried to push his way into the pack and get a piece of squirrel.

"Not today, Grit," said Robert. "You've got to learn, the squirrels don't stay put."

"Oh man! That was so close! Grit's really turning up the heat on these squirrels," said Curt.

"Yeah he is. I only wish he'd learn to watch for the squirrel sometimes," Rob said. He noticed that Grit let many of them get past him, because he was so focused on digging.

"I've been reading a bit about ratting in an old book Papa Ron got me," mentioned the tall blonde, Jon.

Robert jumped up on a stump to stand high above the others and presumed an air of dignity.

"Come one! Come all! Hear the words of the Mighty Papa Ron," Robert teased, poking fun at Jon, whom all called Sasquatch, due to his long limbs and abnormally large feet. "So sayeth The Good Book of Papa Ron, 'Neither shall ye take unto thyself a terrier, but shall hunt hounds continually. Neither shall ye kill the sabertooth chipmunk with thine hound but if ye must kill, kill with a rifle, neither shall a terrier be used for this purpose. Amen'"

"Amen," Curt joined in.

Jon lashed out, "You're a couple of A-holes and you know it!"

"Alright. Alright," laughed out Rob. "What does the book of the Mighty Papa have to say?"

"It was sayin' how some terriers dig and others stand around watching. But none of 'em are useless. The ones 'at do the watching are waiting to catch the bolters."

Somehow, young Jon was always getting his hands on out of print hunting books. The blonde boy's bit of reading was enlightening to Robert.

"Well, that explains a lot."

"Yeah it does," laughed Curt. "Your dogs are great at that sitting and waiting part! Ain't they, Jon?"

All the boys laughed, including Jon who was getting ribbed, "Oh, you just shut your pie-hole, you little Indian girl!"

"No, really though," Rob said. "Coallie seems perfect at that sitting and waiting part. That always kind of bugged me, actually. But now I kinda see how that's important she sits and waits."

While talking, they had been walking toward their bicycles at the bottom of the pasture. The farm hand, George, was leaning over the fence there, waiting for the boys to come down and tell him about the day's hunt. His bottom lip was full of chew. His white beard was stained brownish yellow from nasty spittle.

"Whatchu' boys up to?"

"Catchin' digger squirrels," Curt, the dark haired boy, answered.

"Donchu' know? That ain't p'litically c'rrect no more. Y'all gotta call'm *Degro* squirrels now." George laughed his stupid high pitched laugh. "Well, ye' get any?"

"Yeah, a bunch. A few got away, though," said Curt.

The boys liked George, but he was the village idiot so to speak. He was as dumb as a brick.

"What?! Are you dumb as a brick?" This was his favorite phrase. "Whatchu' goin' lettin' squirrels go?"

"We'll get'm next time, George," said Jon.

"I sure hope you ain't lettin' any of dem squirrels go," George said with a stink-eye. "Dey wreak havoc on dis here place. Dose holes'll break a cow's leg. Don't even 'magine ridin' no horse tru here."

"Yeah, we know. We're takin' care of'm, George." Robert said.

"Eh. Old Gina, she likes you boys. Dat's why she don' poison dem squirrels. She don't wan' yer dogs gettin' into it an' dyin'."

"Yeah," all the boys rolled their heads. They knew George wasn't done with his lecture.

"Y'll jus' 'member, if you don' keep dem squirrels down, I'll poison da lot of 'em. Takin' care of dis here farm is my job and dem squirrels are a nuisance. I got permission to poison dem squirrels if'n dey get too bad. And if dey get too bad, y'all better keep yer dogs the hell outta here or dey'll be *Dog-Gone*!" George laughed out loud again, but the boys weren't sharing in his joke. They knew he wasn't joking, really.

"Alright George. You don't worry. We got 18 yesterday and plenty today. Their numbers'll stay low enough." Robert always felt awkward when George started bossing them around about the right way to have *their* fun. He was taught to respect his elders but sometimes he just wanted to kick George in the nuts.

"OK, I believe ye'," said George. "Now get on outta here. I've got work to do in 'ere."

They tied the dogs into the milk crates that were mounted onto the rear of their bikes and put the shovels and guns in the gun-racks they had on their handle-bars.

"OK, See y'all later."

"Yeah, see ya' later," chimed all the boys.

They rode for a while before talking. They didn't want Ol' George to hear them.

Curt had his feelings hurt by the rant. "George's the idiot," he said.

"Look man, George is just a stupid hillbilly who never learned a damn thing in 'is life! If we kill all the squirrels, all the dog hunting here will be over. Not jus' squirrels but everything," Robert said.

Jon disagreed. "That doesn't make much sense. If we kill every squirrel we catch, they will let us keep hunting here. 'Cause then they don't put poison out that'll kill the dogs."

"That makes sense at first but if you kill all the squirrels, then first of all, there won't be any squirrels left to hunt. But it doesn't stop there. All the small predators we really like to hunt, they eat squirrels. If we kill all the squirrels, what will we hunt? Everything will go where there're rodents, squirrels, rats and stuff. No squirrels means no fox, no bobcat, no mink or weasel. The list goes on."

Curt wanted more George bashing. "Yeah, that's all good and nice. But George doesn't have the good sense God gave animal crackers. So I'm gonna pile the squirrels every day. They're gonna die one way or another."

4. Playing Possum

Fall came too soon and not soon enough for the boys of the valley. Coon season was an excitement but school starting killed a bit of every boy's heart each year.

Grit would need to learn to take punishment from his quarry but this was not the time. If Grit was to become the best dog he could be, the most important step was to get his nose working. This involved taking him on hunts with Lee, Jackson and the hounds. Grit showed great promise when he was taken out by himself but as yet, he didn't know what he was supposed to be chasing. He loved to chase deer, which is not acceptable for a dog meant to catch furbearers. But his success in following deer tracks and his desire to do so, led Robert to believe Grit would be capable of great tracking.

The end of September was near. The rains began to fall and the boys were beginning to hunt regularly for raccoon with the older dogs. Robert and Curt woke early in the morning right before sunrise to get together for a hunt. The two boys lived a mile apart on the same straight road. Fruit and nut orchards grew where there weren't hay fields or vegetable farms. The air was always moist and perfect for hunting in the Fall.

"I think Grit needs to get into some trouble. What do you think?" Robert asked Curt.

"He's young but I guess he's bigger than Lee was when he started."

"Yeah. I just can't control the little booger. He can't be taken out without searching for something. He's kinda saying he's ready on his own without me makin' him go."

"I'd take 'im," said Curt. "Plus, I figur' he's got Lee and Jackson to help him out and protect him from getting too beat up."

"Agreed," said Robert. "We'll be taking him to-day then."

Robert unchained Lee and unkenneled Grit for the day's hunt.

"Aren't you going to bring Jackson?" Curt asked.

"I don't think so."

39

"But Jackson catches a ton of game and will help keep Grit from getting bit when they get a coon." Curt had a soft spot for that brick headed dog but Robert knew better than to listen.

"Jackson takes tracks too fast and searches too wide. I can't control what he gets into. With Grit being so young, he'd get into trouble following old Jackson. Plus, Grit wouldn't be able to figure out what Jackson was running after, the way he just runs off. Grit needs to follow a dog moving slow enough that he can pick up on what the other dog's doing."

"Oh. Yeah, I guess you're right."

"For a while anyway; until Grit figures out what's going on."

The two boys cut through a field and small apple orchard before hitting the road. The plan was to head to where the canoe was laid on the river bank. Along the way they'd hunt. Stout, ruddy haired Tommy Richardson met them along the road near a nut grove. The canoe was placed at his grandfather's house, but he knew he'd be missing out if he didn't meet the other boys half way.

"Let's cut through the field near the hill on the road," suggested Tom. "We might be able to get a fox that way."

It was all the boys' endless obsession to try and catch a fox. For years, Tom and Curt were the only ones of the gang to ever get one. They shot one down as it ran from their two hounds, a bluetick named Roxie and Prissy, Curt's walker bitch.

"Hell yeah! Sounds good to me," said Robert. He and Tom didn't always get along, so Robert tried to be enthusiastic when he agreed with what Tom thought. He wanted to like Tom but Tom was several years younger and just drove him crazy sometimes.

"Agreed," said Curt.

So, about half a mile up the road from Robert's house and a few fields from Tom's grandfather's, they cut off the road and through a barbwire fence. They stuck close to the wooded hill in order to not be seen. There was a neighbor from the city who had bought land out there and would yell and raise Cain if he saw the boys in his neighbors' fields. It wasn't that the neighbor could do anything, so much as the boys thought he could.

That late September day they walked quietly through the maples and cotton woods where the foxes dug their dens each year. The only time to get them to ground would be when they were whelping but the boys hadn't the heart to kill the kits, so they left the fox

41

alone until fall for the most part. If the weather got colder where they lived, then they could dig for fox with the terriers all winter long. But the climate was too temperate, even on a stormy day. This was a cloudy, warm day. The grass was moist and the river low; perfect conditions for a young dog to learn to track and hunt. It had rained during the night, making the animals wet and stinky, easily trackable.

The boys headed past all the fox dens without a peep from the dogs. They didn't truly expect to get a fox, but they could dream. They made it all the way along the small hill to where a large pine tree overshadowed the barbwire fence separating Tom's grandfather's land from the fox-hill. They all slipped through with Grit bringing up the rear, entering a mowed wheat field. About halfway through the field, the boys noticed Lee was not with them and had not been near for a while.

"Where's Lee?" asked Robert. The other boys looked at each other then shook their heads. "I'll head back and see what he's into." Calling Grit, Robert headed back the way they had come.

Back through the fence he went. A short walk into the woods he could hear a faint chopping bark. Lee had found something.

Robert's heart raced. He thought Lee must have caught that Holy Grail of game animals, the fox. He ran toward the dog's voice. He called to the other boys, but they couldn't hear or didn't want to come. He arrived at a log lying on the ground. It had fallen and been dug into by something. It was rotten but provided protection enough for animals to live underneath it. A hole had been dug using the log as a roof for the tunnel.

Robert carried a small shovel, very sturdy and sharp for digging and cutting. Before he started digging, Robert tied Grit back, to make sure the young dog didn't get into a fray too ferocious for his own good.

The dog and his quarry were not deep. The game was giving Lee one heck of a time. Hissing and the sound of grinding teeth came from inside the log. Robert quickly unearthed Lee. Still, Robert couldn't see what he was up against. The wood was rotten in parts but remained hard where the game laid, safely tucked away from Lee's reach. Robert dug out from under the log, trying to open space to maneuver and dispatch the game. The dog whined. The quarry was giving the dog a taste of teeth. With determination, he was able to remove Lee from the hole. He brushed off the dog and looked it over to make sure it was healthy and well, then peered into the hole.

43

"Well, I'll be damned," Robert said to Lee. "If this ain't the toughest possum this side of the Mississippi, then I ain't seen a tough possum."

The damned thing sounded like it had given Lee one heck of a time. Normally, possums can't take punishment without playing dead, but the position this possum had taken under the log gave him just enough protection to feed Lee nothing but teeth to grab.

Possums are the perfect animal for a dog's first exposure to work but Robert didn't feel like going to anymore trouble for this possum. The boy took one more peek at the grinner down the hole.

"You're a tough little bastard. I'll give you that. Farewell. You've earned the white flag today. Go on your way and make some tough possum babies."

Robert leashed Lee for the walk to wherever Tom and Curt had gotten off to. Grit would have to take lessons from another possum, another time.

He reunited with Curt and Tom on Tom's grandfather's place. They were standing next to an enormous blackberry patch, known to be full of coon. The trees were full of gray squirrels jumping from limb to limb.

"Ya'll missed a bit of excitement. Lee found a possum in a log."

"Oh yeah," Curt replied, "huh."

"Yeah. Meanest, toughest bastard of a possum you ever did see!"

"A tough and mean possum?!" Tom mocked. Both Curt and Tom laughed. "Yeah, I'll believe that the day I see it, Rob."

"You would have seen it, if you'd come along to find Lee with me."

"Suuuure," the others said in unison.

"Well, when you two have such fine dogs as mine that can battle a monster possum, then maybe I'll give your opinions a bit of respect."

The boys couldn't help but laugh out loud at such nonsense. Robert let Lee and Grit off their leads and sent them into the brush with a hiss. The dogs shot away, as commanded.

"Oh dear me," Tom said in a high pitched voice, clutching his hands together. "Lord, save my dogs from the Godzilla possums to be found in dem der briarpatch!"

"Oh, you'll get yours Tom," Robert laughed. "You just wait. You attract trouble like shit draws flies."

"Is them fightin' words, Robert? I'm real scared!"

Curt laughed, while the other two wrestled. Robert tried making it a point to get Tom's face into a mudhole but failed. Tom was younger but a strong son of a gun. While they wrestled, Lee began barking a few hundred yards away. Grit started in on the barking shortly thereafter.

The boys forgot their chiding and hopped to. They rushed along the border of the berry patch until they made it to the raucous. The barking was muffled.

"They've got something underground again," Tom spoke loud and excitedly. "It could be a fox!"

They hacked through blackberries with their machetes and shovel until they could see where the dogs had gotten to. The dogs were digging under a buried car. This car had been covered with sand completely. Only the blue top of the cab could be seen. The tight space between the sand and the top of the car had been dug into by something. It was still tight for Lee and Grit. They couldn't quite fit, but were digging madly on their sides. Steam rose from the hole and a musty odour. Kicked by the dogs, sand flew from the hole, spattering the boys with gritty leaf-litter.

Robert grabbed Grit and handed him back to Curt. He needed to see what was in the hole, before letting Grit get into it.

"Tie Grit back, would ya Curt?" Robert asked, then reached under the car again to grab Lee. Handing

Lee back to Curt, Robert shone his light into the hole to see what was hiding there. "Another possum."

For these boys, each dig was sure to be anticlimactic until they could wrap their heads around the idea that they would almost never be digging fox in that valley.

"Oh my! Better not let the dogs get into it with that possum, it might kill them," Tom joked.

"Don't make me punch you, you chubby putz," Robert said. "Hand me Grit. This is a perfect introduction for him."

"No problem," said Curtis. "Grit's going ape. I don't think he likes you tying him back very much." Curtis handed Robert the dog.

Robert dropped Grit at the hole and the dog went berserk trying to shove himself down the hole. Lying on his side, he dug and scrounged for entrance. After about 15 minutes of digging, he was able to make it to the small possum. He didn't take time for nervous baying. He grabbed hold and crunched and shook with devastating effect. The possum immediately played dead. With an older more experienced dog, this ploy may have worked. An older dog would have lost interest in a dead animal. But with a young dog such as Grit, playing dead was the possum's last mistake, a mortal one.

Robert dug to help Grit out. Grit dragged the possum into the open where Lee was allowed a rag on his find. Grit worked himself breathless chewing on his prize. Though he didn't find it on his own, he was mighty proud. Robert petted and praised him, brushing the sand from his coat.

"He did a good job," Curt made mention.

Robert received his praise in turn. "Yeah, I think he's really got promise."

Tom made mention as well. "Nice job for a young dog. You've got a good one, Robert."

"Thanks Tom. What's the chance of a breakfast break?"

"Pretty good, I'd say," Tom answered. "Let's head into my Grandpa's house."

They ate cereal alongside bacon and eggs. Everyone knows to wait 30 minutes before exercising after a meal. The boys didn't care much to keep rules. However, they did stuff themselves to the point that they did not want to canoe across the river. They were so stuffed they didn't want to move. Instead, they went to the front yard of the farmhouse to shoot rifles.

Curt and Robert had semi-automatic rifles that could shoot as fast as they could pull their triggers. But Tom had a meager single-shot .22. When target shooting they took turns shooting one shot at a time. All of them were good shots. There were days of the summer when they'd each go through several hundred rounds of ammunition.

While shooting, something caught the boys' eyes. Out in the field adjoining the yard, a pheasant dodged from clump to clump of grass.

"What's that, 200 yards?" Curt asked.

"Pretty close to that," Robert conjectured.

Pckow!!!!

Tom took an unannounced shot. The other two jumped. He missed and he couldn't reload fast enough to beat the others with a follow up shot. Pckow-pckowpckowpckowpckow!!!! All the shots were missing.

"Wait a minute," said Curt, holding his hand up to stop the shooting. "Let's take turns. At least that way we'll know who's hitting where."

One after the other they each took a single shot. The turf was flying up all around the pheasant but none of them could hit the bird.

"This is bull," Tom decided. He stormed into the house to get a shotgun.

49

Waiting outside for the pheasant's grand finale, Curt and Robert talked.

"Should we tell him it's not pheasant season yet, before he goes out in the field and makes it obvious what's being shot at?" Curt asked, grinning.

"Nah. I don't think he's one to care."

Out came Tom with his shotgun and marched down the gravel road bordering the field. Grit trotted out right beside him. Tom didn't stop to discuss with the others but went out with a determination. He walked straight to where the pheasant was last seen and started kicking the grass clumps and pointing at things for Grit to sniff.

CACACACACACAC!!!! The pheasant erupted from his hide. BOOM! Thud, fell the pheasant.

Grit ran quickly, grabbed the flopping pheasant off the ground and retrieved the bird to Tom. Tom held up his prize proudly. The walk was long and he looked funny, stout as he was, waddling down the road in his rubber boots, waving the pheasant triumphantly, grinning. He never thought to look behind himself and flash for a moment that silly grin in the opposite direction. Instead, he tried to listen but could not hear the warning yells and arm signals of his friends telling him to get rid of the pheasant in the bushes. He could see their hands waving but didn't see the Wildlife Officer driving up behind him in a pickup truck. When he finally turned around and saw the truck driving up, he tossed the bird into the bushes next to the road but it was too late.

"Where's that bird I saw you carrying?" the warden asked.

"What bird?"

"Don't play dumb kid. I heard the cock pheasant, then the gun shot. You killed a bird and I know it."

Tom, feeling confident, put his hand on his heart. "Are you accusing *me* of being a liar? On my own property? The disrespect of. . ."

The warden wasn't looking Tom in the eye but was staring down at his feet. There sat Grit, with the pheasant in his mouth like a good retriever.

Robert and Curtis were slapping their knees laughing. Robert thought he might die for lack of breath.

When the officer was done chewing up and spitting Tom out, he took the bird for "evidence", which likely meant he was taking it for dinner.

There was plenty ribbing to be had from his friends when he got back to the farm-house.

"Wow, the face of a criminal," Robert teased. "I wish I had a camera."

Tom was in no mood. He feared the wrath of his father finding out about the ticket he just received. "Get out of my face."

Robert wasn't letting it go. "Didn't I say you'd get yours. Oh man, this is too much!"

Curt and Robert couldn't stop laughing and running stupid faced and bow-legged, while holding up an imaginary bird. It was still funny when Tom came at them with a stick from behind and started hitting them and shooing them off his family's property. Curt and Robert took the hint and headed home, leaving Tom to deal with his father's fire on his lonesome.

5. Coon In a Pump House

Grit spent the month of October learning to hunt behind Lee. Lee always found game first but Grit was enthusiastic and driven. He often struck before Lee but, in his excitement, would run too fast and lose the track. In these cases, Lee would work out the track to its end. By mid-October Grit had worked several coon, possums and a number of nutria with Lee there to help him.

Evening came and the phone rang at Robert's.

"Hey," came Jon's voice from the line.

"Hey, What's up," Robert answered.

"It rained today. We should be out coon hunting tonight. Perfect tracking conditions."

"Yeah, I'm up for it. You coming out?"

"Sure, I've gotta get my grandpa to drive me but I'll be out in an hour or two."

"Cool. See ya then."

The orchards this time of year were excellent places to catch raccoons. They would be into the fruit in the apple orchards or searching through the leaf litter in the nut groves for worms. The grass was only 2 or 3 inches tall and collected dew like a rag collects water. Tracking conditions could not be more perfect than a moist Autumn evening and the coons were always busy getting fat for the winter ahead.

At 11:00 pm Robert and Jon hit the road. They would spotlight and hunt several orchards within a two mile radius of Robert's house. Their backs were laden with bags full of batteries for their lights, the handlebars on their bicycles were mounted with gun-racks holding rifles. Their baskets were holding machetes and skinning grapples. They were ready for all out war on crop-stealers.

Grit and Jackson were brought that night.

"It's time for Grit to take a track to its end on his own, don't you think Jon?"

"If you think he can do it. Sure"

"I think he can. He's got to learn to slow down. If not slow down, then return and find the track again where he lost it."

They walked through field after field and orchard after orchard. The boys had a goal in mind where they could sit down and let Grit work on his own, while they rested. They took the long route there, stopping at several ponds that raccoons frequented. The night was young when Robert and Jon left the house, so the coons had not yet left their hideouts in the trees. Though they didn't catch a coon on their way to their destination, it gave time for Grit to burn energy and calm down. If he were to catch a raccoon on his own that night, Grit needed to be thoughtful and methodical.

Jon and Robert came to the orchard which was destined to hold the first raccoon Grit would find on his own. Jon parked his bike by the eight-foot tall gate barring the way into the orchard. Grit shot under the fence without waiting for the gate to be opened. Jackson was silent, sitting in the basket strapped to Robert's bicycle. Jackson was a crazy dog, but he was quiet.

Jon unlocked the gate and slowly opened it. The farmers of the area locked their gates but gave the boys keys to the properties. Jon quietly opened the gate. The farmer who owned that particular orchard had built the gate right next to his house. They shut and locked the gate behind them and rode away from the house as quickly as possible. The farmer had a cat that the dogs were more than willing to provide with an economy ticket to hell. Whistling as they rode, the boys led Grit into the 40 acres of apple, nectarine and hazelnut orchards.

"Let's sit here while Grit looks for coons." Jon had spotted some farm machinery to sit down on. It was cold when they sat on the flat metal but their behinds soon warmed the rusty old bars.

"It's nights like this I really miss old Manny," said Jon, reminiscing upon the first terrier the boys had hunted with together. Manny was Roberts first terrier. It was a little black and tan fox terrier type. Manny was no super-star when it came to aggression but the dog found coons by the dozens. He had really come into his own in the same orchard they were sitting that night. Manny and a Jack Russell called Rocky had caught 14 raccoons one week in that orchard.

"I hear ya there, Jon," Robert replied thoughtfully. "I sure loved that little dog. I was a fool to let him go."

When Robert was 13, he had sold Manny to buy a gun. He quickly realized there wasn't a gun worth Manny. He cried the day the dog was taken away.

"Do you remember how he would scream and yell whenever the coon got a hold on him," Jon laughed.

Robert laughed along. "Yeah, that dog was a pussy. I say what. But he could find a coon."

"That's for damn sure."

Just then a screech was heard in the night. It was the squeaky yowl of Grit striking a track. He had moved several hundred yards into the hazel orchard before striking. The boys sat listening for a minute before Grit really got heated up on the track. . . yipe yipe yipe yipe. Grit was letting out three yips a second.

"What the hell are we waiting for!" Robert let out, looking Jon in the face.

They hopped to their feet and took off as fast as they could with batteries, lights and guns strapped to their backs. Jackson was straining on the lead, wheezing and straining but not letting out a single bark. His strong body was taut and stringy muscled, pushing to reach the action.

Grit was moving the track fast.

"Is he gonna over run it again?" Robert wondered.

"He sure is moving it fast," Jon huffed out.

Grit was taking it quickly, barking so fast it was a wonder he could breath. He got hung up on the fence for a while. It was necessary for him to stand on his hind legs and squeeze through higher in the fence where the squares were bigger. The fence was 8 feet tall so there was no jumping it for him, he needed to learn to get through the middle squares.

Robert and Jon got there to help him. Robert put his hand on a higher square to show Grit where to get through. In his excitement it was hard for the dog to focus. Grit knew the coon was gaining distance on him every second. He eventually figured out where to climb through and hit the track running. On the other side of the fence was an open field with a few thin patches of blackberries scattered throughout. The grass was still high. It had not been mowed for hay but had laid fallow for several years. The moist grass served to hold the scent for Grit to follow.

The track was hot, scent dripping on the standing straws, and Grit made the world know about it with all his noise, then. . . silence.

Robert and Jon listened, heads to the side, eyes closed, mouths open to breath with less noise. Seconds passed. Robert was impatient and tempted to release Jackson.

"Just give him a bit," Jon said. Jon knew Robert was antsy and Grit needed time to figure things out on his own.

Soon Grit was heard, "RAAWAAR". It was not the bark of a tracking dog but the sound of a dog that had found its game.

"Game on," Robert yelled.

He let Jackson loose at this point. Grit had done what was asked of him. He found the game on his own. It was not yet time to test his ability to hold the game single-handed.

Jackson was an adept at fences. When he was young he was dumb as a brick when it came to obstacles, now he pushed through obstacles like a wet worm through moist mud. Within a minute Jackson could be heard joining the fray.

The boys left their gear and climbed the fence with nothing but a flash light for vision. They ran as fast as they could. Hearing guided the way. They came to a patch of blackberries that were dark, gnarly brambled. These berries had grown slow and strong.

"Damn! We need the machete," Robert said.

"I'll go back and grab it." Jon ran back.

"Make it quick Sasquatch! There's game afoot!" Robert loved old stories of Robin Hood or King Arthur. At times he let the language slip out.

Robert could only wait. It was wait or tear himself to bits by plowing through the briars. That would be no use. The machete would arrive before he got far.

Jon hopped the fence and got back to Robert in a jiffy.

"Dang boy! You put some fire in *your* ass to get the machete that quick!"

"It sounds ugly in there. Put some fire in your ass and get choppin'!"

Robert beat through the vines. To call what that machete did chopping was an insult to good machetes everywhere. The blade bounced off the thick vines. Robert bludgeoned the ropy briars until they splintered or frayed apart. After a good 15 minutes he broke through to a small pump house, more like a box than a house. It was about 4 foot by 4 foot and a battle was raging within.

"What's going on?" Jon yelled over the din.

"There's a pump house in here. The dogs are in it. I can't get the lid off. There are too many black berries."

"I'm coming in," Jon said.

Robert had to cut a swath out of the patch big enough for both he and Jon to fit. Meanwhile, it sounded like this coon was not walking easy into the night. It was giving the dogs a walloping.

Inside the pump house, dry dust filled the air. The dogs were huffing for air. Their eyes were caked, tears mixing with the dust to make mud coated lashes. There was only darkness inside the box. The dogs fought their adversary by feel alone, a tangled mess of vicious bodies. Pure bravery kept them fighting. Neither Jackson nor Grit feared death.

The vines had grown around the lid of the pump-house like a kraken wraps a ship. It's tendrils reached around, over and beneath the lid. This pump had not been in use for years. Robert hacked and hacked, while Jon pried and pushed at the lid. Jon opened just enough for an arm to go in.

"I can just barely see in there," Jon said. "I think you can get your arm in now."

"Bloody-Hell! You think I'm stickin' my arm in there?"

Despite the question, Robert stuck his arm in. He trusted his dogs more than his leather gloves to keep him from being bitten. A hundred times he'd grabbed a coon while the dogs worked it but that was always with something to see. This time he was putting full faith in Jackson's ability to keep control of the raccoon's head.

He felt for Jackson's rump. He knew it by the tiny knob some fool considered enough tail for a working terrier. That rump told him where the coon's head would be, directly in front of the knob. Robert then felt for the other dog. He expected the young dog would be further down on the neck or chest. His faith was well founded. The coon was on it's back now. Robert felt down it's belly and got hold of a hind leg.

"Can you lift the lid higher, Jon?"

"No, It's stuck. I have to chop some more away."

Robert held the leg of the coon while Jon continued chopping around the lid. Robert had enough of a grip to see the raccoon's foot but he couldn't pull it out further than that.

"My grip is slipping," Robert said. He was begging Jon to move faster to get the lid open. "This coon is big and I can't keep hold of it much longer. My gloves won't grip."

Jon pushed and shoved at the lid. It opened about four inches; not enough for the coon to fit through. The dogs pulled it out of Robert's hand.

"Damn it! I lost it."

The coon was not rolling over to fight anymore. It decided it had enough of being bit, prodded, pulled and slobbered. It gave a mighty beating to the dogs. It was bigger than either Grit or Lee and wasn't going to hold its ground just to be killed. It bull-dozed the dogs and bolted out into the darkness for sanctuary, far away from the dogs and that pump-house.

The terriers tried in vain to track down the coon through the field. They made it a couple hundred yards toward a pond where the raccoon fled. No matter how hard they tried, they couldn't find the coon by scent. The raccoon's smell stuck to the roofs of their mouths and noses. To smell the tiny scent left by feet after having the whole coon in their mouths was an impossible task.

"Well, darn," Robert said, watching the dogs run back to him after a fruitless chase. "I suppose all wasn't a waste, though. Grit did a dang good job finding that coon. He tracked it a good distance for a terrier pup."

"He sure did," Jon agreed. "If anything, that was all your fault we didn't catch the coon."

"Wha. . .? . . ." Robert realized Jon was right. "Well, you weren't much help, 'Squatch!"

6. Learning To Hunt From the Canoe

G rit became a regular part of the team from the day he caught that coon in the pump-house. Robert was foolish, nobody taught him to be otherwise. He did not know to bring a young dog on slowly but instead let Grit do whatever he wished, when he wished, as it applied to hunting. He was not a fool in the way that some are, he didn't feel the need to make Grit "prove" himself by fighting animals to the death. That was not the way Robert did things. Robert knew a dogs job and Robert knew his own job. This was sport to Robert more-so than a service to the farmers, but he felt that sport must be sporting. In other words, he treated his game with respect when he could and treated the dogs with respect as well. Though he respected his dogs and had every wish that they would be great hunting dogs, he didn't have the faintest clue when a terrier should be worked full-bore. So, he worked Grit hard by the age of eight months.

Most dogs this would utterly ruin. But there are a few, very few dogs that can handle the pressure and never let the owner down. Lucky for him, Grit had Lee, Jackson and Coallie always there to back him up. He was fearless with those dogs to help him. He had implicit faith in Jackson and Lee. He put Coallie to shame in the area of tenacity and Coallie was no wimp. Grit was tough as any terrier the boys had seen and they loved him for it. They thought he had an unbreakable soul.

The boys could not yet drive and this created a dilemma for them. They had hunted the orchards and the fields to the point that almost no coon set foot in them. They rarely caught nutria except along the river banks. Many coon and nutria made it to the river before being caught by the dogs and this caused the boys distress. The dogs could easily drown trying to attack a raccoon in the water. Also, there was no way in hell the dogs would out swim a nutria in its habitat.

The boys solved the problem simply. They learned to hunt from a canoe. Most of the boys were terrible in the canoe but Curt and Robert were an unbeatable team. When they rowed, they were like figure skaters on the water. They paddled in perfect unison and could turn on a dime. When they went for speed, white water frothed at the point of the boat. They could cut through the water like a duck, two people with a single mind.

Curt and Robert gave up on taking others on the canoe. Because of this, their days on the canoe were a special thing to them. They were the closest friends of the group, which is probably why they managed the canoe so well together.

Curt and Robert kept the canoe at Tom's grandfather's house. It was about a three-quarter mile walk from Robert's and was smack dab in-between Robert and Curt's homes. They'd meet there early in the morning for the best scenting conditions and game activity. Plus, nutria like to be out at dusk and dawn.

They would load the hounds onto the canoe at night and the terriers on in the mornings. They hunted from the canoe non-stop. They were able to hunt spots that were miles away by road but a short trip by river.

All the good terriers were brought every time they hunted on the water. There was so much game to be caught, they needed the shore scattered with dogs to catch all the nutria. The blackberries grew so thick and high, there was no way to see game through the brambles. Every kind of game lived in the bushes and the roots and in holes along the river; coon, nutria, fox, otter, beaver, everything. Trees grew with their roots dipping into the water's edge. This provided ideal habitat for game. Terriers were by far the best dogs to work the riverside.

The boys would use guns. Guns were not against their code of ethics. But their favorite way to hunt nutria was to herd the nutria up to the dogs by prodding them and pushing them to the point they could not stay in the water any longer. This was Coallie's domain. Coallie could not be convinced to leave sight of Robert for more than a minute or so. This would keep her tied with an invisible lead to the waterline. This made her useful as a canoe hunting dog.

The home-side of the river had been hunted by foot so much, they rarely stayed to hunt that side anymore. They'd cut straight across to the opposite bank. There the blackberries grew thick for miles. The briars quilted the banks, 12-15 feet deep. Curt and Robert had learned to armor themselves and climb the vines like ladders, rather than attempt to hack through with machetes to game. This cut the time it took to get to the dogs from 30 minutes down to about five minutes.

It really made hunting easier on both the boys and their dogs.

One such morning, near Christmas time, Curt and Robert met at the canoe.

"Should be a perfect day!" exclaimed Curt. "Look at how smooth the water is. We'll move up this river like a marble on glass."

"Yeah, I see that," agreed Robert, "and the water is super clear. We should be able to easily move nutria today."

It was necessary that the water be clear and calm to properly push nutria to the dogs. If it rained anytime during the week, the water would get too rapid and murky to properly hunt without a gun.

The boys stood and appreciated the serenity of the river.

Curt broke the revery, "Let's get this boat in the water!"

They pushed the canoe down a sandy embankment and into the water. They sat in the canoe and Robert called the dogs.

"Jackson! Lee! Grit! Coallie! Come!"

Coallie came first, she was always wholly focused on the wants of Robert. She cared only for what he commanded. She was soon followed by Lee, then

Grit and finally Jackson, who zig-zagged his way through the brush he had been hunting before hopping into the canoe. The dogs all piled up together at their master's feet. The boys liked it that way. The dogs kept calm by Robert, rather than running all over the bottom of the boat and rocking the canoe.

The boys knew how best to navigate the river. The water was swiftest in the deep-center of the river. They could not fight the current there. So they aimed the boat at an angle downstream toward the opposite side. They had learned by exhaustion that it was a fruitless battle to fight straight across. Once they hit the opposite bank, they kept the canoe close to shore. The current was almost non-existent there and they could move back upstream and gain the distance they lost. Thus, when they wished to return to dock the canoe, they would again float downstream at an angle, never fighting the current but always working with it.

On this particular day, when the far bank came within view for the dogs, they became excited. Grit thought little of getting cold and wet but jumped into the water to swim to shore ahead of all the other dogs. It was hardly useful, as he was not faster than the canoe. He'd learn that with age. Lee and Jackson waited for the canoe to bump rocks on the shore before jumping into the water just deep enough to wet their chests. Coallie went along by Robert's command.

Grit was already into the brush and hunting. Jackson and Lee were not far behind. Coallie, however, stayed on the sand and grass of the beach. For raccoon hunting, this was not a beneficial behavior but for nutria, it was perfect.

The boys slowly rowed the canoe upstream. They moved at the speed the dogs hunted. They'd listen for twigs snapping and leaves rustling where the dogs passed unseen through the berries and tall grasses. Coallie would trot happily along the bank checking the root clusters along the shore line, sometimes finding what the other dogs would not. But today she was to play as catcher, not chaser.

The boys kept a good look out for V shaped ripples in the water. The ripples would indicate to them where an animal was swimming with head above the water.

"Ripples," whispered Curt to Robert. Curt had the eyes of an eagle. No one could match him in vision.

"Sure enough, is it furred or feathered?" Robert asked, as to say, is it a bird or a mammal.

They watched quietly, so as not to startle whatever it was. The animal swam slowly in half circles back and forth. Perhaps it was also trying to view the boys. Leisurely they paddled toward the game, tensely anticipating a full steam launch as soon as the animal was identified.

"Nutria!" Curt hoarsely whispered back. They drove the vessel with all their might toward the nutria. Coallie kept pace. She knew that something was coming her way when the boys paddled in such a frenzied way.

When they came within thirty feet of the nutria it snapped the water with its tail and dove. But the water was shallow enough near the bank that Curt and Robert could keep an eye on the prey. They let out hollers as they pulled the water with the oars as hard as they could. White froth licked at the prow.

"There's the bubble chain!" Robert shouted, as they neared where the nutria had dodged below the surface. Robert always sat at the front of the canoe and Curtis in the rear. From this view Robert often guided the hunt at this point. Curtis steered, his paddle acting as the rudder. Each of them gave power when needed, where needed. They shot towards what they called "the bubble-chain," (air bubbling slowly out of the nutria's nose.) It would only last for 10 seconds or so before the air in the nose had been purged.

"I see the bugger!" Robert yelled.

The nutria was half swimming, half crawling on the bottom of the river. The boys positioned the canoe right over their quarry, then proceeded to poke and prod as close to it as they could with the oars, herding it back towards shore. The nutria did not want to go to shore just yet. It swam with the current, trying to out-pace the boys. It couldn't. But it could out maneuver them. It would turn in an instant and swim the oppo-site way. The boys were well versed in this tactic and spun the canoe around on the spot, with Robert push-ing water on one side of the canoe and Curt pulling wa-ter on the other. They spun an about-face and kept a look out for the nutria. It could not hold its breath for-ever.

"Thaar she blows!" Curt pointed toward the head surfacing and spouting water from it's nose. They rushed upon it again. The nutria dove and swam as fast as it could, as deep as it could but exhaustion was set-ting in. It dove and resurfaced two more times before it could dive no longer and swam as fast as it could toward the shore. . . and death.

Coallie had been prancing about on the shore in anticipation for the kill. She knew to go wherever the canoe pointed toward the shore. She ran to the spot she knew her favorite of foes would rise from the depths. At least to her they were the depths.

The nutria planted two feet on the shore but was immediately met by a fury of teeth and black fur. Coallie was adept at yanking nutria from the water. She tore it from its supposed safe haven. And savagely dominated the creature. It had no chance in its exhausted state.

The canoe sped onto the shore. Robert was crouching before the canoe had even stopped and sprung to land as soon as the canoe slid up the sand. He was not one to let his dog get unnecessary injuries, nor was he one to let his game suffer. He loved good dog work and took his fair part in the excitement, but paining the animals was not his goal. He quickly grabbed the nutria by the tail and Coallie by the scruff, separating the two combatants. He put a boot down on the nutria to hold it. Curtis tossed him a club and he put the "nuut" down in the blink of an eye.

Coallie ragged on her prey.

"The other dogs must be working a track out somewhere else," Robert conjectured. There wasn't much else they could have been doing, that they would miss all the hubbub that had transpired with the nutria.

"That only means more game to hunt and meat for the dogs," Curt said.

Robert handed the nutria to Curt, who then put the nutria behind himself in the canoe.

Robert grabbed Coallie and put her into the front of the canoe with him. Slowly, they let the canoe drift with the flow of the river. The other dogs had stayed behind toward where they had first come to the opposite shore that day. As the boys drifted, they listened. Over the soft hush of the rapids ahead they could hear yipping, as if a dog was frustrated in its work. Robert and Curtis set their arms once more for the forward press. As they got closer to the yiping, they could tell that it was Grit trying to work out a scent. Something had passed through that way sometime before. The barking quickened as they got closer.

Sploosh! A body hit the water. Sploosh! Followed by Grit. Lee and Jackson soon arrived on the shore. Robert and Curtis sped to the scene. Coallie was commanded out of the canoe to her post as catcher. Lee was quite good at the task as well, if he had been chasing the animal already. Lee and Coallie waited on shore. The bank was covered with roots and tangled masses of debris caught in fallen trees. It was hard work for the dogs to weave through the mess to keep up with the game and the canoe. Grit was swimming in confused circles, wondering where the game had gone. Robert grabbed him up as they went by toward the bubble-chain.

"It's white!" Robert said, looking back at Curtis with wide eyes.

"What? What is white?"

"This nutria. It's a white one!"

This new found discovery only intensified their drive to catch it. Despite it being a rare creature, the boys had no mercy for a nutria of any kind. Nutria were not native, and no matter the rarity of any variety of nutria, they all fell under the variety of pestilence to the boys and to the farmers.

They sped after the white nutria, crawling like a salamander on the rock-river-bottom. The routine was short this time. It went straight for a hideout and took refuge in the exposed roots of a gnarly tree. Coallie and Lee were both in the crowded, clustered roots as quickly as they could cram their chests through. Curt and Robert blocked the game's escape and poked it deeper into the roots, ensuring that it would not bolt to the water again. Coallie eventually got a hold and Lee joined her. But they were not pulling together but against each other. Lee couldn't gain purchase of footing nor balance and was hauled under the water. He was caught by a root, legs dangling in the water, head unable to lift above the surface of the water. Coallie held her game firm, but the white nutria was second priority for Robert.

Robert jumped out of the canoe into waist deep winter cold water. He grabbed and pulled at debris and hacked at roots with his machete to get to Lee. He made room for his arms and shoved his shoulder as far as he could reach into the roots and grabbed hold of Lee's tail. He pulled Lee from the water, nose sputtering but mouth still in grips with his adversary.

"What a dog! Dang near gave me a heart-attack!" Curtis said.

Robert pulled Lee closer along with the nutria, until he could take hold of the nutria in his hand. He pulled it free from the roots and dogs, It had nearly drowned along with Lee. Robert tossed it to shore, where the dogs scrambled to get at it from the roots. Jackson and Grit got their first worry of the excitement. Neither could have gotten into the mess with the other two blocking the way. There was nowhere to fit.

The boys admired their find for a few minutes and debriefed each other on the excitement.

"A white nutria and double the meat for the dogs today," Robert said proudly.

"Yeah. I'd say that was some good dog work done by all today. None of them have anything more to prove." Curtis was catching the drift that Robert wanted to call it a day.

"Why ruin the good luck we've had? Let's go home, skin these and eat."

"Sounds like a plan," Curtis agreed.

That night they went to the local gathering of dogmen in the area. The guys got together every other week to brag about hunts, catches and dogs. Curtis and Robert were in the spotlight that night.

"The exotic and elusive white nutria, huh?" A big man, Doctor Micah, said laughing, "I bet old Hank will be jealous when he gets here to see this. What with him being the nutria expert an' all."

All the men laughed at the boys' stories and patted them on the backs. It all reinforced the camaraderie of the country side to gather together like that. The boys were taught by these men what was proper and sporting and what was merely cruelty.

"Cruelty," the men said, "has no place in hunting. Hunting is the fairest, most natural of ways to manage wildlife."

And it was true. The best hunters were all conservationists at heart. They had more respect for their quarry than any bunny-hugger ever would. They knew the spirit of the animal. They knew its habits, its haunts, its behavior in every season. They understood the balance of predator and prey was natural and a healthful necessity for all creatures.

"Where is Hank anyway?" asked Big Leroy.

Nobody knew.

"Wherever he is, I know he'll want to hear this," Leroy said. "You boys come out and meet Hank and I at the Old Dairy Barns next weekend. We'll give you a taste of some digging with us."

Robert and Curtis were ecstatic to be invited with the older terriermen. They had only hunted with one other terrierman before and he didn't do any digging. For the trip they'd need to get a ride from Robert's father.

That was no problem at all.

7. Big Leroy and Hank

The next week couldn't come fast enough. Curtis and Robert were up all night before the day of the hunt, talking about the stories they had heard about Leroy and Hank's dogs.

Such tales as,

"Did you hear about that dog getting under the slab of concrete with a nuut and needing to be broken out with a sledge hammer?"

Or

"I heard his dogs came from Old-timer Rodger Bars! That guy digs to fox every day!"

And

"Those dogs killed an otter without any help from anybody!"

It was a special time for the boys to be invited by their heroes to hunt.

It was still dark when Robert's father came to wake them and found them out of bed and out of the room already. The dogs were loaded and the boys were decked out in their hunting apparel. William had to wrangle the boys back into the house for some bacon, eggs and toast.

"You've got to eat, same as the dogs before a hunt. I don't want to be digging the dogs out the whole day while you two sit, dead as sacks of flour from lack of sleep and food."

The boys didn't need such advice. They hunted as hard as any man out there, energy was not what they lacked.

Once they got in the truck the boys were knocked out. The ride was long but felt like a blink. They woke and fumbled out of the truck like pups out of a box. Hank was waiting for them at a ferry. They would be crossing to an island near the coast, hunted only by Hank and Leroy. They were paid to hunt there by the farmers whose animals broke their legs in the holes of nutria. One farmer had several hundred acres of root crops devoured by swarms of nutria.

The island was a floating mass of land. If you dug deep enough, you'd always hit water, no matter where you were on the island. In the winter time, you'd only have to dig a few feet to hit water. Because of the water saturation, farmers had created a grid-work of canals to drain the water off the land. Hank was always fascinated by this and wondered how the island didn't just break apart and float to sea.

Hank was a short man with long hair, tattoos and heavy gold earrings that sagged his earlobes. There was no use wondering where he had been in his life. . .

"I've been everywhere man!" he said when asked about where his wild tattoos and taboo fashions arose.

Big Leroy was a different sort of man. It was a wonder he and Hank were cohorts. Leroy was soft spoken but obviously contained immense strength under the canvas jacket and overalls he wore. It became known that he was known as Big Iron by some, due to his strength as a wrestler in his younger days. The name carried on into his profession as a gunsmith. He was a lot like an older version of Curtis actually, soft spoken unless provoked.

They had also invited along a man who had never hunted with terriers but wanted to join the brotherhood so to speak. His name was Dallas. He liked motorcycles and guns but really seemed a city person by all other means of knowing. He wore a baseball cap, blue jeans, leather boots and a nice canvas jacket similar to what Leroy wore, if Leroy had just bought the whole getup at the store the day before. Dallas' clothes were spotless. But he was a nice guy. Everyone in the group got along fine while they walked across fields on the island to reach a particular field that was full of problem holes.

Robert had brought Lee, Jackson, his hairy brown dogs and Grit for the hunt. He kept them leashed for the beginning of the hunt. He wanted to see what the other men's dogs could do. Hank brought a tiny little black bitch called Cindy. Leroy brought two dogs, a shaggy white dog called Sassy and a black wire-haired dog with a head like a gator. He called the black one Jon the Strong. And strong that dog was.

Leroy let both his dogs run ahead when the group first entered the field. The white dog was off like a rocket. Jon the Strong stayed close but worked a thick patch of berries. It was not long before the white Sassy could be heard working away.

"That was quick," Robert said.

Leroy nodded his head and smiling said, "She may not be the toughest, youngest dog out there, but she never fails to find first."

Hank wasn't gonna stroll leisurely like he was too cool to run. He ran past the gang with his pony-tail waving in the wind behind him and his big clunky boots flinging mud in front of him. He looked like a juju wizard chasing demons with a shovel. Robert and Curtis would learn that the man never failed to entertain, though by no means intentionally.

He got to the embankment where Sassy was baying away about three feet out of arms reach into the bank. Hank was a whirlwind of dirt. . . but a tidy whirlwind. He sliced at the bank quickly opening a cavity to reach the dog. He piled his dirt to one side, so he could fill in the hole the best he could. Leroy followed the gang with Jon the Strong in his arms. He hopped down the bank and into the shallow muddy water near the hole. He called to Sassy and she came shuffling backwards out of the hole.

"Some people will tell you that a dog that comes off game when called is useless," Leroy said, handing Sassy to Hank to leash to a tree. "That's all nonsense in my opinion. Who wants to dig, if they don't have to?"

The boys saw his point. It did not look like an easy dig ahead to get that nutria Sassy had been barking at.

Leroy could see that the boys were wondering if they were just gonna spend the day passing game up because Leroy didn't want to dig, "But don't worry fellas.

There are other methods to get game out of a hole." He winked and let the dog in his arms loose. It squeezed into the hole without hesitation. In a short time the dog was making some noise.

"He always screams," Hank remarked. "That doesn't mean he's getting bit. It doesn't mean he's not doing the biting either."

These guys were obviously proud of their team. And for what they were hunting, they could be. The dogs were working in a wonderfully orchestrated fashion. The one found and bayed, the other grabbed and beat.

"Aaaah, Aaaaaah," the sound of a nutria was coming from under the earth.

"Yaaar, Raaw," Strong Jon was making contact and telling the underworld about it. He was that nutria's Grimm Reaper.

Soon the sound subsided into a quieter "Rgh, Rgh Rgh" Coming in a rhythm of about one per second. Not too long a wait and Leroy reached into the hole and pulled the dog by the hind legs out with a nutria in it's mouth.

"That nuut's as floppy as a flat inner-tube!" Robert said surprised.

"More like a sack of water I'd say," Robert senior said.

The nutria looked like it was nothing but porridge held together by a furry sack. Leroy handed it to Robert.

"I don't feel a single bone in tact!" Robert said with wide, disbelieving eyes.

"Now you see why we call him Jon the Strong," Hank said. "That's what they call a draw dog back in England. The dog helps make the work lighter when used properly."

Next up was Jackson. He was a pain in the ass, obedience wise, but Robert knew that Jackson would come through and find for them. When he let Jackson loose, he found even ahead of the Sassy bitch. That impressed all the men.

He located inside a drain underneath a farm road. Jackson was no weakling. He liked the kill as much as the find. He didn't wait for any draw dog to arrive and help him. He set his teeth and made the defender of the drain cry. It doesn't take long for a nutria to die, but it seemed Jackson was not finishing in there.

The men tried to look into the culvert but only saw darkness.

85

"I think he finished one and is on another," William said.

"Can your dogs work together fine?" asked Leroy.

"Yes, they can," Robert informed him.

"Well, it's frowned upon by the men who make all the rules, but that dog might need help down there. You might want to go ahead and let another dog off the lead."

Robert felt like this was a good time to let Grit show how tough he was. He sent him in and he barreled down the pipe screaming for action.

Curtis was standing at the other side of the road listening where it was less crowded. The entrance to the pipe from that side was covered with reeds. Curt couldn't see into the pipe but could hear fine. He was tuned into the noise when Grit shot down the pipe.

"Raaawaar," yelled Grit.

The mighty war cry of the little dog scared the hell out of a nutria and it shot out of the reeds straight at Curtis, who was taken by total surprise. He swung the hatchet he held for cutting roots with and met the nutria square between the eyes with it. The hatchet sunk deep through the skull. Dallas, who had been on the road watching both sides, couldn't stop laughing. It had taken him by surprise as well.

Curtis slowly held up the nutria stuck to his hatchet. He was in a state of surprise.

"I didn't think," Curtis said, still not believing his reflexes. "I just saw that thing lunging toward me, so I swung at it!"

Dallas was still laughing, "You'd like to have thought it was coming for your manhood, the way your eyes popped out when it bolted. Priceless."

"Hey folks! The dogs are still working," Robert reminded the gang to keep some level of focus.

Grit and Jackson were both full on fighting. The ruckus in that pipe was enough to raise Cain.

"That's got to be at least three big nutria that were in that tube. I killed one, Jackson had to have killed that first and Grit and Jackson are still fighting something." Curtis was trying to fathom why it was taking so long for the dogs to finish their job in the drain. The only possible explanation was that their were more than one nutria in the culvert.

"I think there are more than just one still alive in there," Hank chimed in. "Two dogs on one nutria wouldn't take this long."

"I can send Jon the Strong in," offered Leroy.

"That's playing a dangerous game," Hank said, reluctant to mix the dog with unknown dogs. "Jon could start a fight and there's no digging the dogs out. That could end in a dead dog."

"It could end in a dead dog with a gang of nutria beating on them," Leroy retorted.

Hank wasn't happy with the idea. "I wouldn't do it. But that's just my two cents."

"It's up to you Robert," Leroy said. "I don't need to let him go, but he'd make short work of trouble in there."

Robert hadn't had any problems with terriers fighting before. The choice was easy for him. "Let him loose."

Dallas handed Curtis a .22 rifle to shoot any bolters. "Just don't go trigger happy and shoot a dog." Dallas was a little worried about that boy's reflexive killing. He didn't know Curt had shot nearly as much as he had. Curt took gun safety very seriously. He would not be flippant with it. He had plenty of experience shooting over dogs as well. Nothing new for Curtis.

When Jon the Strong went into the culvert, he scared out three nutria to Curtis who quickly shot the bunch. But Jon the Strong was not so keen on nutria as he was the dogs blocking the way. A fight ensued.

"Wo!" Said Robert the younger, "Jon sure livened things up in there. He's probably killing the heck out of those things."

"That's not game he's fighting son! He's got another dog." William informed his son of what the younger Robert had no experience.

"Damn!" Hank yelled, getting down onto his hands and knees. "I knew this shit would happen!. . . Knock that shit off!" he yelled at the top of his lungs. "Knock it off you damned son of a bitch!"

It didn't sound pretty down in that dark metal pipe. One of the dogs was getting a beating and it sure as heck wasn't Jon the Strong. Neither Jackson nor Grit could have stood up to him. Both of them, maybe, but a nutria was still moaning, meaning one of the dogs was working and the other was being worked.

"Oh man!" Robert put his hands on his head and spun on his heel, "I should have listened to Hank. I didn't expect a dog to choose to fight another dog when game was there."

Grit was squealing like a whipped puppy. It was not a good situation. But the sounds were getting closer. Jon was drawing Grit out, luckily before killing him. Soon Jon's rump could be seen. He was pulled out by the tail with Grit, yelping, in his mouth.

Hank was quickly on the scene with a breaking stick. "I always keep one of these in my pocket. You never know when you're gonna need one. These aren't just for fighting dogs. Shit happens and you gotta be ready."

He broke Jon's grip on Grit. Leroy leashed the dog up.

"I'm so sorry Robert. I thought like you, that he'd go for the game not the dogs. I really should have known better and not talked you into letting me drop him."

"That's alright." Robert was an understanding sort. "By the look of it, Grit really needed to get out of the fray. He's worse off than I've ever seen a dog."

It was true. Grit was torn to pieces and not by Jon. Jackson finished off the remaining stragglers in the culvert. All accounted for there had been seven nutria in that pipe and they had made mince meat of Jackson and Grit. The dog's shoulders and faces had gashes all over them and both dogs had tattered skin covering their jaws.

"That is definitely a mess," Hank agreed. "Let's get those dogs doctored. They've done enough work for the month, let alone today."

Jackson and Grit were doctored on the spot using Hank's field kit. He poured salt water over the
wounds to clean them of sand, mud and blood. He then
poured iodine on the wounds and sewed them shut with
fishing line and a needle. He had obviously done these
field dressings many times. He then gave the dogs fatty
hamburger meat for energy to recover.

"Our day would be finished, but we haven't yet
got the group of nutria the farmer was really wanting us
here for today." Leroy was a bit bashful in bringing this
up as it was evident Grit and Jackson needed rest. "You
all can go home, if you like."

Jackson and Grit had done well but Lee was the
best dog of the bunch and Robert wanted to let the dog
shine at what he did best, nutria underground. Lee was
smaller than either Jackson or Grit but he had a neck as
big as his chest and strength to back it up underneath
his thick coat of red wire.

"No, Lee still hasn't seen his fair share today,"
Robert said.

Robert senior knew his son would be disappointed to miss the rest of the hunt, so he took the
mantle of responsibility.

"I'll take Jackson and Grit back to the trucks.
No sense in them being left out here to shiver while

they're wounded. I'll just meet y'all when you get back from hunting."

Nobody needed to be convinced. With the dogs leashed, the group set off to the far end of a 40 acre plot. In the corner of the field was a large tree with exposed roots reaching as far as it's branches into the field and into a gravelly stream bed. Underneath the tree was hollow earth. A group of nutria had dug under the tree for what must have been years.

"This is a big sette," Hank said. "We can send in Lee and see what he's made of."

That sounded good to Robert. He let Lee loose. Lee could smell game and ran around swiftly with his head to the ground. He found a hole at the topside base of the giant tree. He stuck his head in the hole first. Lee was a brave dog but always went to ground with a level of caution. His tail went straight and quivered with excitement. Something was definitely home. He proceeded into the darkness beneath the earth.

It was not long till he could be heard baying right beneath where Robert had released him. He bayed only a few times then made contact.

"This is going to be a son of a bitch!" Hank swore.

Roots were never an easy matter but this gang of nutria were going to undermine the bank causing the loss of valuable soil. They had to be exterminated. Hank liked the challenge and so did the boys.

Robert quickly started digging.

"Wait a minute," Leroy told him. "Sometimes the game will move. Just give it some time to settle. That is a rangy place down there and there's a chance Lee may not quite be able to hold the game."

Robert listened and obeyed but he had undying faith in Lee that once contact was made, he wouldn't be losing his grip. On a coon he might need some time to wrestle it down but nutria were no match for Lee. Once he got a hold of a nuut, it was as good as dead. Lee had never found a nutria he couldn't kill.

"I'd say he's settled," Said Hank, who was listening to Lee work from the entrances at the bottom of the bank.

"It sounds to be about six feet down," Leroy said.

The boys looked at each other uneasily. Six feet wasn't what they bargained for.

Robert put metal to soil and lifted the sod out in several large pieces to put back on top when the dig was finished. It was an ordeal of digging and hacking roots with the hatchet. At about two feet they broke through to a giant cavern with a ceiling suspended by roots. It was a nutria hall fit for a nutria king. It really was a spacious den. But Lee was further still down into the ground.

"Let me get in there boys." Leroy pushed his way into position with a pair of post-hole diggers and got to work. "I figure we'd have to really open a gaping hole to get down deeper with the shovel. I don't want to ruin this whole place."

He dug a narrow hole with the diggers for about two more feet and opened right on top of the action. Leroy looked at Robert, "It's your dog. You do the honors."

Robert had to get into the hole and lay down to reach the rest of the way. He could see the brown back of the dirty dog. He scruffed the fur in his hand and pulled. It was no dog but a live nutria.

"Whoa!" he yelled throwing it up on the bank.

The nutria hit the grass and bared it's orange teeth to the gang of men and dogs standing around. That was foolish. It would have been smart to run. Strong Jon was on it in a flash and had it put down in no time. It was a big nutria, probably 22 pounds but

Jon the Strong took no thought of a thing's size. It was easy work in the day of that dog.

Everyone was laughing. Dallas chuckled and nudged Robert with his boot, "Those big teeth got a little close for comfort did they?!"

"I could have sworn that was the dog." Robert stood up for himself, but he was already blushing.

"Well, the dog is still in there. He hasn't come out on his own." Leroy was wanting work to commence.

Robert reached down again, feeling safe now that the nutria was out. He put his hand in and felt fur. It was limp and dead. He pulled out another large nutria, dead as a door nail. But Lee wasn't present. It was quiet beneath the roots of the tree.

Looking out of the hole Robert spoke to the onlookers, "Lee's not here. He must be going out a different way. He was here when I pulled that nutria out."

"I hear him breathing down here," Hank yelled over the bank. He was crouching in the shallow water beneath the tree with his head stuck up a hole.

Lee soon came out ass-forwards drawing another sizable and dead nutria.

"Dang boy!" Hank said handing Lee up the bank to Curt, "I'd say you've got yourself a damn fine dog in this Lee."

Robert knew it and Curt felt pride in the dog as well, it was practically his dog too; he hunted with Lee so much.

Hank sent Cindy through and she pushed another nutria into the cavern where she killed it and left it just out of reach. They couldn't get Strong Jon to pull it out without it picking a fight with him first. Considering it was dead, Jon didn't have much interest in it.

"Ah hell," Hank said, brushing hair back from his face, "Leave that bastard as a warning to Nutrian-Kind to never come back."

They made the long walk back to the trucks with pride, carrying their catches for the day with them and the dogs plodding alongside tiredly.

Dallas spoke up during a silence, "I sure like your dogs Robert. They were a lot tougher than you gave them credit."

Robert knew how to take a compliment. "Thank you", he said.

"I would like to have dogs like that someday myself," Dallas went on. "I liked that Jackson dog. he put on quite the show."

"If you like him that much, he's yours," Robert said.

Curtis couldn't believe his ears. He stopped walking and gaped at Robert. "But that's one of our lead dogs!"

"I know," Robert replied, "but he's not in the breeding program and never will be and Lee's got pups coming up for next year's hunting dogs and Grit's gonna be just as good and better than Jackson. So, yeah. . . Dallas you can have Ol' Jackson."

"Wow. That is really generous. Are you sure? He looked like your best dog today." Dallas was already bragging the dog up before he even owned him.

"Ha. No. No dog can beat Lee. You just didn't have your eyes screwed in right today," Robert said. He was actually a bit insulted anyone would think his second best dog did better than Lee. There is a pride in one's favorite dog that shouldn't be spoken against. "I'm sure I won't need the dog and you'll like him better than I will. That dog's nuttier'n squirrel shit."

"Alright. I guess I'll thank you then."

"Yeah, no problem. Just let him heal with me for a while then come get him."

They arrived back at the trucks near the falling of darkness. They had parked near an old farmstead. They told the tale of the feats of Lee under the hollow tree to William and had a renewing of making fun of

Robert for grabbing the live nutria unawares. They laughed about Curtis and his Indian-Warrior hatchet chop.

Hank went back behind a truck to check himself for ticks. He got stark naked with nothing but his long pony tail covering his backside. Just as he was doing so, some women came out of the farmhouse, saw a tattooed, long haired man naked in the drive, blushed, maybe shuddered a little bit and rushed back inside.

Hank dressed and came back around to where the men were all talking.

"What were those women in such a tissy about?" Curtis asked.

"It's the long hair, boy," Hank said grinning. He winked at Robert, who had quite long hair for a boy of the time as well. "They just can't control their animal instinct when they see a man with locks."

"A thousand women can't be wrong, Hank!" William chimed in. He took every opportunity he could to say that phrase.

8. Parting Is Sorrow

Jackson was not fully healed when Dallas came to pick him up. Robert felt the dog had healed enough to be cared for by an amateur, so he let him go. They hunted and had a good day out with all the dogs. Grit really shone that day. Dallas offered Robert any sum of money to buy Grit but Robert wouldn't consider it, not even for a month's wage. Some dogs are irreplaceable. Robert may have been generous with Jackson but he felt another like Grit wouldn't be coming along anytime soon. He would come to feel that another better than Grit may not have existed.

Lee and Grit were really the best dogs left. Robert's father had some terriers but Robert hated them. He felt they were too soft and all of them seemed to need another dog working beside them or they were useless. While Grit, Lee and Coallie were often worked together, they did not need each other. They could all do fine on their own. Coallie was problematic at times, because she did not range far to search but she had her uses.

Some time passed after Jackson left. Grit came into his own and soon was even outdoing Lee in many areas. Though, Lee was still the best earth dog of the two. Grit would never quite equal Lee there. Robert turned 17 and spent a lot of time hunting the hounds. Grit and Lee were brought along for coon or grey fox in the rocks. Grit was never a useful dog for grey fox in the rocks. He was too big for the small cracks the foxes sought for refuge. Lee had a son that was used for this more often than any of the other dogs. He was called Horsefly. His career was not long, however. He was used mainly because nobody valued him as a great dog. The rocks were a dangerous spot to put a dog and the young men didn't care to put their favorite dogs in after a fox.

One hot summer day Robert and Curtis went with Lee and Grit just to let the dogs run. They drove along a farm drive with the dogs running along the oak hill searching for game. The grass was high and dry along the road. All the weeds and thistles were dry. The dogs' coats soon filled with burs, seeds and thistle pricks. It really was too warm to be running the dogs but they planned to run them down to the river where they could cool off.

Robert pulled his truck up to a closed gate and shut off the truck to listen. He hadn't seen the dogs for a while and needed to find out what they were doing before proceeding. He could hear, not far up the hill, some barking.

He and Curtis ran up the hill. The hill was covered in oak and madrone trees. The ground under the oaks grew no grass as the leaves fell and smothered the understory vegetation. The hard cracked clay under the leaves was ruddy yellow. Up the hill, under an oak tree, Lee had fit down a tight hole in the roots. Grit couldn't fit but was trying to squeeze through. Robert ran back and got the tools, while Curtis held Grit. He brought up a hand saw and small shovel that was good for digging while on one's knees.

The hole was just a skunk hole. It was a tight squeeze. Lee couldn't be heard anymore but they knew he was close. Skunk holes rarely went deep and were often just a straight pipe from four to six feet in length. Robert would just trench under the tree toward Lee.

It took only five minutes to dig to where Lee could be reached. But Lee wasn't moving. Robert tried pulling on Lee to get him out of the hole but Robert couldn't budge him. Lee was caught on something and it had cut off the dog's air supply.

Robert kicked into high gear. Lee was his most loved dog. Truly, Lee was Robert's father's dog but Robert worshiped him as the end all of terriers. There was no sweeter a dog and no more clever a worker. Lee was attached to Robert by the soul. To lose him would be devastating to the young man.

He continued to dig and came to the roots that had blocked Lee's forward movement and trapped him. Lee's collar had snagged on a root he had bitten off in order to pass. He had made a barb of it and it hooked his collar. He couldn't back out and he couldn't pass forward through the roots. He had squeezed his chest too tight and the collar strangled him.

Robert cut away furiously at the roots. He wouldn't let Lee die like this. He had gotten to him as fast as possible. He'd done all he could do but Lee was removed from the hole limp. Robert wasn't giving up so easily. He lifted Lee up and blew into his nostrils, filling Lee's lungs with air.

The dog sputtered to life. Relief.

Robert, still on his knees, lifted his head to the sky, "Thank God." He laughed, not because he thought it was comical. It was a laugh of pure relief, a release from the burden of grief. "Thank God," Robert said again.

Curtis had stood quietly watching. There had not been room for him to help and he knew there were no words that would have consoled his friend in those moments that had passed just before.

They peaked down the hole to see a possum just a foot ahead of where Lee was caught in the roots.

"What a little punk!" Curtis said, "To think we almost lost the best dog we've got to a stinky possum. That's hardly a dignified death."

"A working death is better than going out slowly, I'd say, even if it's a possum." Robert, having thought just minutes ago that Lee was dying over that possum, felt he needed to defend his dog's willingness to sacrifice itself.

They rested under the shade of the oak trees for a while. The heat was not enjoyable.

Lee seemed refreshed and ready to move again, so the gang picked up and moved toward the truck. The river was next on the trestle-board. It was just down the drive a little further, through a gate. Robert didn't even bother putting the dogs in the pickup bed. They could run there. He saw Grit running up ahead toward the river and figured Lee was ahead of him.

Curtis opened the gate and waved Robert through. As soon as the truck started moving, horror struck on Curtis' face. Yelps were heard sharply, even over the rock 'n' roll playing on the radio. Robert could see Lee running frantically down the gravel drive yelping every breath.

"What happened?" Robert asked.

"You ran him over!"

"Why didn't you tell me he was there!"

"I didn't see him there."

"Damn!" Cursed Robert, "I thought he was up ahead with Grit."

Robert got out of the truck and ran down the drive after Lee. Curtis was right beside him running.

"I guess him running so fast is a good sign," Robert said hopefully.

"I guess." Curtis tried to be optimistic. The fact was that Lee was such a little dog, the truck rolling over him could do a lot of damage.

They found Lee lying under a rhododendron, working to breathe. There was no fixing him. Robert's heart dropped as he got on his hands and knees to call Lee out of the bush. Lee couldn't even pick his head up.

"Lee," Robert whispered, trying to choke back tears. "Come on Lee."

Lee didn't move but to breathe hoarse breaths. Robert crawled into the bushes to be with his dog. A long moan came from deep inside Robert's turning stomach. Lee had coughed up a pool of frothy blood. His lungs had been punctured.

Robert laid in the sticks and leaves with his beloved dog and held him to his face. He moaned with grief, he shuttered and cried for the little warrior who had moments before been playfully trotting alongside him in the forest.

Curtis sat down outside the bush and tried to comfort Robert quietly. He said nothing, only put his hand on Robert's leg to let him know he shared the sorrow of parting love with him.

Robert laid there long after Lee's last breath. The farmer who owned the property came walking down the road and saw Robert crying. He was a kind Austrian man who had fought in World War II as a fighter pilot. As strong minded of a man as he was, he was the kindest Robert had ever known.

"What is wrong my dear boy?" Came the farmer's soft voice. Robert moved to reveal Lee's dead body. "Aaah." sighed Franz. He got on his knees and held Robert. He had known Robert since Robert was an infant. "Look at me," Franz said. Robert looked. "We all have great sorrows in our life. Death comes to every-thing we love. I know your sadness." Franz wiped the tears from Robert's face and hugged him. His hands were softer than doe-skin gloves. Robert would always remember how soft and kind those hands were.

It fell dark before the boys left for home. Curtis gathered up Grit and tied him in the back of the truck.

Robert drove home with Lee draped across his knees. He would finally stop crying only to start again as soon as tears had replenished.

They arrived home where William and Robert's mother met them in the driveway. They had seen Robert get out of the car, with Lee limp in his arms. Lee was also William's favorite dog. He did not cry but he was distraught. Robert's mother hugged him. There is no real conciliation for the sadness following the loss of loved life, whether human or animal.

Robert grabbed a shovel and buried Lee beneath a crooked trunked black walnut tree on the family farm. The spot is still marked by that leaning tree. It will al-ways be sacred.

Robert couldn't fathom the saying, "Parting is such sweet sorrow." For him there was nothing sweet. For him, parting was sorrow.

9. The Weeks After

The weeks after Lee's death were empty for Robert. He didn't hunt the other dogs. He contemplated never hunting again. Sometimes friends act like a leg on a chair. If one is missing, the whole chair falls. Lee was the leg on a chair for Robert. When he was removed, Robert hit the ground.

Robert would take the dogs out to run but didn't take them hunting. William was in the terriers for Robert the younger's sake. Once he saw that Robert would be leaving home soon and that he loved only Grit, he was done with terriers and returned to his true loves, pigeons, sheep and plants. Eventually, he sold and traded what dogs he could. Only Grit remained. Robert gave Coallie to a friend from school who wanted her to help with his hound pack. Grit was another leg on the chair. And though Robert hadn't known it, so was Jackson. With one leg of his chair, all he could do was let it lie there.

Robert eventually hunted again with his friends. Grit wasn't catching anything. Several nights Robert hunted until the early morning hours with Curtis and Jon. Their hounds were treeing and carrying on business as usual but Grit moped along at Robert's heels. His spirit for hunting had left him as soon as Lee's spirit left it's body.

Robert gave Grit one last chance after many attempts to get his hunting spirit on fire again. He brought him to a spot he knew would have nutria. In a blueberry field, a marsh 30 yards wide and a mile long ran through the middle. Tall grass and cat-tails grew all along the marsh. Usually, Robert would drop the dogs there and catch a load of nutria. But he needed to check Grit's drive with an easy job. There were drains underneath a road where Robert could check with a light whether nutria were in the pipes or not. He left Grit in the truck and checked each pipe with his light. There was a pipe with a few small nutria in it; nothing Grit couldn't handle by himself. All Grit would have to do is walk down the pipe and work the game, either scaring it out the other side or fighting and conquering the game.

It would not have been hard for him in his normal mental state.

Robert went back to the truck. He released Grit to run free and walked toward the pipe with the nutria in it. He called Grit and sent him down the pipe. The dog entered without hesitation. He was still obedient, whether his drive for hunting was gone or not. Grit went down the pipe, barked twice, turned around and came back out.

"Go on Grit," Robert said excitedly, trying to get him to do what came naturally. "Get 'em Grit. Go on, Get 'em!"

Grit made a movement like he considered going for it but then went and sat on the road looking at Robert.

Robert couldn't control his emotions. Only months before, his hunting dogs were everything to him. Now it seemed as if everything he loved had slipped from him. He loved Grit but Grit wasn't acting like himself. He mirrored Robert. The sad state of both man and dog were apparent to anyone.

Robert yelled at Grit, "Get in there and do your damn job!"

Grit cowered at his master's rage.

"Don't cower you stupid dog! Do your job!"

He went toward Grit but Grit ran away, tail tucked. Robert picked up a rock and threw it at his dog.

"Son of a bitch!" Robert cried. It came time for him to realize Grit had more emotion than some would wish to believe a dog capable of. Grit's chair had also been pulled out from under him.

Some dogs are raised in a lonely fashion. For dogs like that, there never was a pack beyond their master. But Grit was not such a dog. He relied on his pack-members. Now that Jackson, Lee and Coallie were gone, Grit did not care much for his old enjoyments. He needed healing time. And so did Robert.

∘ ∘ ∘

A couple months passed. Robert had spent the day with Grit at the river, swimming and fishing. He walked home slowly, strolling through the warm walnut groves. Two years later when he would return home, those trees would not be there. He did not know this at the time, but he appreciated the lovely trees none-the-less. He cut across fields and along berry lines to get home, eating blackberries with Grit and enjoying what he could of the simple life he knew the military would take from him. He was not depressed any longer concerning Lee. Though, he'd always remember the dog with a feeling of nostalgia and love. He chuckled and kicked rocks with lighthearted flicks of his feet while he walked and thought about the funny antics of that little dog.

Robert was free-spirited, shirtless and stained brown with dust when he arrived home. When Robert entered the house it was full of girls. There was a party of his sister's dancing friends there. At the head of the kitchen table stood a stunning blonde. Robert was for a moment speechless, until he recognized his state of nakedness and uncleanness in the presence of this new found beauty. Robert was no man to show his fear. He wore his dust and ragged cut off jeans like he was clothed in gold. He was lean, tall and strong from ranch work and the sun had turned his hair to a coppery sheen.

All the girls, except the blonde, knew Robert when he walked in. They all smiled and laughed, teasing him for his get-up, calling him "Huckleberry" and "Hillbilly".

"Now, now girls," Robert said, holding his arms up in a sign of surrender. He closed his eyes to make it all the more dramatic. "I am not a hillbilly!"

"Could have fooled us!" One of the girls teased.

Robert pointed at the girl who mocked him and raised an eyebrow, as if he was an authority pointing the shaming finger at her to quiet down.

"I am not a hillbilly and I will tell you why," Robert continued. "I am a mountain-billy."

"A what?" The girls all laughed; all except the new girl.

"What is the difference then?" she asked.

"Yes please shower us with your wisdom, Mountain Man," another joked. All the while the beautiful blonde looked bored.

"You see, a hillbilly can't read," Robert stated matter-of-factly, "and I," he pretended humility and bowed to the girls seated and standing around the table, "know how to read."

Robert could not get the blonde girl to laugh all night. It drove him mad. Eventually, he separated himself from the group to clean up and change clothing. He did not go into the kitchen or living room again that night, *to make a fool of myself,* he thought. Though, Robert did learn her name. . . Hero.

10. Departure

September came. When Autumn fell, it was time for Robert to leave.

"I do not mean to be heartless," said Robert's father, "but I agreed to keep Grit, only if he hunted. He hasn't hunted in months now."

Robert understood. This was not unexpected. His father had never kept anything on the property that he didn't like for his own uses. Grit had outlasted any dog or animal of any sort that wasn't part of William's personal plans. Now that Robert was leaving indefinitely, his father would not have use for Grit. This did not stop Robert from feeling miserable. He went out to the kennels, empty of terriers or hounds, and kicked a wooden post. Leaning against the kennels Robert cried. His life was bleak at that time. He would be leaving everything behind. Moving forward was frightening.

Normally, Grit would have gone to a friend. But Grit was no longer his normal self. Grit would not hunt. Therefore, none of Robert's friends would keep him either.

When Dallas heard Robert was leaving, he begged for Grit. Robert had no reason to not give the man the dog. Though he warned Dallas, "Grit doesn't work," but Dallas did not care. Dallas was after the lineage of dogs Grit came from; strong workers.

Dallas had recently obtained a cousin to Grit. As far as Robert was concerned, she was trash. Robert hated to think Grit would be used to produce a rubbish heap of worthless terriers, but he wanted to have him near enough to hear about. The only other hunters who wanted him were too far removed for Robert to let him go to them.

"I bet I can get him hunting. Who knows," Dallas said. "Maybe you ruined him."

Robert was too young to ever be insulted by Dallas' rude remarks but such remarks came often. *Maybe I did ruin him.* Robert thought. It is common for an amateur terrierman to start his dogs too young and ruin them on game too hard for them. Robert was not so proud that he didn't contemplate the possibility that he had ruined Grit.

Robert carried Grit to Dallas' truck. "Old buddy, I hope we meet again." He scratched the terrier's head and looked him over. Robert's mother came outside with a camera and asked Robert to hold Grit for a picture. He posed with Grit held under his arm. Robert kept that picture through his service in the military and looked at it everyday. As much as he missed his family, he missed the dogs.

Dallas packed off with the last vestige of that glorious era in Robert's life. Truly, the trio of Lee, Grit and Jackson would never be bettered. And Dallas would never respect the value of the gifts he received. Grit and Jackson had been cursed to a life of maltreatment and boredom.

After Dallas drove away with Grit, Robert sat in the walnut tree under-which Lee was buried. He thought of his beloved dogs, releasing each one from his emotions the best he could. It was time for another chapter in his life; a chapter without dogs.

He left shortly thereafter and was quickly sent out on duty. His years away were full of longing for the green valleys and river bottoms of his home. But it was not he who fared so poorly. Grit had his own trials. Robert went by choice, but Grit had no power over the direction of his life, except to conquer whatever was put before him.

11. The Miserables

Robert was gone, as far as Grit could tell, forever. When he last saw Robert was when Robert put him in Dallas' dog-box. He thought at the time that he was going on a hunt. Instead, he was brought to Dallas' home.

Dallas was a man of appearances. He worried about image rather than practice. His kennels were immaculate. He had runs built off of a lovely wooden building. Each run had a hole connected to the building where the dogs could enter the wooden building and stay warm. What the kennels were all missing however, were dividers to keep the dogs from getting at each other through the bars.

Dallas kept a number of terriers there that he collected in his short time keeping dogs. They were all "bred well" or had been great workers for somebody else. He had not raised a single one of the dogs himself. As great as the breeding he had or the workers he had obtained, none of the dogs looked as if they'd seen work since the day he had obtained them. Grit recognized Jackson by smell, as he was walked to his own kennel. Grit's kennel was next to a dog named Garvey. Garvey was no wimpy looking dog and a wiseman would have kept him well separated from other dogs. His face was pocked white where wounds had once been and the toes on one foot were missing where they'd been chewed off by a raccoon he had been stuck with inside the walls of an abandoned house. The issue wasn't that he was stuck with the raccoon, so much as he wouldn't leave his job. Garvey was a veteran worth having in any hunter's yard. But Dallas wasn't really a hunter. He didn't have business owning a working dog of that caliber.

Aside from Jackson, Garvey and Grit, Dallas' dogs were good looking dogs of various lines that looked good but hadn't done a day of hard work. All had been tried and failed at being workers; young dogs that Dallas insisted he could get working, despite much better dogmen having given the dogs ample chances. Dallas' wife liked to show dogs and that was really what those terriers were there for. They wanted show dogs they could claim were workers. That was the plan for

Grit and his pups. Grit wasn't yet truly marked by the amount of work he'd done. He still retained clean lines and the majority of his teeth. Jackson and Garvey would never make show dogs for Dallas and his wife in the sense of winning ribbons, but they were show dogs in the sense that Dallas would show them to people and brag about what workers they were, as attested to by their scars. They weren't going to be put to ground anytime soon, at least not by Dallas. Poor Jackson had already grown plump and his nails long from being kept in the prison of a fancy kennel. Some dogs live on chains, others in kennels that cost thousands of dollars to build, some inside mansions with their owners. Much of the time, its that old dog on the end of a chain that gets more freedom than all the rest. His master may not have the money to give that dog a fancy lifestyle but the dog gets set loose to do the work it loves day after day, living to a ripe age doing what it loves to do. Dallas' dogs were no more than miserable inmates in fancy cages.

Grit hardly settled in long before trouble started for him. Garvey left Jackson alone for the most part, because his food bowl was attached to the side of the kennel farthest away from Garvey. But Grit's food bowl was attached onto the bars between he and Garvey.

For weeks, when feeding time came, Grit slunk back into his shelter. While he was trying to eat, Garvey would growl and lunge at Grit through the bars. Grit was not one to pick a fight nor to retaliate aggression without much harassment. Thus, he tried to avoid Garvey as much as possible.

If the dogs were let loose in the yard, Garvey would nip and growl at Grit. Grit being the younger, less dominant dog, he took his lashes. Eventually, the day came he could take it no more. Garvey attacked at him through the bars of the kennel. Normally, Grit let Garvey have his way but not this day. Grit made no noise about it, he simply went into attack mode. He reached his head under the kennel divider where Garvey was snapping and snarling and grabbed the other dog by the side of its face. Teeth met teeth along each dogs top jaws. They laid on their sides to do battle. There was no way to gain dominance in this fight. The fight was to the pain. One had to give up from pain, die of blood loss, or be separated by a human. Garvey was the bigger dog, but this gave him no advantage. His head appeared stronger but it took damage much more readily than Grit's. Appearance doesn't mean much.

Grit bore in with his teeth. They scraped along Garvey's pallet, grinding the dog's nasal cavities into hamburger. Grit twisted and shook to set his teeth deeper. His teeth got into the roots of Garvey's and pried them from their sockets. It was mere flesh and lips holding the upper teeth in Garvey's mouth. The fight lasted well over an hour. Anytime the dog's lost hold of each other, they fought through the fence, bashing their faces against the mesh.

Dallas returned home from work and heard the raucous in his kennels. All the dogs were going mad. He ran through the gate and saw the cement pad in Grit and Garvey's kennels stained with drying blood. The dogs were still in grips with one another. He rushed into Garvey's kennel and pried the dogs' mouths apart. Both dogs' faces were tattered. Garvey had gotten the worst of it. Grit's top lip was split all the way to his nose and his nose was ground up badly. His left top canine had been broken as well.

Garvey was a wreck compared to Grit. Over the next week, meat sloughed off Garvey's face. Many of his teeth fell out on one side and the infection took half of his nose. The dog looked monstrous. This only increased Garvey's value in Dallas' mind but he began to hate Grit that day. He blamed Grit for the fight.

Dallas began advertising Garvey as "Garvey-Two-Face" and pretended his wounds were from hard work. The Garvey dog became quite popular and people hearing of him would travel far to breed their favorite bitches to him. Dallas made more profit off of that mangled dog than any of his flashy looking show dogs. Not that Garvey hadn't been a decent worker at one time, but the dog didn't deserve the fame it received as a stud. Nor did Dallas deserve the reputation he garnered as the breeder of fine dogs. Garvey had not been produced by Dallas and Dallas wouldn't have known how to produce another like him.

Jackson was the real gem in that kennel, but he went unnoticed for the most part. He grew fatter every day and his nails grew longer. Until one day a man came by Dallas' place and wanted to see the magnificent "Garvey-Two-Face" work. Dallas was apprehensive, but he conceded, after much harassment from the local terriermen, who were catching on to the fact that he never actually hunted.

The man who came to harass Dallas into putting actions to words was a hillbilly named Timmy Waler. Timmy was a gruff sort. He had a full-Manchu mustache, the bottoms of which were stained yellow brown from chewing tobacco. His voice was deep and gravelly. When he pulled up to Dallas' house the day of the hunt, he had a fat cigar in his mouth and was drunk as usual. Along with him came his drinking buddy. They were like two alcohol soaked worms from the bottom of a tequila bottle. His friend was Morton Twist; an ugly old sheep-farmer with a face and head shaved as clean as Elmer Fudd's. His eyes were always squinted wherever he went and he spoke with an accent only heard in very remote western hill communities. It was high-pitched and nasally.

Dallas took the two of them back to his kennels to show them Garvey-Two-Face.

"Fine looking dog, that," said Timmy, when he saw Garvey.

"Dat don't mean shit!" spat out ugly old Morton. "All I hea' is 'Two-Face, Two-Face Dis, Two-Face Dat'. Damsumbitch! Horse Shit!" He looked at Garvey with squinty eyes. "Let's see what dis damsumbitch can do f'real. Hell, d'mess on dat dog's face could be from anyt'ing!"

"He's the best dog in these parts and I'd bet even America. There may not be a better dog in the world!" said Dallas. Garvey wasn't bad but Jackson was thrice the dog Garvey ever had or would've been in any man's care. If Dallas had ever actually worked the dogs enough to compare them, he would have known right away.

On the way out the men saw Jackson.

"Looky-he'e," Morton nudged Timmy.

"Ugh-huh," graveled Timmy's agreement. The two stood and stared at Jackson. Timmy Waler looked at Dallas and pointed back at Jackson. He spoke with the cigar in his mouth. "Look here at this dog. He's too fat to roll out of his box, but here he is, running on his little stick legs like he's gonna go huntin'. What the hell? You never let this dog out or somethin' Dallas?" He was fat and out of shape. Well, as Twist spat out, "Dat don't mean shit!" The dog still had heart, if only the right man had him.

Dallas clenched his jaw and rolled his eyes. These fellas, he knew, would be out spreading the word that he was too chicken to hunt, if he didn't go with them that day.

"I don't have anything to prove to anybody," Dallas said. "I know I've got the best dogs anybody's got and Garvey'll prove that today!"

Timmy took the soggy cigar out of his mouth and stared at Dallas for a while, then snorted, "Whatever you say princess."

Dallas would've liked to trounce those two but he didn't have the balls for it.

"Wha'd'at kennel der on it's lonesome? Sum po' sumbitch dat nebber getta go hunt?" It wasn't easy for anyone to understand what Morton Twist said, but his gestures helped make it clear. He pointed and swaggered over to where Grit was kept alone, away from the other dogs.

Grit was still young and fresh but his battle with Garvey had made him look hard and used.

"What's this dog?" Timmy asked.

"That's Grit," Dallas said. "He's one special dog. I wouldn't let him go for any amount of money. Great dog." Dallas was so full of shit, it was a wonder his breath didn't knock out the two drinking worms, Waler and Twist.

"Collar that dog up then!" growled Timmy.

"Oh no. Garvey and he don't get along. Another time maybe." Dallas knew he couldn't back up his bullshit when it came to Grit. He had taken Grit on purely for the sake of bragging, not doing.

"Hell no!" Timmy said, "We didn't drive all this way to hear stories and bullshit. You're gonna show us some dog work. We've heard 'nough of your stupid ass tales. Time for the shovel to meet the earth. Hear me? You been prancing around like the princess of terriers, now's'en you show us what all the talk's about."

If Dallas were a tougher man, he would have told those two to bugger off. But he wasn't a tougher man. In his own way he'd been as big an asshole to Robert as these two were being to him. It was his turn to take ridicule. The difference was, Waler and Twist weren't passive aggressive. They were just plain aggressive. Not much different from that ugly Garvey dog.

Dallas took Grit out of the kennel and put him into the box. Luckily, there were two compartments in his dog box or they wouldn't have made it to the hunt without a fight.

"So, where are we going?" Dallas asked the two gruff men who got into his truck with him.

"Hell if I know!" scoffed Tim.

Dallas had been hoping that those two would suggest a good place to hunt. Dallas had no places of his own. He didn't want to admit that of course, so he drove them to a spot that he knew Robert and Curt frequented, a slough of about one mile in length. To one side of the slough were marshy fields, sometimes drained for alfalfa. To the other side was a thin strip of blackberries running along the waterside. The water there was muddy, full of algae and water-loving plants. The plants grew so thick over the water that a small man could be held by them, only sinking about two feet into the muddy water. There were muddy slides into the water, coming from all directions. These indicated where nutria traveled daily.

"Dis' a damn nice spot," said the fuddish looking Morton.

"Sure is," agreed Tim. "It'd be sure disappointing, if your dogs fail in a place like this, game everywhere about."

"Yes," Dallas nodded his head, "I save this spot for when I've got people wanting to see the dogs work." Dallas hadn't actually ever been there himself, he just knew these were Robert's stomping grounds. Robert had every permission in the area.

The men let both dogs loose at the same time. The tradition of one dog at a time had not quite reached the western united states. Most men let all their dogs go at once and let chips fall where they may. The dogs ran wild for a bit. Neither of them had had freedom beyond Dallas' backyard for months. Meanwhile, the men found a bridge to cross to the blackberried side of the slough. They crossed the bridge and climbed down an embankment to the marshy path between the water and the berries. The vegetation was riddled with trails eaten out of the marsh grass by nutria. The men were quick to find a large sette dug into the bank.

o o o

Meanwhile, Grit, far from the men, dove into a hole. He smelled composted turds. There was a nutria home. Grit would have shown his value there in that hole, had not Garvey shot in behind him. Grit heard the slopping of Garvey in the mud but paid him no mind. There was game up the tube and Grit was going to kill it. Garvey pushed up next to Grit and tried to squeeze past. There was not enough room. Garvey snapped at Grit, as if to say "move out of my way." Grit didn't wait for the other dog to get an upperhand, he latched his mouth over the top of Garvey's face. His top canine set into Garvey's eye socket. Jerking backwards he twisted Garvey into an awkward U-shape. Grit had the upperhand now. Garvey couldn't gain power from that position. Grit felt the space of the tunnel around him. He had room to fight, now that he wasn't wedged against the wall. He pushed forward into Garvey, keeping hold on his face. Garvey's legs folded under the pushing weight of Grit. He rolled onto his back. With speed, Grit changed holds to Garvey's throat and ground his opponent into the slop. Garvey squirmed and kicked. He swiveled his head with open mouth, seeking purchase for his teeth. All that entered his mouth was unclean water. He sputtered, gasped, kicked, scratched.

∘ ∘ ∘

Dallas called, "Garvey! Come on boy!" but the dog didn't respond.

"Looks like your dogs took off for the next county, there Princess," Tim teased.

"If you can't see them, they're doing what they're supposed to be doing." Dallas took a line he had heard Robert use when describing Jackson. Jackson had a tendency to always be out of sight, due to his constantly hunting through the brush or being to ground. The dog simply was never visible. Tim raised his eyebrows at Dallas, then nodded his head. *That's right, I know what I'm talking about*, Dallas thought.

"Grit!" Dallas called out. He hoped Garvey would come, but any dog to save him the embarrassment would do. He'd not worked with them in the field enough to have them respond to recall.

They waited and waited for a dog to come, but neither did. Listening, they heard no barking.

"Whe'e dem dumsumbitches?" cursed Morton. "Whe'e dey at?"

"Maybe they caught something up ahead," Dallas conjectured. He did have a lot of faith in Garvey, even though he had not hunted the dog himself yet. The men walked up the slough. Old Tim Waler and Morty Twist were not terrible company when they weren't haranguing a person. In fact, they were quite jovial fellows for the most part. They joked and laughed, mostly at Dallas' expense, for about half a mile. At which point, there were ripples in the water just ahead. Timmy spotted it first and ran to see what was going on.

Tim stopped to inspect the water. He took the cigar out of his mouth. "There's blood here in the water!" he yelled to the other fellows close behind him.

Sure enough, when the other two men came to the scene, they saw the blood-mingled ripples surging out of a muddy nutria hole.

"Hot Damn!" hooted Timmy Waler, slapping his thigh and stomping his foot. An excited smile plastered across his face.

Morton was all business and set to digging. Nothing could be heard, so he guessed where the action was happening and stuck in the shovel.

"I told you," Dallas started into his bragging, "this Garvey dog is something else. He'll hunt every day of the week like this, beat up or no."

"You gonna jabber er he'p dig?" barked Morton.

At that Dallas began to help. They got about two feet down and broke into a very wet, muddy pipe. The mud was soupy and there was plenty of blood to prove a tussle had taken place near by.

"This must be one tough nutria, if Garvey hasn't finished off yet," said Dallas.

They trenched the pipe until they came to the commotion. The pipe floor was drenched in blood, but none of it was of nutria. Garvey-two-face lay near death, his body pushed deep into the mud, which was formed like a cast around his body. Grit had Garvey by the throat and was drilling him quietly into the mud and death. Garvey's head was encased in the mud. He couldn't even let out a gurgle.

Dallas yelled and cussed and screamed. He grabbed Grit off of Garvey's body. Garvey choked in a breath of bloody air. Dallas began to kick Grit hard. A few of those kicks would send a dog into the next life.

"Now! Now! Ye dumsumbitch! Stop dat!" Morton grabbed Dallas' coat collar and pulled him backwards into the mud. "Seems t' me dat's a fine dog!

Whooped d'hell outta dat wo'ldbeater ye got dyin' in dat muddy hole."

"I swear, I'll drown that dog!" fumed Dallas.

"Naw, Naw ya won't." Tim interjected, mouth open, stroking his stained Manchu, deep in thought. "I'll trade you some fine tobacco for that fine dog. He'll be off your hands and you'll be richer some of the best tobacco money can buy."

Dallas' head cooled a bit with the prospect of a deal. *Waler does get his hands on the best tobacco*, he thought.

"I want two bales of your finest for the dog," he declared.

"Hold on now! You were gonna kill him just a minute ago. I'll give you a single bale of the finest stuff for a dog that's as good as dead in your hands."

The deal was struck.

"Now get your ass outta the mud, Princess," Tim said. He offered Dallas his hand to help him onto his feet.

12. The Waler Squaller

So it was that Garvey-two-face lost his eyes and had to be put down. Grit had done quite the number on poor old Garvey. It was a damn shame, as Garvey was an honorable little dog. Had a man with some wit owned the dog, he would've never been placed on the ground with Grit.

Grit turned a new leaf through his experiences with Garvey-two-face. No longer did Grit depend on Jackson or Lee or Coallie for confidence. Grit was full of his own confidence. His new found confidence was swift, furious and unshakeable. Dallas didn't realize that Grit's gears were beginning to turn, sitting there in the kennel all day, everyday. Grit was fully grown and his mind was prepared for the work of a terrier.

Old Tim Waler and Morty Twist weren't the best dog men but they gave their dogs some work. The work wasn't the issue for the dogs there. Unlike Dallas, Tim only kept dogs for their purpose. He liked a good dog but treated them like he treated all his possessions, with very little care. These fellas were hillbillies. They were lucky enough to inherit land where their forefathers had planted a homestead. Waler and Twist themselves were pretty trashy when looked at as a whole. Though Timmy Waler was worth more as a friend and Morton as a business partner, neither of them were worth much. The two of them farmed for income. Morton kept his farm clean and running as smooth as was his bald head, which did little to influence his drinking buddy Tim, who kept a ramshackle home.

Tim's house was guarded by bull dogs chained to the front porch. Traps hung from the side of the house on hooks. His home was littered in trash a foot deep. Beer bottles, boxes, bits of left over meals, years worth of old newspapers and blankets, pissed and shat on by generations of pups, laid all over the floors. As one can imagine, his dogs were kept in poor conditions. The house and structures were trashy but Tim lived up one of the most beautiful valleys, pastures, streams and ponds settled in the bottom of two fir covered mountains. The streams led down to Morty's place on the foothills of the mountains, beautiful, lush grassland.

Grit was chained out like the rest of the dogs. Some had wooden houses, some had barrels made of metal. Grit was in a barrel. His chain space was grassy, indicating that the dog that once occupied it must have died, 'cause Tim never moved his dogs.

Most of the dogs were hounds. The hounds were a motley crew with long faces and longer ears. They were lean and hunted regularly. Tim liked to run anything the hounds could catch. He was especially known in the area for catching coyote with his hounds. Tim was not a terrierman but he liked ferocity. Thus, when Grit knocked the hell out of Garvey, Tim saw a dog with real sand. He liked that. Hounds aren't known for being gritty.

When Tim traded the bale for Grit, he figured he'd use him for getting coyote cubs out of holes for the hounds or guarding his chickens or rabbits. Grit was far too small a dog to handle an adult coyote. Surely, a coyote would be his undoing, if they were to meet face to face. When Tim had a bout of sobriety, he realized he'd be better off continuing to use his bull dogs for the job of getting coyotes out of holes. Sure, Grit could have handled pups but a man never knows if the parents are home or not, unless he's dispatched them already. Thus, Grit fulfilled his days guarding fowl and bunnies.

Grit's first task with Tim was unexpected. Grit heard a commotion in one of the coops. He kept quiet but left his barrel to see what was going on. No scent was flowing his way, so he couldn't perceive what was happening. He kept quiet because he didn't want a whipping for waking Tim in the night.

Tim came running outside wearing nothing but his underwear and a pair of rubber boots. He had a strong metal flashlight he used to light his way. Grit caught drift of alcohol on the air. He cowered into his barrel, fearing the worst. Tim got to Grit, reached into the barrel, patted the dog on the head and unclipped Grit's chain.

"Now, let's see how useful a dog you will be," Tim said. He pulled the dog out of the barrel and held him to his chest.

He ran the dog toward the chicken coop. Grit was nervous. He'd been broken off of chickens by Robert. He didn't plan to kill chickens even with coaxing from Tim but when he got near the coop another scent wafted toward him. . . Raccoon.

The embers sparked in Grit's bosom. He remembered what he was born to be. The fire began to rise.

"YEOW," Grit screamed. He was stoked. He couldn't hold in the fury.

"Good boy! Get 'im! Get 'im!" Tim patted Grit's side to set the dog off more.

Tim got to the coop door with Grit and threw him in, hoping that he found the coon and not a chicken.

From outside the hen house it sounded like murder. Grit had found the bandit and was giving him a walloping to remember. Meanwhile, Tim tried to push the hatch at the top of the coop shut, in order to keep the raccoon from climbing out. But it was too late, a second raccoon was already there. Tim caught it in between the hatch and the coop but he couldn't squeeze the hatch tight enough to hold it in place and grab the raccoon with his free hand. The raccoon got away. But Grit still had his in a lock on the floor of the coop.

Tim hopped down from the hatch, now safely latched, and got himself into the chicken coop to help Grit. There Grit was, doing as Robert had always hoped him to do. Grit had the coon by the side of the head and was working it into exhaustion. Grit wasn't in good shape, as he had been sedentary for some time. The coon was fat from farm raids but was still a worthy opponent. Tim grabbed it by the tail, stepped on Grit's snout to get him to release his hold and then whacked the raccoon on the head with his flashlight. He killed it with a single blow.

"Damn fine job, dog!" Tim was pleased. "You earned your food this week. Keep it up and you'll have a place here!" He scratched Grit between the ears.

Grit was exhausted, mouth full of fur, face scratched and bleeding but his tail was wagging. Grit loved the positive reinforcement from Tim.

○ ○ ○

Grit was not often hunted. His job was to protect the poultry and rabbits from pests. When Grit was not guarding, he was chained by his metal barrel, cold and damp. The mud was better for warmth than the cold metal that Tim called a shelter. It wasn't that Tim was a terrible man. Tim loved his good dogs and culled the poor ones, just as all men claimed they did at that time. Tim's problem was that he was a drunk. He was too drunk to care for himself, let alone animals. He wanted to be a good dogman and prided himself in keeping only proper hunting and working dogs, whether they be hound, terrier or cattle dog. Sadly, the dogs he was so proud of were sorely neglected.

Coldness to the bone became the norm to Grit. He was always soaked and covered in filthy shitty mud.

Being so well acquainted with the cold and damp, it was like entering heaven for Grit to be called on for guarding the rabbits. Inside the rabbit shed Grit had dry straw in a corner to lay on. Though the air was thick with ammonia from rabbit feces and urine, Grit was content to stay in the shed, sheltered from the draft and icy western rains.

The shed was not well made. It had plywood sides, much of it rotting, the boards separating. The walls were built to within a foot of the sloping roof. The extra foot was open space for ventilation. The shed really needed much more ventilation than that. Such concerns were not over thought by Tim. If Tim could get away with it, he'd always do the minimum amount of work on any undertaking. The rabbits were kept in four different stalls, many rabbits to a stall. The doors were made of ply wood, hinged to swing and came to the height of a man's waste. When the stalls got too filthy, Tim would throw down more straw on top of the old muck. He shoveled the shed out only once a year, if he got around to it.

It was in this shed that Grit found comfort, while living with Tim. Grit had free movement within the shed. He could jump the doors separating each stall, but he never bothered the rabbits. When he was not resting, Grit would spend his time digging up rats that made their systems of tunnels through the peat-like rabbit shit. The supply of rats seemed to never end. Between the rabbit shed and poultry coop there was enough food to feed the denizens of rodents for as long as Grit could stand to kill them. Grit could only be in one place at one time. Thus, whenever he had dug up every inch of one building's rodent tunnels, all the rats needed to do was move to the next building.

Grit denting the rodent population was a plus that Tim considered when valuing Grit but Grit's real purpose in those buildings was to keep predators from killing the livestock.

The gaps between the walls and the roof allowed for raccoons to get into the building. On occasion, skunks were also able to burrow under the building and pop through to the inside of the coops or rabbit shed. Sorry mistake for them when they found Grit there. He made quick work of skunks or any type of weasel.

Raccoons are a tougher lot than skunks but Grit could handle them well enough. Even if they got away after a tussle, Grit hit hard enough to not be forgotten. There was one night in particular that Tim would always remember. He never expected such a feat from a single dog, but Grit pulled it off.

One night, while Grit was watching over the rabbits, a band of raccoons came marauding. He lay sleeping on his hay, when he was awakened by the thudding of bodies hitting the floor. The entire band was climbing through the ventilation space between the roof and walls and dropping without grace into the rabbit stalls.

Grit jumped to action. He leapt the door of the stall in which the raccoons planned to make massacre. He immediately latched to the first enemy his teeth could find. But there were more than one. Grit could not count but knew he was outnumbered. He remained focused. He had killed coon by himself before but one after another without pause for breath, that was a task he wouldn't have ever been expected to perform. He set his teeth for a tussle. At first, the raccoon hissed and spat, snarled and growled. It thought it could intimidate its assailant. Grit pulled the coon hard by the side of the face to keep it off balance. Grit shook and tugged, eventually knocking the bandit off its feet. Grit set his own feet and plowed his jaws into the raccoon's throat. The rabbit-killer knew there was no hope, if it had no help. It wrapped its hands and legs around Grit and formed a ball, trying to control the fight. It was no use, Grit would not relent nor relinquish his hold. The raccoon squalled in fear. It knew it would die.

What happened next, some hunters claim does not happen. Others say it does and claim that those who do not believe it to happen are numpties without real world experience with raccoons. Whatever the case, it did happen this night. It happened to Grit. The raccoons, hearing the squalling of their comrade, came to aide in the fight. The whole band jumped upon Grit with tooth and claw. They rolled him off of his feet but he kept his hold on the throat of the raccoon he had already subdued. The raccoons bit and clawed at him, chewing him. He had no way to defend against injury. If he were to fight one, another would be grinding its teeth into him. He ground his teeth together, meeting them in the windpipe of his primary opponent. Grit felt the fight go out of the first raccoon. He released his hold and was rolled onto his back by the remaining raccoons.

His back was the last position he wished to find himself but he had little choice. He had two enemies upon him, both larger than he. He immediately went to defending himself. The tables had turned. Though he had killed one of the band, the other two were not nursing any wounds from the previous round, as was he.

Grit was tough, but not stupid. He knew merely biting anywhere would not end in a dead enemy. He planned his attack, knowing which holds might give him dominance. One of his attackers' armpits was within grabbing distance. Grit curled his body and neck up to reach it. His mouth found purchase. It was enough to cause the raccoon to leave it's overbearing position and try to remove itself from the fight. But Grit wouldn't have that. The other raccoon gnawed at Grit's hind leg, while the one Grit held by the armpit bit at his snout and ear, trying to get free. The raccoon could not free itself but rather was entangled more with Grit, who had taken an opportunity to set his teeth into the raccoon's chest. Grit bit and bit with as much force as possible, causing internal bleeding and trauma to vital organs. The squalling began anew, this time with one of the defenders of the first. This sent the third raccoon into a frenzy of machine gun bites and chewing. It found Grit's foot and began tearing at it. The pain was too much even for Grit. He let out a scream of pain, in affect letting go of the raccoon he had a hold on.

The raccoon he had been holding ran for the beams in an attempt to escape. The third, unharmed raccoon let go of Grit and ran for an escape as well. But Grit was not finished meting out doom. He tore the unharmed bandit from the beam as it was trying to scuttle out of the rabbit shed.

This fight was one on one. Grit was winded and wounded but the pain that seared his foot put him in a berserker like rage. He made quick work of tearing his enemy to death.

The other raccoon made it to the refuge of open air but did not make it far before collapsing. Despite all the air in the world to breath, only blood filled its lungs. It dropped dead no more than 5 feet from the rabbit shed.

∘ ∘ ∘

Tim walked out to his rabbits the next morning and found the dead raccoons. First he saw the one lying outside the shed. He knitted his eyebrows, *That's odd,* he thought. When he got inside the shed, he just stood with raised eyebrows, mouth open. Grit was curled up sleeping the work off. The dead raccoons were stiff on the floor.

Finding the three dead raccoons increased Grit's worth in Tim's mind. As far as he was concerned, Grit would always be a valuable part of his farm. Despite Grit's amazing accomplishments, Tim didn't take good care of the dog. The day after Grit did battle with the three raccoons, Tim did not clean nor dress Grit's wounds. Lucky for Grit, despite the muck and infection that got into the bite wounds, his immune system triumphed and he healed well.

In time the neglect began to show. Grit's coat grew shaggy from lack of going through brush, his nails long for lack of digging hard earth or running, a bit of the light went out of his eyes. Grit was bored and lonely most of the time he lived on that farm. There were times he was used in conjunction with hounds but for the most part he was delegated to tasks around the farm. He was not socialized as the hounds were but rather left to himself in the sheds, barns or coops. This led to Grit turning into quite a somber animal. When he was not set guarding a building, the cold of his environment kept him hunkered over and sickly. It seemed as if death would gather him up.

On an especially cold winter night, after a year of living in terrible condition, it seemed life could take no worse. Grit became desperate. Grit was desperate for warmth, for comfort, for camaraderie. So, he began to bark. He barked and he barked. There was nothing to bark at but he didn't know how else to get what he needed. He was suffering and needed peace. Several times, Timmy yelled out the door for Grit to be quiet.

Normally, Grit was an obedient dog and would be silent when told but he needed Tim to address his needs. Morty was with Tim that night. When they got together, the drinking would go all night. Each time Tim yelled he sounded angrier and drunker.

After several hours, Tim stumbled out of the house drunk. Grit thought for a moment that Tim would aid him. Those thoughts vanished quickly when he heard the tone of Tim's voice cussing and muttering under his breath. Grit cowered and crawled into his barrel. He knew he was going to receive punishment, not assistance. But he kept barking. He knew he was mad to keep barking at Tim but the fear added to his suffering made him crazy.

Tim stumbled as fast as he could go toward Grit's barrel and kicked it.

"SHUTUP!" he yelled, then grabbed the barrel, shaking Grit out like straw into the mud. Grit kept barking and snapped at Tim. He had truly lost all respect of Tim. Tim kicked Grit in the face to quiet him. Grit in defense ran to Tim and bit his leg. Grit had simply had enough. It was a life or death struggle and he knew it. He would die, if he submitted or quieted. He would die, if he fought. So, he fought.

Grit had no chance at beating the drunken man nor did he have a chance at bettering his life by barking. Tim would never care for him the way he needed care.

Tim stomped the wind out of Grit. Grit let go and choked in the shitty mud for breath. He lifted his head, barked, then a club came down on his head. Everything went dark. Grit felt no more. . .

13. Redeemed

There was a tumult after Tim hit Grit in the head. Old Morty Twist liked the Grit dog and saw what transpired from the door, where he was stooped over and drunk. When he saw Grit get hit in the head he ran out to defend the dog, though he feared it was too late.

"Ye dumsumbitch!" he yelled.

He tumbled out of the doorway and stumbled toward Tim. One mighty blow from Morty's fist found it's mark under Tim's ear. Tim dropped into the muck of Grit's chain-space, unconscious. Old Twist was drunk but still strong from all the work he did day in and day out. He dragged his unconscious friend back inside, otherwise Tim would freeze to death. Then went to take Grit.

He gathered up the twitching little dog and un-chained him. Morty stumbled down the mud road to his own home. Grit ceased to move after a quarter mile but Morty kept on going. He didn't discard the little fellow. Morty had felt sympathy for Grit for months but hadn't felt the right to take him from Tim. When he saw Waler hit Grit with the stick and possibly kill the dog, he couldn't stand it anymore. Morty, similar to Tim in vice, was very different than Tim when it came to animal husbandry and cleanliness. Morty kept a clean house. His sheep were kept fat and sassy. And though he cussed endlessly and kicked half-heartedly at his dogs all day, he kept good care of them. His "dumsumbitches" he called them.

When he arrived home, he set Grit by his fireplace, though it seemed the dog would die. Morty sat himself in an armchair and fell into a drunken slumber.

When he awoke, Grit was lying with his eyes open. It would seem he couldn't be put down so easily. Morty was pleased to see the dog was at least alive, though possibly brain damaged.

Morty went to brew himself some coffee to clear his head. When he went to put his hand on the grinder to grind his beans, he saw that the pinky finger on his right hand was broken at the base and dangling like a snapped twig from his hand.

"Holy Hail!?" Morty exclaimed, staring at his hand. His punch the night before had been strong but evidently his fist struck with the wrong knuckles. His pinky looked like hell, and he didn't have the means for a doctor to fix it. He was a tough old man. He'd get through the pain for the time.

He ate bread and cheese for breakfast, downed some coffee and set some morsels in front of Grit along with water.

"Sure as shit chye-dumbsumbitch, ol' Timmy bopped you good in d' head. An' ye ain't halfway t' starvin', neither."

Morty put on his cowboy hat and left the house to feed his sheep and look over his flocks. Grit laid by the fireplace that day, until old Morty Twist came back in for the day. Twist brought with him a jar of sheep's milk. He poured half for Grit and drank the other half himself. Grit lapped it up from a laying position.

Morty leaned against the counter and stared down at Grit, "It ain't go'n' do, havin' ye stink up d' place like dogshit!" he said. "Time t' getchye all cleaned up."

He walked over to sit near the dog. He cuddled Grit into his arms by the fire and began to strip Grit's ragged, ugly, dead coat. He pulled the long hairs off in clumps. It was easy to do. Much of the hair had been dead for a long time and was merely matted into the rest of the coat. Grit sometimes winced when too much healthy hair was grabbed with the bad. Otherwise, he sat through it without a peep. Slowly, the shape of the dog began to appear under all that muddy mess of a coat.

After stripping the dog's coat, Morton prepared warm water for Grit in a tin wash tub. He carried the little dog over to it and placed him in. Grit didn't fight. He simply sulked and let the old man scrub him clean. The old man was gentle with the little dog, despite all the exterior harshness the man boasted. Morty kept shaking his head as he looked at the terrier that stood shakily and emaciated in the tub. Morty peeled old scabs and sores off of Grit that had not been attended to. He cleaned anything that still ran blood.

After the bath was done, he lifted Grit from the tub and dried him with a towel, then placed him again by the fire in a box full of wool to dry thoroughly. Grit's true sandy-golden color now could be seen in the fire-light. When drying was done, Morty cleaned Grit's wounds and sores with alcohol. He then made a paste from lard and honey to anoint the injuries with. This would act as an antiseptic and healing agent.

Grit began to feel warm and cared for as he had not felt since leaving Robert; what seemed an eternity to him.

∘ ∘ ∘

Tim Waler wasn't long in missing his dog. He came storming down the mud lane in his big truck. Morty heard him and went out to meet the fury in the yard.

"What the hell you think yer doin' takin' my dog like that."

Morton stood calm, staring at Tim through squinty eyes. The two were good enough friends that it wouldn't turn into anything violent.

"Feels like I been hit with a brick!" Tim said with a slight grin on his angry face.

"Shut t'hell up. I wa'n't go'n' sit and see dat dumb dog die. Ye can't tell the difference 'tween raisins and sheep shit! He's un helluva good sumbitch and I be damned if'n I sat and watched yer dumb ass kill 'im!"

"Well damn it Morty! He's my dog and I'll be havin' 'im back now!"

"Like hell! Ye dumb sumbitch. You shur's hell don't deserve such an animal."

"Jesus Christ!" Tim took off his hat and threw it on the ground. He was flustered but coming to his senses a little bit. He knew Twist would put his fists up again for that dog. "Well. . ." Tim paused to think with his hand on a fence post. He looked at the grass at his feet. "Well. Take the dog if you like him so damned much. He's of no use dyin'. Jus' as you said." At that he picked up his hat, climbed into his truck and drove slowly home without a goodbye or a wave.

14. An Old Friend

Ol' Morty Twist took good care of Grit. He nurtured him through the spring and got Grit's coat back to a glossy sheen. Grit pranced around the farm with his head and tail held high. Most days he just followed Morty wherever Morty went. Sometimes he'd sit in the fields or follow the sheep around. He'd catch a critter here and there but Morty never took him out with a purpose to hunt. Every now and again, he'd still go down and lay on Tim Waler's porch. Just as most dogs, Grit let go of a grudge quickly. He'd mostly visit Tim while Morty was off doing business away from the farm.

One such a day, in sunny June, found Grit lying out on Tim's dusty front porch. The porch was the coolest spot to be on both farms, when the heat of the day came around. There Grit lay, waiting for the sound of Morty's truck to come bumping down the road, ushering him home. Soon enough the bumping and thunking of that old truck came rattling down the dusty road. Grit sprung up and shot down the road full speed to meet Morty in the drive.

Morty opened his truck door to a springing terrier. He grabbed an armful of bags and walked into the house with Grit trailing his steps. "Howdy-do, sumbitch?" Morty said to, more than asked, Grit. As he put away foodstuffs, he kept talking to Grit, who sat in the middle of the kitchen floor staring up at the man. "I seen some-un in town I think y'd like t'know. He kinda tall-like an'a big injun sumbitch." Morty stopped to look down at Grit.

The dog was staring back intently as if to say, "Go on. I hear ya."

"Anyhow," Morty continued after the short pause, "I think ye'll like 'im a lot better'n ye like me. I ain't got no time fo' no little sumbitch hunt' dog." At this he reached down and patted Grit on the head. No matter how much he liked the little dog, he didn't have use of him on the farm. He knew there were folk who could appreciate the talents Grit had better than he did. "Yer ol' friend'll be here anytime naw."

Morty sat down in a rocking chair he kept on the porch. He smoked his tobacco pipe there. With Grit by his side, he waited for Curtis to arrive. He'd seen Curtis in the Co-Op and recalled having heard he was part of Robert's gang. He approached him about the dog and Curtis said he'd take the dog back no problem, as long as it wasn't going to cost him anything.

"The dog wasn't hunting last I saw him," Curtis said. But after some small convincing from Morty that the dog was still yet "a firecracker" Curtis complied. "I know Robert will be glad he's back in my care." The two men agreed on a time for the pick up.

Curtis was a bit late but Morty didn't care. It was too hot to be working and truthfully, he wasn't sure he wanted to let little Grit go. But when Curtis did arrive, Morty knew it was time to say goodbye for good. No more would he be smoking his pipe with the little dog as his companion on the porch.

Morty put on his tough guy demeanor for Curtis.

"Hey," Curtis greeted Morty with a firm handshake. Curtis had grown to about 6' 3". The boy he was just a short time before was long gone. A black and red beard grew on his face now. "Hey there little buddy," he said, upon seeing Grit. With one hand in his pocket, he bent over and scratched Grit around the ears.

"Don' go mushy 'round me!" grouched Ol' Morty.

Curtis only laughed.

"Ye wan' a drink?" Morty asked.

"No. Thanks though," Curtis politely declined. He'd sworn off drinking as a little boy. He saw the affects alcohol had on his father and he wasn't going to have any part of it.

"A'right den. I s'pose ye can have the sumbitch den."

"Thanks for letting me come and get him. I know Robert loved this dog. You did him a great favor talking to me."

"Meh Meh," Twist just waved his hands at Curtis, as if to say, "You're giving me too much credit, I just want rid of the animal." Morty looked at the ground, looking anywhere but at the little dog. He thought he'd go soft if he looked at Grit.

"I guess I'll see you around sometime." Curtis offered Morty his hand again. Morty gave him his in return. "Whoa?!" Curtis looked astonished, "What happened to your finger?"

The old man's pinky still dangled stubbornly. He couldn't get it to heal right, no matter how he set it.

It reminded him of just how much he really did like that little dog.

He shrugged, "I dunno."

15. The Pack

When Curtis arrived home he took Grit into the house to look him over. It was cool and shady in the house. There were maple trees keeping the sun blocked on the east and southern sides of the house. Grit remembered Curtis and took to being at his house well. Curtis sat down on the cool steel of his fire-stove. Holding Grit in his lap, he looked the dog over for any health issues. Curtis had stayed at the local college, while Robert was off at war. He was studying to be a veterinarian.

"You look good little buddy," Curtis said, checking Grit's teeth. "You've earned some new battle scars, I see. That's good. I don't want a cull eating all my dog food." He chuckled at this. "I wouldn't have the heart to cull you anyway. Plus, all my dogs are useless mongrels. You'll fit right in."

It was common practice for all dog men in the area to talk down their own dogs, as if they were no use. Truth be told, Curtis had a couple of fine hounds. Granted, they would run trash when bored, but they never really ran it whole-heartedly. Many men's hounds in the area ran nothing but trash. Curtis' hounds at least caught a respectable number of cats. Bobcat were Curtis' favorite quarry. He would have liked bear hunting too, if he had the money to supply a larger pack with dog food. He knew he could catch a few bear with his two hounds but he'd rather not subject them to that sort of danger. Especially considering his financial state as a student, he couldn't afford taking a dog to the vet for a major injury. So as it was, he wouldn't run his dogs with bear packs. Almost everybody ran bear with their hounds.

After the examining of Grit was done, Curtis got up with a grunt and sigh from his seat on the stove. "Let's get you in a kennel dog." They walked out back. Grit ran ahead. He had been to the kennels here many times before. He knew the hounds and remembered well the good hunts he had with them. He stuck his nose through the mesh to smell Curtis' main bitch, Prissy. She was a black and white walker hound. She was something of a wunderkind as a pup. She was already trailing and treeing coon at four months old. Curtis arrived at the kennel. His hounds were roaring.

"I swear, you better shutup or I'll shoot the both of you!" Curtis yelled, but the hounds never listened when he told them to be quiet. That was Prissy's biggest flaw; she never wanted to be quiet. Curtis banged his hand on the kennels but that only ever excited the dogs.

Curtis' second hound wasn't really a hound-hound but more of a white cur dog. He called that one Burdog. Old Burdog had the body of a spaniel and a head somewhere between a beagle's and a terrier's. His tail was short and stumpy. He wasn't the prettiest of dogs, but he had all it took to be a great dog. He'd do anything Curtis told him to. In fact, Robert and Curtis had their first experience using a dog for hunting with Old Burdog.

Both the boys, when about 10 years old wanted to catch a fox for a pet. William had told the boys that if they wanted a fox, they'd have to find it's den and dig up the kits in the spring. Only if they raised the kits from the point their eyes were closed could they tame them. That winter it snowed deeper and colder than either boy could remember. Early one morning before everyone else was awake, they met at the hill midway between their houses. Curtis had Ol' Burdog in tow. They kept Burdog on a leash and looked for tracks in the snow. It wasn't long before they found a fresh line. Burdog was interested and took the line; not making a peep. He pulled Curtis along at a slow and steady pace, Robert close on their heels. The scent led them through pines and firs and back into the fields again. Lo and behold, at the bottom of a hill Burdog stopped. There in the snow was a fox den. They planned to come back in the spring to get kits from the den. This wasn't to be, however. Never did those boys dig that den up, not even with terriers.

Grit was put in his own kennel next to Prissy. Only the hunting dogs were kept kenneled. There were great danes and a few mutts running loose on the farm. A few kennels were empty just in case the farm dogs needed to be put away but as it was, one was available for Grit.

"I know I can't trust you, you little punk," Curtis spoke endearingly to the dog. "This aughta hold you though." He wrapped a chain around the door and snapped it to itself to keep the door closed.

○ ○ ○

Staying with Curtis was easy for Grit. Because cat season wasn't going, Grit didn't get to hunt, nor did he get let out of the kennel very often. Curtis lived in an area where hunting dogs couldn't just run loose. If another farmer caught sight of the dog or if Grit got into the wrong gang of dogs, it could be the end of the terrier. Sometimes, Curtis brought Grit fishing with him or out to scout the mountains for elk and deer sign. Most often, however, it was Burdog that Curtis took with him. Burdog had what hunters call "an off-switch," meaning when he wasn't supposed to be hunting, Burdog would not hunt.

Grit did get to go with Curtis to the seed farms owned by the Richardsons. It was there that Curtis saw Grit really had turned on to hunting again. Curtis brought him to the seed farm to take care of a few problem nutria. Grit took care of them in a jiffy. There wasn't any backing up for Grit on nutria, he killed everyone of them without needing help from Curtis or the Richardsons.

The end of the summer was Grit's first time getting to hunt like the old days he had with Robert and Curtis, with the hounds. Grit was allowed to run with the hounds when Robert had him, because he made so much noise going through the woods, Robert could keep track of him. Lee and Jackson were not hunted in that way. Neither Lee nor Jackson had the speed to keep up with hounds nor did they speak on track. Grit wasn't a big terrier but he had long legs and stamina to spare.

It was middle September when it finally rained. That was Curtis' cue to get the hounds out and running cats in preparation for the actual hunting season. Before season actually opens, the hound hunters take their dogs out to exercise and chase game but they don't shoot anything. The pelts would be worthless, so soon after the summer.

Thomas Richardson was going with Curtis on this particular morning. Thomas was a wild sort. He was nearly as tall and big as Curtis with a ruddy-brown beard and an already balding head at the age of 20. He loved ripping through the country-side like a bootlegger moving moonshine. Curtis couldn't help but laughing at the Richardson boys' antics. They'd jump trucks like they were jumping motor bikes. They were reckless fellows but knew how to have a damned good time. Not only did they know how to have a good time but they were about the best lot of people a person could be acquainted with. What was theirs was yours, so long as you were a friend. Salt of the Earth, those folks.

Thomas had recently bought and souped-up a powerful truck. He wanted to give it a whirl.

"Let's take my truck there Curtis. It's the first rain of the season and I got a feeling there's some mud just waiting for tires." Thomas spoke with a constant grin and a mischievous twinkle, almost craze in his eyes. He just couldn't help the insane excitement he got for driving dangerously. Curtis had to think twice about hopping into that truck but at last consented.

"Alright," Curtis agreed to the perilous ride, "but we'll have to load my dogbox into your pickup. Don't trash it with crazy driving. I can't afford to build another one right now."

"What?" Thomas gave a disbelieving look, "Me drive crazy? I'll drive like a grandma on Sunday, I promise." The raise in pitch when he said "I promise" made Curtis all the more nervous.

"And keep the guns in the cab. I don't want you shooting everything in the woods right before deer season starts. I want there to be some game for those of us who actually follow the law." Curtis was usually not one to be bossy but in the case of Thomas, he was going to make it clear that this hunting trip was on his terms. Thomas didn't have to be invited.

Thomas rolled his eyes, while he helped Curtis put the dog box into the truckbed, "Now you're just spouting crap."

Curtis laughed. He really wasn't any better about poaching than any of the other fellows. But he liked to pretend he was anyway. Laughing still, he said, "Hey, I'm trying to be good here!"

Once the dogs were loaded. Thomas hit the road with a heavy foot and tires spinning. Curtis shook his head, "There'll be trouble today, I know it."

On the way to the forest, Thomas drove all over the windy road at high speeds. Curtis had a firm hold on the oh-shit-handle. "Are you suicidal or do you just like driving on the wrong side of the road?"

Thomas was quick in his reply, "I pay for both sides, don't I."

By the time they got to the woods, Curtis was ready to settle the mood by dropping some dogs to road. Thomas begged to go mudding in his new truck first but Curtis reminded him that this was a hunting trip first, a mudding trip second. "We'll go mudding when it gets later and the scenting gets worse."

They roaded Prissy and Burdog by letting them run ahead of the truck on the road. In this way the dogs could directly strike a line. This was easier for the dogs than searching for scent while riding on top of the box. It also gave them the exercise they needed, whether they chased anything on a particular day or not. Curtis did not let Grit run on the road with the hounds. Memory of Lee's death would not allow him to feel comfortable with a terrier on the road ever again. Though Robert would eventually make him accept the practice, whether he liked it or not.

It was an hour or two into daylight when Prissy struck a track. The day was cool, it was moist and overcast, scenting was great. Prissy roared and Burdog joined in with the chop chop of his bark. Grit went into a frenzy inside the dogbox. He screeched and scratched at the door. Curtis wasn't going to let him out on this run. He didn't have complete faith that the terrier could endure the race to its end without getting lost in the woods. Curtis had to walk around a bend in the road to hear the dogs in the race. Grit wouldn't shutup no matter how much Curtis shushed him.

Listening to hounds when they are in a large pack is a pleasure unto itself. With a large pack, the catch is almost insignificant, when compared to the thrill of hearing a warlike raucous blow through the woods. At a long distance, through echoing woods, the sound changed from warlike shouting into a soft singing chorus. On the wind the hounds could sound of anger and excitement or of sadness, longing and disappointment but always, the feelings of the hounds voices were raw and honest.

A single hound may have a beautiful voice. This is a joy to listen to. But for the most part, when one goes out with a few hounds rather than many, the enjoyment is in understanding exactly what is happening. Whereas listening to many hounds is to enjoy a song, listening to a few hounds is to enjoy a conversation. The hunter knows every voice, what every tone means. He can hear the dips and the rises in the ground, the heat of the track in the hounds' noses. The hunter's ears are translators of terrain and animal intention.

The woods were older where the hounds struck than in the surrounding forestry units. The sound was clear and the earth was pithy. It was easy walking to keep within hearing of the hounds. Curtis called Thomas on. Usually, a hunter would wait for the dogs to tree before setting off into the woods. A race could last all day and go twenty miles. But in the older trees and with the hot track, Curtis thought the hounds would tree quickly.

∘ ∘ ∘

Grit could hear the hounds bawling in the distance. He screeched to be let out. Dusty light was shining through an airhole in the dog box. Grit swiveled his head around the hole to get purchase for his teeth. A canine caught the edge of the hole and splintered the wood. Grit wasn't going to wait idly in the box while the hounds had all the fun.

∘ ∘ ∘

It wasn't a poor race. Actually, it went ideally. It was not so short that the hounds didn't have to work for it. It was not so long that men and dog wished for an end. It landed somewhere in the sweet middle of the two, making it an ideal race in ideal terrain. The hounds left the thick trunked old growth and moved the cat through some 10 year old re-prod, thick and branchy young trees. The men waited outside of the unit, listening to the bark bark and yowl of the dogs. The cat wound them through the thickest parts of the wood for 30 minutes before running down into a gully. After running a short way down the gully, it turned back to head uphill and back toward the road again. His circle was going to take him into a unit nearer to the truck. Curt and Thomas started moving in the direction they predicted the cat would go. They needed to keep ahead of the hounds as much as possible, if they wished to go the entire race on foot.

It was their luck that the cat treed within a couple hundred yards from the road, in forest not too thick. Prissy had a distinct locate and tree bawl. Curt's friends all had good ears for hounds but they could never quite get a handle on Prissy's different voices as did Curt. Try as they may, everyone but Curt heard but one song from Prissy.

"They're treed," Curtis announced. "We can take our time getting there. The dogs need a little time learning to stay treed. It must be closer to the truck than I thought, I can hear Grit right near the hounds."

Thomas was practically hopping out of his boots, when Curtis finally decided to head into the tree. When they got there, there was a surprise awaiting them. Not only was there a nice sized cat up the tree but Grit was at the bottom of the tree jumping up and down.

"What the? What are you? A little Houdini?" Curt said.

Thomas put his hands on his hips, looked at the dog and looked at Curtis, "Well, you shoulda let him hunt. He musta pulled the latch through one of the airholes and popped the door right open."

"I wouldn't believe it, if I didn't see the dog sitting here at the bottom of the tree," Curtis said.

"It sure is a pity there's no gun here," Thomas said. He had an insatiable blood lust. All of his learning concerning conservation went out the window anytime he saw something he could shoot.

"Exactly why I didn't bring the gun. I'll catch that cat later."

"Why later? Let's have some fun now."

Thomas grabbed a stick and beat the trunk to agitate the cat and rile the dogs. The dogs renewed their fury. The noise was almost deafening, even with only one actual hound there. Thomas wanted the cat to jump out of the tree and give them another race. Instead, the cat pissed down the trunk of the tree. The strong scent riled the dogs up even more than they already were.

"He ain't coming out this way, is he?" Thomas said, looking back at Curt.

"Nope." Curt was curt.

"Climb it Curt! Let's see those coon hunting skills."

"No way. The tree is too wet and the branches old."

"Gutless. I shoulda known you were full of hot air." Thomas winked, then started up the tree.

He got right up to the cat about thirty feet high in the tree. He tried shaking the branch the cat sat upon but the cat wasn't going to budge. It flattened its ears and silently hissed at Thomas.

"He won't jump!" He yelled over the hounds, down to Curtis.

"Use a branch and poke him out." Curt suggested.

Thomas looked up the tree for a thinner branch he could break off and fashion a poker with. It was easy to spot one. He started to climb the short distance to his poker. He reached up to the branch. . . SNAP! It wasn't the branch he was reaching for that broke but the one he held in his left hand for balance. He toppled down the tree. His feet acted like a fulcrum and swung Thomas head first down the tree. He fell some distance before hitting a branch. It hit him right where the neck hits the back. Crack! It snapped. He crashed right through it. Crack! Crack! Crack! He hit more branches. They planted themselves on his neck, head and back every time. Curtis looked on helplessly, awestruck. Fwoomp! Thomas hit the ground with enormous impact. He slid down the hill a small way. His descent was stopped by a stump.

Curtis leapt down to Thomas. He was sure his friend would be dead. Thomas was not breathing and completely unconscious. Curtis turned Thomas so that his head was uphill. At this, Thomas started spitting up white foam, but did not awaken. One or the other of the dogs would come and lick at Thomas face, to be quickly kicked away by Curtis.

Curtis knew Thomas needed to get out of the woods and into the hospital as quickly as possible. He left the dogs barking on the cat tree. The cat still sitting up the tree staring down on the couple fools down below her.

Curtis knew which direction the road lay. He braced Thomas around the chest and started the descent through the woods. It was not easy. Thomas was fit, but 200 pounds of dead weight is hard to carry down a mountain safely no matter it's shape.

Curtis got Thomas to the road without incident. He had to leave Thomas in the brush by the roadside, while he ran up the road to get the truck. It was three quarters of a mile up the road. He ran to get there as fast as he could. As soon as he got to the pickup, he jumped in and started down the road to where he left Thomas.

Rounding a corner, he saw Thomas standing dazed in the road. Thomas had the look of a lost and thoughtful man. Curtis pulled up next to him and pushed the passenger door open to Thomas.

"Get in! I'm driving." Thomas didn't question him.

"Oh hey Curt. Fancy finding you out here."

"Yeah? Life is crazy ain't it?" Curtis could tell Thomas was completely out of it. He couldn't pass up the opportunity to tease him, despite the seriousness of what had happened. Once he realized Thomas was not in immediate danger of death, it loosened Curt up considerably.

"How do you like my new truck Thomas?"

"This is your new rig? Wow, I like it. It's pretty nice." Thomas started looking at the cab more carefully.

"Yeah, I like it a lot." Curtis grabbed a handkerchief and polished the dash.

"Where are we?" Thomas was starting to come to, enough that he realized something wasn't right.

"We're in the woods up Strong's Ranch. You just fell out of a tree and have been unconscious for a long while."

"No way? How'd I fall out of a tree?"

"You were trying to shake a bobcat out."

"Wow. I feel fine."

"That's good, but you are not fine. You need a doctor."

"Naw, I'm fine. I think I just need some rest."

"Don't fall asleep, Thomas. Stay awake."

"Geez, You don't have to be so serious Curtis."

Curt made fun of Thomas the whole way back home. He figured the laughing would be good to keep Thomas alert.

When Curt pulled up to Thomas' family home. He told Thomas to stay where he was. He didn't know if Thomas could stay standing if he walked. Curtis called into the house for Mrs. Richardson. She quickly came to see what was going on. The story was recapped and she went to get her own car immediately. While she was gone, Curtis helped Thomas out of the truck. Right before Curtis opened the door for Thomas, he teased him once more before saying goodbye.

"Uh, Thomas." Curtis talked with some hesitation to bait Thomas.

"Yeah? What is it bud?"

"Uh, I didn't want to tell you but. . . You sorta had an erection when you got knocked out." Thomas just stared at Curt. "Yeah, uh, it kinda made me nervous that you were so happy touching all that wood on your way down the tree." Curtis couldn't help but laughing at his own wit.

"I ain't the one staring at my knocked out buddy's boner, Curtis."

At that, Thomas got in the car laughing and went to the hospital.

∘ ∘ ∘

Curtis drove back to the woods as soon as Thomas was off to the hospital. His dogs were still treeing when he arrived. *I suppose they got the practice treeing that they needed*, thought Curt. He grabbed a number of chain-leads and headed toward the dogs. Their excitement had died down, since he left them. It had been a couple hours job, treeing on that cat.

When Curtis got to the tree, he looked up at the cat. It was calm as a pond on a windless day.

"You, cat, are lucky I am a gracious man," Curtis said. "My friend almost died trying to shake your sorry butt outta that tree."

He stared at the cat a while, before snapping up the dogs and leading them from the tree.

He arrived at the truck and opened the tailgate to yet another surprise. It should have crossed his mind earlier, as there was no way Grit could have opened the dogbox door with the tailgate shut. Grit had chewed a gaping hole in Curtis' brand new box. He stood gaping for a bit, before touching the ragged edges of the hole.

It was as if he couldn't believe what he was seeing, he had to feel with his hands too.

"You punk. Are you gonna pay for that?. . . No?. . . I didn't think so."

The hounds hopped in the box without complaint. They were tired and ready for rest. Curtis let Grit ride shotgun in the cab. There was no point trying to keep him in the box. Grit slept sound all the way home.

"You don't have a shred of regret, do you? Shameless little mutt." Curtis scratched the sleeping dog behind the ears.

16. The Weary Traveler Returns

For one year Grit stayed with Curtis. Curtis hunted him every now and then with the hounds but not much. He liked the dog but didn't like the idea of it dying in his care. Grit was a much better hunter than when Robert had last seen him. He'd be happy to have Grit back and working to his full potential. The night Robert returned home was a snowy, icy night. Curtis paid that no mind. As soon as he was able, he went to Robert's home. Robert opened the door and gave Curtis a hug as soon as he walked in. Curtis was never one for hugs but he caved in this instance.

"You're huge!" Robert said.

Curtis had grown half a foot and 50 pounds since Robert had last seen him. Robert on the other hand had lost twenty pounds, since they'd seen each other. Curtis chuckled at Robert, who had to look up at Curtis.

"You look pathetic," Curtis replied.

Robert laughed at his friend's usual candor, "Thanks bud. Come on upstairs. We'll discuss the times we've missed together."

Curtis followed Robert up to Robert's bedroom. The room was as much a library as a bedroom. Robert loved to read. They told each other stories of what had transpired to each of them over the period of separation. Curtis told many stories of his and Thomas' adventures. Robert told of his problems following commands and his hatred for being so subdued while in the military. Curtis understood.

"I figured that's how it would be. That's why I just couldn't do it," Curtis said, shaking his head.

"It ruined me in a way Curtis. I don't know what to do with myself. Nothing seems appealing to me anymore. I don't even want to hunt anymore. I just don't want to kill anything."

At this, Curtis got wide-eyed. "Oh no," he said. "You're not changed that much. That's not even possible. You're just not in the swing of things."

"No. Really Curtis, I haven't even thought of hunting for the past year."

Curtis couldn't believe his ears. For a while, he let Robert give his reasons for not pursuing his most loved passion any further. He couldn't take it.

"You go ahead and sit here thinking you are done hunting. I am going to get something from my place. We'll see how you feel after you've seen it."

Curtis left Robert and drove home. He threw Grit in the dogbox and grabbed some pictures from the last few month's hunting. He drove back to Robert's house to talk some sense into him. Curt left Grit in the box and ran inside, with the pictures in hand.

"Alright, let's see what you've got for me," Robert said.

Curtis sat down and first showed Robert some pictures of fox that the hounds had caught. Robert hadn't talked about hunting much for more than a year. He couldn't help it, his eyes got wide with excitement to see the hounds treeing and game up a tree, even if they were only pictures. When Curtis showed him pictures of a bear and some lions, Robert had to admit to himself that the hounds, the fields and the forests did send energy through his veins.

"Damn! Those are some fine pictures you've got there. I might follow your dogs every now and then, but I think I should start a new chapter in my life."

"You're going to be a punk about this, aren't you," Curtis laughed.

"Man, I'd be lying, if I said I do not get a thrill just thinking of hunting, now that I am back around you. But I feel very disconnected from who I used to be. Hunting is like something from another life."

"I thought as much. Now you can see what it is I brought you. After you see this and if you still don't want to hunt, then I'll know you are brain damaged."

"The pictures aren't it?" asked Robert.

"Nope. Put on some clothes and boots and meet me at my truck."

Robert changed into his work clothes and coat to go outside. It was his first time wearing them in years. The clothes felt so comfortable and natural to him. He felt stronger and healthier in his own coat and pants.

He arrived at Curtis' truck. Curtis was sitting on the tailgate waiting with hand on the latch of his dog-box.

"I got a new dog," Curtis said. "I think he'll tempt you back into the woods." He opened the door and a sandy red dog came out to greet him.

"Grit?" Robert couldn't believe his eyes. "What are you doing with him?" He reached to let the dog

181

smell him. Grit became very excited when he heard Robert's voice and smelled his hand.

"I ran into an old hillbilly at a feed-shop who had him. He asked if I wanted him. I figured it was a bit odd that I'd be offered the dog. Too big of a coincidence. So, I took him, so you could have him when you got back. He's a good dog. He was in on all those hunts in the pictures."

"Wow. That's great. Thank you Curtis." He scratched his dog's ears and head. All the feelings and memories of hunting flooded Robert at once. He sat down on the tailgate to be closer to the dog.

Curtis got a grin on his face, "Grit, give Robert a hug. Hug, Grit."

Grit stepped up onto Robert's chest and nuzzled his head around Robert's neck.

"Alright! Alright, you sappy bastard! You've convinced me to hunt again. There's nothing that could have pleased me more than Grit. Except maybe my sister's friend Hero. You haven't got her somewhere in this truck do you?"

Curtis helped Robert set a kennel up for Grit. Then, he headed home. They agreed to meet in the morning for a run to the woods with the dogs. They were successful and treed a big tom bobcat. Robert was back to his old habits.

◦ ◦ ◦

When Robert returned the winter after his twentieth birthday. There had been some worry for him. Many heard he was ill, others that he was wounded mortally. His arrival home put the community at ease. He had been wounded. A limp was noticeable in his gait. Whenever he was asked to tell the story behind his limp he would rarely say much. Very few would he converse with about his experiences. Anger and sadness were in him where they had not existed in him before. His family could not understand. Robert's sister and Curtis were the only two he felt at ease with. Curt did not need to get to the bottom of Robert's feelings. He merely said, "I am just glad to have my friend back."

Robert got away from all worry of pleasing others when he was with Curtis. There were times when Curtis would pick him up to hunt and they would not say a word to each other the entire day. Robert felt that was a testament to the concrete friendship Curtis had for him. Robert needed to prove nothing to him.

While Curtis comforted Robert silently, Robert's sister, Lara, comforted him with joy. She arranged a party every weekend. Robert always joined in the festivities. Though he was unable to relieve himself of all his anger, he was always able to let loose at his sister's gatherings. There was one major attraction that ensured Robert would be present, Hero. Lara, had written to Robert every week in detail about how wonderful Hero was. She told him that he and Hero were a perfect match and must be married. Robert teased her to set the date for the December of his return. Hero had only gained in beauty and talent, while Robert was away. He was completely enamored with her. She had only turned 17 by the time Robert saw her again. But he cared little that she was younger. He loved every moment of time he spent in her presence. He spent the next year courting her with poetry, songs and wildflowers. He would bring her family venison, mushrooms and fern fiddleheads. But he eventually realized they weren't country folk. They couldn't appreciate the fine flavors of the woods. But Hero fell in love with his mountain spirit. When she turned 18, her parents finally consented to her dating Robert, "That uneducated hillbilly".

17. New Dogs

Robert was fully obsessed with hunting again. As it says in the bible, clear a house of a single devil, invite it back in and you'll have seven more along with it. Robert had a demon for hunting and it was as strong as ever. He hunted Grit as much as he could but it was not enough to satisfy him. He wanted more dogs. He made some calls and got some agreements from fellows who would give him dogs. Rowdy Hank had a bitch Robert took but she didn't work out. He went searching for a more familiar type of dog.

Robert's next couple of dogs was a natural choice. He loved Grit so well, he went calling upon Joseph the goatherd for more.

"I have some I can loan you," Joseph offered without hesitation, "but they are fine dogs. I'll want them in my pack again after the season is over and you've gotten yourself some more dogs."

"No problem. I'll come to get them as soon as I can gather the funds for the journey."

Joseph lived 1,000 miles from Robert but it would be worth it. Once a person has worked with excellent dogs, he cannot go back to mediocre. Keeping poor performing dogs eats at a hunter's nerves.

∘ ∘ ∘

Robert wasted no time. He worked as swiftly as he could to gather the money for the trip. By mid-January, he and Grit were on their way to see Joseph and bring some dogs back.

The Idaho-Oregon border was very different in January than in the late Spring when Robert had last been there. No the alfalfa fields were only stubble and dusted with snow. The canals running with water in the spring, were frozen.

Joseph met Robert at the gate. Red collies were swarming around his feet.

"It's been a while since I last saw you," Joseph said, offering his hand to Robert.

"It feels like yesterday I saw you," Robert said, smiling.

"If it was yesterday, you grew a foot overnight," Came Joseph's memorable raspy voice.

"It's been known to happen."

"Is that Grit in the cab?" Joseph asked.

"Sure is. I didn't want you to go to the grave without seeing the best dog in the world." Robert winked.

"Don't you worry about that Robert. I've got the best here. Let me show you some real dogs." He shot the wink right back.

The dogs were all in handmade kennels of wood and wire. There were about eight spaces in all. Joseph limped to the first kennel. His arthritis was chewing his joints to bits. That didn't stop Joseph. He was as rough and ready a man as any. "Tough as barbwire" some would say of Joseph. There were stories of Joseph, even in his old age, lassoing a mountain lion and fixin' to hogtie the cat. Well, that was the idea. He ended up climbing the tree to avoid branches that would snag the rope. He had a bit of a slip and ended upside down with his leg caught in a crotch. Even in his old age, he was tougher than most men.

Joseph pointed to the red dog in the first kennel, "That's Goldie. Coallie's sire. The best dog in the world." Joseph had a good laugh at that.

"I've heard of him," Robert said.

The Goldie dog was big for an earthdog, but Joseph hunted mostly above ground now. He didn't want to be bothered with digging fox anymore. As far as looks went, Goldie was as well built a dog as anyone could dream of. His head was a sledge and his muscles as dense as concrete. He looked sculpted.

"Yeah. He's no fox dog. I gave that digging up a few years ago. I ain't as young as I once was."

Joseph went through naming each dog and telling each dogs strong points and weak points. The man was honest to his own detriment when it came to dogs. He could never pull of being a salesman. He finally came to the two he was lending to Robert.

"This here is Sandy. You'll remember him." Joseph pointed to an enormous terrier covered in thick wiry hair. The head on the dog looked much like an English bullterrier's head. Sandy was Grit's littermate brother. "I'd like to say he's an excellent dog. I've been hearing a lot about Grit and how good he's gotten. The truth is, I just haven't worked him very much. I've got more dogs than I can handle right now and he is always the one that gets left behind. I'd like to see what you can get out of him."

"I've got no problem with that. He looks well capable of the job."

"And here's old Scrapper." Joseph pointed out a long legged, lean black and tan dog. The dog was not actually old, four or five years at most. But to call a dog "old" or "ol'" is a matter of respect for the dog. "Old" is like a title that a dog or a person earns. "Scrapper, he'll hunt. The problem is, he won't stop. He won't come when you call him either. He just goes until he finds something and you take him off of it."

"That sounds familiar. That's how my old Jackson dog was."

"I don't know if you want to take him. But you can use him for the rest of the season, if you like."

"Oh yeah. I'll try him out. Thanks again, Joseph. I am in a pickle for dogs right now. This should bolster my success."

"Sure thing, Robert. You're doing me a favor. You came all this way. Do you want to do some hunting?"

"Sounds good to me," Robert replied.

Joseph loaded Goldie up. He wanted to show off his best dog. He also loaded up a black bitch he called Snake, Coallie's half sister. And Sandy was brought along as well. Joseph left the Scrapper dog behind. He didn't want the hunt to last too long, if they didn't catch anything. They drove only a mile or so down the road to a hillside covered in very tightly packed, thick vined blackberries. The snow weighed them down in the winter, packing them tight and causing the vines to grow stronger to support the weight. Their was a deep stream bed at the base of the hill. Only a little water trickled underneath the thin ice. Water plus blackberry bushes is an equation for coon, no matter what state you're in.

"I have saved this hunting spot all year to take a guest to. This is as good a time as any."

"I'll have to agree with you on that, Joseph."

"A couple years ago, my dogs ran three coyotes out of the brush here. If I'd had a shotgun, I would have blasted the yotes."

"Man, I bet they could tear up your dogs."

"Oh, No doubt about it. They could kill one of these little dogs in the blink of an eye. It worries me to hunt them here sometimes. That's why I usually like to have my bulldog cross with me. I don't think we'll run into coyotes today though."

The dogs were dropped and searched the brush, while the men talked. Grit and Goldie shot like arrows to the thickest berry patch.

"What is the oddest thing you have encountered while you were hunting with the dogs? Have you ever seen sign of Bigfoot?" Robert asked Joseph.

"Can't say 'at I've seen Bigfoot. But the weirdest thing I've seen while following dogs was when I was trying to catch a lion. It was a very cold winter. We were getting temperatures well below zero every night. There was a lion coming in to kill farm animals. Could have been finding shelter under the barn too, 'cause that's where we scared him up the first afternoon. We ran him with the dogs until the sun went down. We knew it would be too dangerous to keep the hounds out overnight. And I was already colder than a witch's tit on a north slope. I gathered the dogs and decided to catch that cougar the next day."

"Your dogs didn't catch him right off the jump?"

"No," answered Joseph, "the snow was very deep and the cougar seemed to be gliding through it. My dogs' pads got shredded to bits in the ice. But I brought some fresh hounds the next day and we started the track again where we had left off. As I said, the nights were incredibly cold. After a few hours of cold trailing, the hounds found the cougar. But he was dead, frozen as stiff as my pecker!"

"So he was pretty limp, then?" said Robert.

Joseph grinned. "Boy, I aught to drown you in this creek."

"You're welcome to try old man. I wouldn't want to force your family to collect on life insurance so soon."

Joseph took playful jabs with his fists. Robert dodged them.

"I'm old but my knuckles'll still knock a fool out. . . If I was looking to hit you."

They heard a dog bark and stopped to listen.

"Was that Grit or Goldie?" Robert asked.

"Not sure. I never thought there'd be a day I had to question," Joseph answered.

Goldie had run across the field and through a marshy patch and shot into another patch of blackberries. Snake and Sandy had been content to march around the blackberries waiting for Goldie and Grit to do the work. That often happens when a person continues hunting young dogs with a better old dog. It is better to let the young dogs figure hunting out for themselves. The raccoon snorted and houghed. Goldie barked his raspy low bark. *The dog sounds like Ol' Joseph*. Robert thought. *Where the heck is Grit?*

Snake and Sandy bulldozed through the brush as fast as they could push. The men marched across the field to catch up with the action. Screeching and yelps told the men that the two "me-too" dogs had made it to the fight. When the men arrived at the briar patch, Joseph handed Robert a pair of clippers. Robert preferred machetes for thick berries but he wasn't going to complain. He put his gloves on and walked on top of the berries until he was right next to the dogs with the raccoon. One thick vine at a time, he clipped a hole into the dogs. The coon was getting all it could take. The dogs were nearly silent, their mouths full of fur, while the raccoon strained to make frightening noises to scare it's attackers away. Compared to these big terriers, the raccoon was small. Though it was 18 pounds at least, a strong coon anywhere else. Robert got a hold of it's tail and pulled it out of the brush. That was no easy task with about 70 pounds of dog latched to it as well. Joseph helped Robert by grabbing the dogs one at a time and leashing them. Goldie was the last dog to be taken off of the raccoon. Robert stared at his head, while he continued to hold tight onto the coon. His head was incredibly strong. Thick muscle bulged between Goldie's ears. His snout was wide and thick. It would take quite a coon to put any hurt on that dog. Grit was not to be seen.

"No Grit? I'm gonna have to hang on to the champion's belt this year Robert. Try again next January." He gave Robert a teasing nudge.

"Hey. If you don't see Grit, it's cause he's doing what he's supposed to."

Joseph laughed. "We'll see." He paused to look the raccoon over. "I know the dogs put a hurt on this coon but let's let it go. I think it can make it alive."

"As you wish," Robert replied. He helped the raccoon up ontop of the blackberries. The sorry animal slowly moved across the top of the patch. The dogs had put more than a little hurt on that raccoon. Joseph was a sportsman. He always tried to give the healthy raccoons a chance to live, if he didn't have to kill them. With such big dogs having bitten the raccoon, Robert didn't quite feel comfortable letting the coon go to suffer and die later but it was Joseph's raccoon to do with as he wished.

They took the dogs to the nearby stream to drink and cool down. All three of the dogs had very thick coats. Each of them got into the stream and laid in the water. Robert was surprised that the dogs didn't mind the cold of the water at all. There was still ice covering parts of the stream.

Robert stood quietly listening for Grit, while the dogs took a short break to catch their breath. There was a faint "chop-chop" in the distance, all the way back near the truck.

"You hear that, Joseph?"

"Can't say that I do."

"Grit's got something bayed back by the truck."

"Huh. Let's head back then."

"That'd be funny."

"What'd be funny?" Joseph asked.

"Oh, just Goldie being the best dog in the world an' all but he passed up the coon closest to the truck." At that Robert widened his eyes in a mocking face of surprise, then ran to get to his dog. He could hear Joseph laughing far behind him.

Grit had another 18 pound coon pushed up into a dead end in the blackberries. It was equally as big as Grit and taking shots on him. Each time the raccoon lunged for Grit, Robert could hear it snort. Grit's barking would get higher pitched every time the raccoon tried to run past him.

"Get 'im, Grit!"

As soon as Grit heard his master's voice, he locked teeth on the raccoon. The snorts of the raccoon turned into a growl like the zzzz–zzzz rhythm of a saw dragging back and forth across the trunk of a tree. Joseph arrived shortly and let Goldie loose to help Grit lock the raccoon down until Robert clipped through to them.

Once again, Robert was astounded at the strength of the Goldie dog. He was a magnificent animal. As soon as the men got through to the fray, Robert broke the dogs off and carried the raccoon at arm's length to a tree. Up the tree the coon went, up to safety.

"Up for one more round?" Joseph asked.

As always, Robert was ready for more.

A little walk and a little talk and another coon was caught by Goldie.

"Sometimes I wonder if that dog keeps the coons in a pocket and pulls them out when he's in the bushes. I can't believe how good he is at locating," Joseph said of Goldie.

"Maybe he carries a pouch of dehydrated raccoons. He just needs to add water and poof, there's a coon," said Robert.

The third coon played out just as the first but Grit was there this time. Robert didn't let this one go. It looked even worse off. Robert preferred to only let the very robust go. Hunting with one dog often kept the coon from receiving too much punishment. But four large dogs can kill a coon fast.

"I'll give Goldie the title of champion this year, but Grit's gonna pull through as champ next time you see him."

"Grit's as fine a dog as you say he is, Robert. Another day here and Grit may have shown old Goldie up."

"You come out my way sometime, Joseph and we'll have a good time. We'll see if Grit can't show Goldie a thing or two on his home turf."

Joseph had chores to perform and Robert had arrived late in the day, so Robert left soon after arriving. He took Scrap and Sandy in a couple of crates and headed back the way he had come. He drove all the way home without stopping at a hotel for the night and arrived back the morning of the next day. He had himself some new dogs.

18. River Hunt

Robert spent the first week with his new dogs bonding with them. Sandy was a very shy animal. The first night Robert had him, Sandy somehow made it free and nobody could catch him. Robert drove after the dog in his pickup truck. He herded Sandy through fields and back onto his father's farm. There, he lured Sandy into grabbing range with a piece of cheese. Scrapper needed bonding as well. He was not shy in the least, only aloof. He did not mind being petted or picked up but he acted as if he were deaf, completely ignoring commands. So Robert would sit with them every day in the kennels. He'd call them to come to him a short distance and give them food. As they became accustomed to that, he began taking them out on a lead and commanding their attention, while out on walks. And from there he graduated them to lunge-lines. Lunge lines are often used for horse work but Robert found them useful for training his dogs with basic commands. A lunge line is a lead that allows the animal to get distance from the trainer. Robert used a 35 foot long lunge line.

By week's end, Robert could wait no longer to try the dogs. He hunted Scrapper alone first. Scrapper was an excellent dog, every bit as good as any Robert had owned himself. On the first day out with Robert, Scrap caught five raccoon. Some in the brush, some he put into holes in trees. The dog was a machine, pro-grammed only to find raccoons. Robert was very im-pressed by the dog.

He took him again the next day and Scrap ran and bolted a fox from cover. Robert couldn't have been more pleased. Robert didn't carry a gun to hunt on these days out with Scrapper, so all was let live to hunt again another day. Though Robert was very impressed with the dogs hunting abilities, he couldn't get the dog to come when called. It was just as Joseph said, if he didn't catch anything, he wouldn't come in. It would be the dog's doom.

Sandy was not acclimating so well as Scrapper to the hunting. Scrapper had been one of Joseph's main dogs whereas, Sandy was a back-burner dog. Joseph thought if anybody could get the most out of Sandy, it would be Robert. And Robert gave it his all but it became quickly apparent that Sandy had "me too'd" it too long. Robert walked him along riverbanks and through brushy areas but Sandy wouldn't leave Robert's heels. Robert came to the conclusion that Sandy was a great help when game was getting out of hand for another dog but was of no use solo.

Robert worked with the dogs individually for three weeks before he took them along with Grit as a pack to hunt bigger game than coon. Robert and Curtis slid the canoe into the water, near where Grit had swam across the river as a puppy.

The water was low for the time of year. It hadn't been an especially wet Autumn or Winter. The banks were steep and covered with willow and blackberry. Every thirty feet or so there were cottonwoods sprouting up in groups of three or four trees above the willow.

Robert dropped the dogs to hunt before the canoe was put into the water. Grit and Sandy stayed close to Curt and Rob but Scrapper immediately took off to hunt on his own. The salmon were running at the time, which made Robert and Curtis nervous to have dogs down near the water. Fish that travel from the ocean to the rivers to spawn carry with them a deadly parasite that, if ingested, can kill a dog inside one week. But it couldn't be helped that the run coincided with hunting season. As they floated onto the mirror-like surface of the river, they could see Scrap pop in and out of the bushes every now and then.

There were loads of sign on the closest bank; otter slides, used by both otter and beaver, beaver chews, willow wands. Grit ran the bank and zoomed up the slides to find where they began. On one of these short excursions up the banks, Grit found Scrapper eating a rotting salmon that had been pulled up into the brush. Grit was focused on his hunting and passed by without second thought. He wasn't hungry.

After about one quarter mile of floating, they came to a major den site. The willows were heavily burdened by a thick layer of berry vines. Inside the dark tangle, holes had been dug deep into the bank, deep and wide. Rob tried to call Scrapper. He knew this sette would hold game. He also knew that his calling would be in vain. Scrapper was a free agent.

Grit slithered his way through the unearthed roots and branches. In time, he found his way into the system of holes and dens dug into the bank. Sandy was too big in the chest to squeeze through all the brush. He went down the bank and swam around the barriers and into the hole the same way a beaver would enter.

A raucous was soon heard. A small tussle ensued and ended quickly with a few gurgles. Curt shined a light up into the hole.

"Looks like a nutria," Curtis said.

"Dang. I was hoping for something special. A mink or something cool that is small, not a nutria."

"Sorry to disappoint."

Just then, Grit and Sandy both lit up into a hard bay. The baying went silent. Muffled biting could be heard through the sand and brush. *Thump Thump Thump Thump Swoosh! Splsh!* An enormous beaver hit the water. The willow branches pried Sandy and Grit off of the beaver. The tree-chopping rodent looked the size of a small sheep. For a second, Robert couldn't discern what he was seeing. The head was that enormous.

The beaver surfaced only meters from where it had plunged. It looked as if Grit and Sandy had winded it, at least. Robert quickly shot a bullet toward it's head. Sploshlap! The beaver rolled and slapped it's tail. It dove into the dark weedy depths but never surfaced again.

"Darnit! Did I miss?"

"I don't think so," Curtis said with a questioning look, "I think he was just too big for a .22 to take out."

"That sounds like bull shit. A .22 bullet to the brain would kill a moose."

"Maybe, but you might have hit it in the neck. That's all flesh. Would've hurt it but not killed it."

"I guess so. He's got to come up for air sometime. We'll wait." But the beaver never surfaced again. "Might as well hack in and see what it was they killed in the hole," Robert said, after waiting longer than any beaver could hold it's breath. "If that big beaver isn't dead floating on the bottom of the river somewhere, he's found a hole to hide in under the water."

Rob hopped out of the canoe and whacked away branches until he could slice away at the den with a shovel and reach to grab the game. He reached in and felt around for fur. The body was not far from the entrance of the hole. It had probably tried to bolt but was caught in the tunnel by the dogs, while it was on its way out. Robert lifted a 16 pound body from the den. It had a small, wide, flat tail. It was a yearling beaver.

Robert held it up for Curt to see, "Dog food.".

"Better than a nutria," Curtis said, shrugging his shoulders.

Robert got into the canoe with Curt and called the dogs. Sandy and Grit hopped into the canoe within 5 minutes. But Scrapper couldn't be heard barking or rustling through brush. He hadn't come to help with the beavers at all. The men floated back the way they came to search for Scrapper but he wasn't to be seen or heard.

"I don't want to spend the day searching for a dog," Robert said. "He'll eventually catch something and we'll find him then. Until that happens, let's paddle across and try to catch something on the other side."

Grit and Sandy laid at Rob's feet in the canoe as they floated across. They hadn't worked hard, but they were calm and easy dogs when in the canoe. Robert loved that about them.

The opposite bank was opposite in more than direction. It was bare, covered only in grass, sand and some giant cottonwood trees and maples further up the bank in the fields. Rocks were apparent on the shore. There was a maple tree up in the field with fox dens dug all through its roots. Grit was dug to a coon and a nutria on different occasions up in that sette. On this day, nothing was in the ground there. So, the men let the dogs run the bank checking washed out roots. A mink ran the short way from the water and into the roots of a giant cotton wood. Robert and Curtis pushed into high gear and paddled to where they saw the mink go into the roots. They called Sandy and Grit to take a look.

Neither dog had ever hunted mink before. They both approached and sniffed but showed very little interest. They had both been broken off of skunks and other trash. The smell of mink gave cause for the dogs to halt and wonder if they should be pursuing it at all.

"It's probably better that they don't want to catch that mink," Curtis said. "There's no way I want to cut through all those roots. It's so small too. Who knows if we'd ever actually get to it?"

"Yeah. You're right," Robert agreed. "Plus, this is the cottonwood the eagles nest in every year. If it fell over from us cutting through its roots for a mink. . . Oh hoo ho. There'd be trouble from Gina."

"Let's leave it then and head back across. We'll hunt our way back down and try to get that Scrapper dog back."

They did as Curtis suggested. They grabbed the dogs up and paddled upstream a bit further, then crossed back to the other side. They put the dogs to shore on some rocks at the base of a hill. There was thick grass and a maze of water going through rock and weeds. The dogs went charging into the labyrinth. Curtis and Rob didn't hear anything but rustling of the coarse saw grass for 10 minutes. Then,

"RAWAAH!" Grit was on something and pushing through the grass and into water. *Splash! Splash! Sploosh!* "Yiieee! Yiiiieee!"

"Holy Hell! Something is really putting the hurt on Grit!" Robert said. He didn't have to tell Curt to paddle like mad, he was already on it.

More splashing and then quiet.

"There's a bubble chain!" Curtis said. He leaned forward and pointed. There was bubble after bubble popping up to surface in a straight line down the river.

Curtis, as rudder and rear drive, directed the canoe and together the men paddled after the otter. It surfaced twice. Each time, the canoe shot in its direction, pressuring it to go on land. Each time it had less breath. When the otter surfaced for the third time, it had made it to where the beavers had been caught. Into the holes it went. The dogs were still behind in the water maze, swimming and searching for the missing otter.

"You stay and watch the hole. I'll go and get the dogs," said Robert.

Curtis hopped onto land and placed himself, crouching in front of the hole. He wanted to block the exit and keep the otter in. Luckily, the otter didn't want to leave.

Robert was back with Grit in hand within 10 minutes. He snapped Sandy to a bar in the canoe to await a time when he would be necessary.

Curtis spoke up, "We can put just Grit in and we'll get an easy bolt, as usual. Or we could put Sandy down the other side and block off the retreat and dig to it."

"Other side?"

"Yeah, there's another hole that joins all these. I saw it when we floated by earlier. It's hidden by grass, but it should connect. Check it out."

Robert handed Grit to Curtis, then swooped the canoe back around all the willows that were hanging about ten feet out over the river. Sure enough, there was a sandy narrow trail through the grass. A hole was possibly up there but Robert couldn't be sure. He parked the canoe and walked up. The trail did lead to a hole.

"There's a hole," Rob told Curt through the thicket.

"I'll drop Grit here," Curt said. "You let Sandy run through that side. We'll bottle him. It's unlikely you'll be able to get a good shot on him bolting."

Robert put on airs, "Are you calling me a bad shot? I could shoot a feather in the wind."

Curt laughed. "I won't say you're a bad shot. But I might bring up the beaver that isn't sitting in the canoe."

"We can't all be as fantastic a shot as you."

"Nope. That's the truth." Curtis ducked his head to see Robert through the brush and grinned.

"Whatever, Curt. We'll do it your way."

"We'll need to let the dogs in at the same time or we'll have a bolt anyway."

"Just say when," Robert answered.

Rob went back to the canoe and unsnapped Sandy. He also grabbed the .22, just in case of a bolt. He took Sandy straight to the hole and let him get a good whiff. He patted the dog and tried to excite him over the new smell.

"Ssssk, sssssk Get 'im, get 'im boy sssssk." The dog started whining and straining on the collar. "Ready on this side." Robert called to Curtis.

"Letting Grit go now," Curtis said.

Robert let Grit get a bit of a lead. Sandy wasn't a dog that liked to meet game head on by himself. He'd want Grit there before he'd really lay down the hammer on the otter. Also, if the otter gained momentum bolting in the direction of Grit, the otter may just push right through the smaller dog. If Grit went first, it helped ensure that the otter would bolt toward Sandy. Sandy was a much bigger dog. He'd block a large portion of the otter's way out.

Grit was in and on and Sandy moved down the pipe toward the fight.

"Yieeee! Yieeee!" Grit was taking serious punishment from the otter. The old-timers liked to say that the otter has the speed of the fox and the power of the badger. Grit was feeling the affects of that dynamic.

"Yhooowaa!" Sandy was on and taking damage as well. Both dogs tussled with the otter. Both were taking what sounded like hard damage. After five minutes of the otter staying put, it was time to move.

"I'm coming back your way Curtis. That seems the best place to dig."

"Okay. You want me to switch you places? Make sure there isn't a bolt from that side."

"Actually, I think I'll want your help digging and hacking through all the brush," Robert said.

"Alright. But we could get a bolt, while we're digging."

"I'm not worried about it. Sandy is so big, how could the otter pass him?"

"It's not like Sandy has proven himself. But, I guess now is as good a time as any to test his metal."

Before Robert got around in the canoe, Curtis was already hacking away at the brush to clear the area for digging. The earth was pure sand. It could easily collapse onto the dogs and suffocate them. The willows didn't give the men much room to move but they hoped that the roots would create a structure to hold the sand up. They did. Curt and Rob cut away at the sand for about three feet before they hit a bundle of roots too thick to hack through. The interweaving wood would take hours to hack through. Lucky for them, they had a hole large enough to fit Grit through and Grit was just up the tunnel another foot or so. Curtis was who broke through to the pipe. The sound of barking grew more clear with open air to grow into.

"Can you tell what the situation is?" Robert asked.

"I can tell Grit is right within reach here. The tunnel is inclined upward. I think the otter has the high ground advantage."

"Dang. That's tough on the dogs. Is the otter sitting up on a ledge and just taking jabs?"

"I can't say. The incline is too steep to see more than a bit of Grit's feet every once in a while."

"Can you grab Grit and get him out of the way?"

Curt imagined reaching into the den and pulling his hand back out with bloody stubs for fingers. "Are you kidding me? You reach your hand in with that otter. These are your dogs. Remember?"

"Geez! Have I got to do everything around here?" Robert mocked. He laid down on his belly and shone the light into the hole. He could see loose sand get kicked back now and again by the baying terrier. When Robert looked into that dark hole, he couldn't tell what would meet his hand when he reached in. His stomach went into his throat. Robert looked up at Curtis, "I think that otter could snap right through my fingers."

Curtis chuffed, "See why I wasn't going to reach my hand in there?"

"Okay. You can shutup before you start," Robert said. He peered back into the hole. "I'm just going to have to wait till I can get a good view of something to grab. I'm not fumbling around in there blindly with my hand."

"Geez!" Curtis teased.

"Didn't I tell you to shut it?"

"You'll only lose one, two fingers tops. Just reach in and grab it. Or do I have to do everything around here?"

"Hearty Har Har. Hand me the machete again. I'll try to get some of these roots cleared and get a better view." Robert hacked at the roots for a while, but the space he had to work in didn't give him enough room to really swing and get the chips flying. "We're gonna have to dig out more, so I can have room."

Curtis hopped to and dug around the hole, widening it some but not much.

"There are just too many thick roots. We'd need a saw to do this properly. And that clump there, blocking our way to Grit, that'd take a chainsaw. There are just too many thick roots in there."

The men sat still for a while, listening to Grit and Sandy baying away. The otter had taught them their lessons and they didn't want another tutorial.

Robert spoke up, "If we could just get an extra six inches of vision, we could pull Grit out and maybe get a clean shot on the otter."

"To do that, you'd need to take off that six inches from the bottom of the roots. There's no room to swing like that." Curtis pointed out.

At that, Robert laid on his belly again. He'd wait for Grit to come down the pipe a way and then grab him out.

"Thump on the ground over where the otter should be sitting," Robert told Curtis.

Curtis cut some more brush out of his way, then went to thumping the sand with the shovel. The dogs got noisier. The Otter pushed at the dogs a bit, to test their determination. When the otter pushed at Grit, Grit slid down the pipe to within Robert's view. Grit went from barking to muffled growls. He got a hold of the otter when it tried to bolt past him. Robert quickly shot his arm up the pipe and grabbed Grit's hind legs.

Robert got excited, "Get the gun quick! This may be our shot!"

Curt jumped over Robert and leaped for the gun. He went back to the hole and hovered over Rob, who was trying to slowly pull Grit into the open with his quarry. Sandy was still baying from the other pipe.

Robert needed to wait to know whether Grit had the otter mouth to mouth. If Grit did have it by the mouth, any pulling could cause harm to Grit. Pulling could cause the otter's teeth to strip Grit's pallet. While Rob waited, he held onto Grit's legs and looked up to talk to Curt.

"It's nice that I don't have to worry about pulling the weight of the otter and Sandy out of the hole with Grit, but I've got to say, I'm disappointed that Sandy is baying when Grit has taken the otter's attention."

"Yeah. I wouldn't expect great things from that dog."

Sandy continued to bay from behind the otter, while Robert slowly made progress pulling Grit out of the hole with the otter in grips. As Grit's hind-end made an appearance, Curt readied the gun.

"Whooo doggy! That otter will be within reach any second now," Said Robert, still gently pulling the dog from the hole. But he spoke too soon. The otter must have twisted and pulled loose. Grit lost his hold. Robert pulled Grit out to inspect him. There were chunks taken out of Grit's lips and face. These were not puncture wounds in the way other animals wounded Grit. These bites looked like the otter had bitten the dog and twisted.

"Tie him back in the canoe would you?" Robert handed Grit to Curtis.

The otter had shot back into the back of the holt and met Sandy there. It hit Sandy like a whirlwind. Screeching and growling could be heard, mostly coming from Sandy. Curtis hitched Grit to the bar in the canoe, then stood waiting for what was inevitable. Sandy had moved into the open space inside the holt and let the exit tunnel go unguarded. The otter won his way past Sandy and shot out the hole and through the grass to the water. He torpedoed through the water right under the canoe and into the deeper parts of the river. But the otter was too tired to stay under long. Sandy came out of the hole looking tired. But when he heard the otter surface and let out a watery "Spphhh," Sandy jumped into the river to pursue. Grit strained on the chain and screamed in excitement. He wanted another piece of that otter. PKOW! PKOW! Curtis sent two bullets through the brain-pan of the otter. The shot game rolled and thrashed in the water. It was in it's death rolls.

Curtis smiled back at Robert and winked. "That's how we do it in Dixie!" He pushed the canoe out to grab the otter before it sank or hit the rapids. Sandy was already on the scene trying to get a hold on the thrashing otter. Curtis got to the dog and quarry. He lifted Sandy in first. Along with the dog came the otter.

19. The Search

After some back slapping and grins, the otter was inspected, it's weight guessed to be about twenty pounds and it's age guessed to be young. It was now time to search out and find the Scrapper dog.

Searching for him on the way back was easy. They had to float back down the river anyway. But there was not sign of hide nor hair of that dog. Robert called for the dog, screeched like a distressed raccoon but the dog came to nothing. The men loaded the canoe on top of the truck, tied it down and put Grit and Sandy battered and scarred into the box.

They walked along the edge of the brush, quietly listening for any rustle in the brush. There was only silence. They walked back past the truck and listened for barking. There was none. They looked from high vantage points over the rocky river-land below. The dog was not to be seen.

"There's nothing for it Curtis. I'll have to come back tomorrow and search for him."

"Alright. If that's what you think is best."

Robert left a sweater at the base of a tree where the truck had been parked. He hoped the dog would come back and stay where something was familiar. The men then drove off to home.

∘ ∘ ∘

Robert went back to search for Scrapper the next morning but once again was unable to find or hear any sign of the dog. For three days he walked the river and the woods of that area, searching for Scrapper but he could not locate him.

On the fourth day Gina, the woman who owned the land along that portion of river, called Robert's home.

"Robert, have you been missing a dog?" Her voice was always so motherly. She had known Robert since he was a boy and knew about his hunting dogs.

"Yes. I am missing a dog." Robert was excited to know Gina must have seen Scrapper.

"Well, I just saw the little fella wandering around down by the river. He doesn't look very good but he wouldn't let me catch him."

"OK. Thank you for calling Gina. I'll be there in 10 minutes. Can you show me where he was?"

"Yes, I can. You've got to train your dogs better or something Robert. You can't keep losing them like this." Gina had found one of Robert's dogs a few years before that had been missing for several weeks. That particular dog had come home fatter than it had left, living off of small game it caught for itself. Robert expected that Scrapper was every bit as capable of taking care of himself. Though Scrapper was a much more determined working terrier than the other dog, which worried Robert. Scrapper had on one occasion stayed to ground on a fox for 27 hours. When he was finally dug to after all that time, he was given a drink of water, then he tried to shoot back underground to find more fox. If anything, Robert expected the dog had been to ground most of that time and was tattered by some animal.

When Robert arrived at the ranch, he walked through the fields with Gina right to where he had parked his truck the day of the hunt. There was Scrap, hanging around the sweater Robert had left. But it was quickly apparent that the dog was knocking on death's door. Gina looked sadly at the dog.

"Really Robert, you need to care more for these dogs."

"Yes ma'am. Thank you for your help." Robert knew there was no explaining to her the nature of what he did. She was by no means anti-hunting. She wanted the boys to hunt on her property to protect her crops and livestock but she didn't understand that sometimes the dogs just couldn't or wouldn't be found at the end of a hunt.

Robert drove straight home with the dog and called up Joseph the goatherd. Joseph's woman friend answered the phone. Robert asked her to let Joseph know to call as soon as possible.

Robert was in over his head with the situation. He had not yet been taught how to hydrate a sick dog, nor did he know what the dog was suffering from or how to cure it. The dog was deathly dehydrated. Scrapper could barely stand. Robert loaded Scrap into the car and drove him to the veterinarian. This would be the last hunting dog Robert trusted to a veterinarian's care. He realized after his experience with Scrapper that veterinarians just were not willing to sacrifice time or effort for his hunting dogs. When he arrived, a female veterinary assistant took the dog back to be inspected immediately.

They put Scrap on the table.

"How did the dog get to this point of dehydration before you decided to bring him in?" asked the assistant.

"He was lost, while out hunting. I searched all week for him and just found him today."

"It looks like he has not eaten nor drank in that entire time."

"You're telling me what I already know. Now tell me what the problem is," Robert said. He had brought in dogs before and the conclusion was always the same, the dog needed to be put down. Every time, Robert took the dogs home and tried his own methods and never did it fail that Robert revived the dogs to full health. This time however, the sickness was too long overdue for treatment. The assistant took samples from the dog and ran tests. After sometime the woman returned.

"My best guess is salmon poisoning," the woman said.

"Your best guess? The tests didn't confirm that?" Robert asked.

"No. The tests didn't show any recognizable disease."

"What's to be done then?"

"The best thing to do is put the dog down."

"No. That's not an option. That's what you all tell me every time. Fix this dog. I don't care what the price is."

The woman looked at Robert with some sympathy, perhaps real, perhaps feigned. "We can try to hydrate him but don't get your hopes up. There's nothing else you can do, so I'll keep the dog here and let you know what's happening if anything goes on."

Robert didn't know what else to do. He left the dog with the clinic and went home. Joseph called him shortly after he arrived. His raspy voice was immediately recognizable. But it was the first time Robert had ever been nervous to hear it.

"I heard you called," came the old man's voice.

"Yes, I did."

"What's the news then?" Joseph sounded happy and excited. Usually Robert only called to tell him hunting stories.

"The news isn't good Joseph. Your dog Scrap is in the veterinarian's right now."

"That's not good. What's going on with the dog?"

"The vet isn't sure but they say it's probably salmon poisoning."

"Salmon poisoning? What the hell is that?" Joseph wasn't speaking angrily. Salmon poisoning is almost strictly a disease caught by dogs along the coast of the United States.

"It is caused by a parasite in the blood of salmon and trout."

"That sounds awfully quick Robert. Scrapper must have caught something from my place and is just now showing that he's sick."

"I won't rule that possibility out, Joseph. But the salmon are running now and the ones that are spawned out have washed to shore. I've been told the disease can take a dog out pretty fast."

"Hmmm." Joseph thought for a bit. "What's the advice of the vet?"

"They want to put him down. I told them I'd foot whatever bill."

"Don't do that, Robert. He's a good dog but I know you don't have the money for that. If they need to put the dog down, just let them do it."

"I am so sorry Joseph. I just didn't know how to handle this situation. I haven't had a dog go sick like this so fast before. Do you want me to pay for the dog?"

"No. You don't worry about that. Shit happens. Nobody could've helped it. I'll let you off the phone. You give that vet a call and tell them to do what needs to be done."

Robert got off the phone and called the vet's office right away. They asked if he wanted to see the dog before they put it down. Robert didn't see the point in petting a dog doomed to die. He stayed home and felt sorry for old Joseph.

20. A Stint With the Hounds

The year after that passed normally. It was seen that Sandy would never hunt as Robert expected of a dog in his care. So, Sandy was sent back to Joseph with an honest report of what Robert thought of the dog. Joseph felt that Sandy would still do just fine for his own needs. Robert was down to Grit as his only dog by summertime. With less time working terriers, Robert went hunting with Jon and Curt and their hounds.

Curt still had Ol' Burdog and Prissy. Jon was always going through new hounds. He never seemed to find satisfaction in the dogs he worked but at this particular time, he had the ugliest treeing walker coon hound the world had ever seen. He called the dog Smoky and what a fine dog it was. You didn't want to look at it long or it would hurt your eyes but to listen to the hound track and tree was a pleasure. Young as it was, the hound had a lot of potential.

Jon and Robert spent that summer hunting raccoons in the oaky hills and fir covered mountains. There was one farm in particular that the two young men enjoyed hunting. It was very dry there in the summertime. There was never water in the creeks there that time of year. One hunt was especially memorable to Robert and Jon. One summer evening, the hounds treed a large raccoon up an oak tree that grew along the creek. The creek banks were tall, about 15 feet above the stony bottom. Jon shot the raccoon out of the tree and it fell onto the stones below, dead as could be. The hounds and Grit ran down the bank sides and went to mauling their catch. But one by one they'd yelp as if bitten. Eventually, every dog but Grit and Smoky had run from the scene. Jon and Robert stood above on the bank cursing at the dogs for being cowards.

"Stupid dogs! The coon is already dead!" Robert yelled down to the hounds.

"For crying out loud! I thought our hounds were over any of this puppy shit," Jon said. "I guess I better go down and get the coon."

So, Jon went down to retrieve the dead raccoon. He was carrying a heavy spotlight and several leashes with him when he went down. He got to the coon and reached for it.

"God damn!" Jon cursed. "Shit!", he yelled and slapped his neck.

It was dark, so Rob couldn't see what was going on. "What's happening down there?"

"Shit! Damn! Mother!" was all Jon replied. Robert was shining his light down at the Jon, who was leaping around like a marionette. He couldn't see what was bugging Jon. Robert was bent over laughing. But then he heard it. Jon dropped all the leashes, the coon and his brand new spotlight and ran down the creekbed as fast as he could, the meanwhile, slapping his head and arms. A swarm of hornets came flying for Robert's light.

"Holy Hell!" Robert yelled. He was laughing hard until he saw those angry masses coming at him. He ran top speed out of the woods and into the fields. He met Jon in the field, at which point they stopped to assess the damage. The dogs were running to their masters one by one at this point.

"I think we out ran them," Robert said. But he spoke too soon. The swarm was on them again and the dogs were yiping and tucking tail. There was no relief from the unseen attackers.

"What the hell?" yelled Jon as they ran. "We're at least a quarter mile from the nest of those bastards." All Robert could do was laugh and ran. The sight of Jon cussing and slapping himself was a highlight of Rob's summer.

When they got back to the truck, they had finally outran the hornets. There were still dozens of the insects clinging to the dogs and to the mens' clothing. Jon and Robert cleaned the dogs off, then hopped into the truck. They didn't even think to go back for what was left in the creekbed. When Robert finally got home an hour later, he undressed. Live hornets fell out of his clothes. That much later they still clung to him. But Robert suffered not a single sting. He squashed his would be attackers and showered before bed.

o o o

Near the farm where the hornets attacked, there was a creek the size of a small river. The creek was further into the mountains than the farm and the water ran there year round. Jon, Curt and Rob hunted in the mountains there almost every weekend of the summer. It was a long drive from their homes but they'd sing country songs on the way and that made the time fly. They caught a decent amount of raccoons along that creek. The most fascinating wildlife that lived in that area were the ring-tailed cats. These are creatures in the raccoon family, but much smaller and with longer tails. They're a beautiful, communal creature. But most of all, the reason for hunting in that area was the grey fox population. There were fox all over that creek. Grey fox are different than red fox in several aspects. Their color is different. Their size is much smaller than red fox. And they climb trees.

There were many fox living along that creek. The high population of game gave Grit a good chance to use his nose on a regular basis. He eventually became a highly trusted member of the pack. Grit's nose was extraordinary for a terrier. He often struck scent before the hounds and because of his small size, he could move the tracks faster through the brush than the larger dogs. He was more easily broken off of bad game than the hounds as well. This quality made him invaluable to the young men. Anytime the young hounds would strike. Grit would be used to test whether the scent was game or trash. If the scent was that of trash, Grit would not run it. If it was game, he would speak and move the track. He was a great assistant in training young hounds.

Though there were many fox, there was a single fox that always outwitted the hounds and the men. Every week, the hounds would strike the track at the same place. The fox would lead them on a chase through heavy boulders along the riverbank, through thick brush, under the road and onto the mountainside where the elderberries and viny maples made such a strong network of brush that the men crawled ten feet above the forest floor on top of the branches of the plants.

The terrain and plant-life were the blessing and the curse of that mountain valley. Everything gave cover for the foxes, which allowed the large population of game to survive. But, the cover allowed the foxes to jump out of trees, whenever the men came close to shoot them out for the hounds. The fox they hunted every week had mastered the game and could not be caught. It took several weeks before the hounds and Grit were even able to solve the fox's scent puzzles and follow it beyond the road and onto the mountainside. Eventually, the dogs knew to get up into the thick brushed mountain and push the track there. Finally, Grit was able to push the fox hard enough to tree. The hounds were close behind and they stayed treed for a good while; long enough for Curt, Jon and Rob to begin the climb. Rob led the way. He was the smallest and thus was better supported by the maples and elderberries. He climbed the vines and shimmied up fallen logs and got right within sight of the tree. Then the fox jumped out of the tree, over the dogs and back to the ground.

"He's jumped!" Robert yelled to the other two men.

It took a while for the dogs to be convinced to leave the tree and start the track again where the fox had went down. The brush was so thick, the dogs had no idea the fox had left the tree. After some time chop-chop-chopping treed, one of the dogs left the empty tree and found the fresher track. The dogs were off again after the fox. This turned into a tradition with the men and this fox. That night alone, they treed it three or four times. Every weekend, they'd return and do it all over again. The best way to have caught that fox would have been to net the culvert that it used to run under the road. But that didn't seem sporting to the men. They wanted to catch it without traps and tricks. They never did catch that fox.

○ ○ ○

For several years Grit was hunted with the hounds. He was as good as any hound the young men had. He would stick to a track to its end and tree until the men arrived. He was rare among terriers in that he could do it all. Though, there was one hunt with Grit that turned Robert's head around.

Summer was ending and turning toward fall. The heat was still high and the forest dry. Bear hunting was well underway that September. Curtis and Robert kept their hunting to the night time during the hot season of the year. The heat of the day could cause dog or man to have heat stroke and drop dead in the woods. The nights were cool and the dew on the ground caused scenting conditions to be better.

Curtis had brought Prissy, his hound bitch, and a young pup called Crotch. Robert brought Grit and a couple other terriers. Not having much experience hunting bear, they mostly wanted to tree raccoons and possums that night. But plans don't always go as planned, so they say.

Robert drove the mountain roads for several hours, to no avail. The dogs weren't making a peep. There wasn't a track to strike for many miles. They left the creeks and valley-bottoms and moved into the "reprod" and deep forests. The ground got drier and the air hotter up there. They drove by a section of forest so dark that even they, who were well acquainted with the night, were frightened of the deathly looking place.

"Let's turn around and head down that road we passed to the right," Curtis suggested.

"No problem," Robert replied, "this place gives me the creeps."

Robert turned the truck around and drove the few miles back to the fork in the road and took the dogs and truck down the mountain. Halfway to the end of the short road, the dogs struck scent. The hounds yelled out.

"It's about time!" Robert said.

The men hopped out of the truck to let Prissy and Grit loose. The older dogs would test the track. If it was good, then the men would release the rest of the pack.

Prissy and Grit went straight to searching for the line. Prissy stood high on her hind feet trying to catch wind of the scent, which was evidently above her head. First she went one way, then the other. Up the hill, then back across the road and down into the thick "re-prod" firs. In the dank forest, Prissy gave voice. The scent hung low there. She crouched through the thick brush. Grit was close behind.

The track wound deep into the forest. The track heated up and Grit and Prissy could be heard giving cry every breath.

"Let's try to get closer," Curtis said.

They hopped into the truck and drove to the end of the road they were on. No roads were any closer to the action than where Curtis and Robert stood.

"Any chance of getting closer than this?" asked Robert, who did not know the mountains so well as Curtis.

"I don't think so."

"You wanna drop the young dogs?"

"Sure," Curtis answered, "but leave Crotch. He's not ready for this kind of race."

Robert released the two remaining young dogs. They ran into the forest without hesitation. It was time to listen. The two friends stood at the forest's edge with ears tuned to the action. They knew every dog by it's sound. Prissy, the hound, of course was easily discernible over the terriers' squeaking barks.

"This could be anything," Robert surmised.

"Yeah. It's run too far as a hot track for it to be coon or possum though. . . Cat, maybe?" said Curtis.

"Could be."

The track was getting hotter and further away.

"They may have reached a lower road by now," Curtis said. "Let's try to find a way around and closer.

Robert drove them back down the mountain and tried to find a way around. There was no luck for them. The dogs couldn't even be heard from the lower roads.

"We could see if that road through that creepy part of the forest will get us any closer," Robert suggested.

"That's our only other option. Might as well."

They drove through the dark, dead forest. They had went a few miles when they finally decided it was not hopeful. It didn't turn in the direction they needed to go. It just went on and on, along a different ridge.

"Looks like we're stuck walking from the end of the road where the dogs struck," Robert said.

"Yep."

They arrived at the dead end of the road where the scent was struck and listened again.

"I'd say they're treed." Curtis could always tell by Prissy's sound, whether she was treed. No matter how often Robert hunted with that hound, he couldn't hear the difference between her tree voice and her tracking voice.

"I'll take your word for it." Robert said, wondering to himself how, in all these years, he hadn't yet been able to hear her switch over to treeing.

The young dog, Crotch, was barking like mad to get loose and get to the tree.

"Not this time, El Crotcho," Curtis said, patting Crotch on the head.

"We can leave him tied to the truck, instead of putting him in the box," Robert suggested. "He's not going to shut up and that will give us a beacon back to the truck."

"Ha, Nice plan. Plus, I don't need another dog eating a hole in my box."

So Curt left the dog tied to the rear bumper of the truck, to give them a guiding sound back to the truck. And the two men started into the woods.

The trek was not a short one nor easy. The men had to descend hundreds of feet down to a stream, then back up and equal distance before they would come to the treeing dogs. The terrain was covered in fallen mighty firs, trunks large enough that two men would not be able to reach around. The drop was almost sheer and the majority of the climb had to be done with hands and feet.

Crotch howled and barked the entire time the men climbed. And, though the dogs were stationary, the way the sounds echoed off the mountains, it became difficult for the men to know if they were going toward the dogs or away from them. They knew where they needed to go from when they had listened at the truck. The sound had been clear there. The climb up to the dogs on the opposite mount was arduous. Viny maples were thick and large rock faces blocked their path at times, causing them to alter course. Eventually, they made it within 30 feet of the dogs. The dogs were just above them over a large rock. They couldn't see through all the foliage and rocks, so they went around. But as they crested the rock, whatever was in the tree jumped out, making an enormous crash through the understory.

"Bear!" both men exclaimed.

∘ ∘ ∘

Grit got a mouth full of musty dark fur. The bear smacked the terrier off itself. The hounds each took fearful grabs at the bear but were not courageous enough to pull it to the ground. It was no more than 80 pounds but that only gave it more speed to inflict pain. The bear lunged at Prissy, she attempted to dodge but was caught against an elderberry bush. She let out frightened but ferocious cries. The other hounds took courage and bit at the bear's hind end. It turned to them. Prissy was the only experienced hound there. The two young dogs let the bear pass right through them. Its small size gave it speed to out pace the dogs. Grit clung onto the shaggy hide as long as he could but the thick foliage brushed Grit off like a cockle-bur.

For a time, the dogs could hear the bear crashing through the forest ahead of them. But as the noise of the bear's escape went quiet, the dogs had to turn to their scenting ability to continue the hunt. Like a dumpster with legs, the bear left plenty of scent for the dogs. They ran hard to keep up but soon were forced to pace themselves to continue tracking.

o o o

The black brute ran the dogs further into the mountains, further away from roads. Time and again, the bear treed, the men ascended and descended mountains and the bear jumped as soon as the men arrived. The trek wore Robert completely out. It was well close to morning by the time they caught up with Prissy. She laid near the third tree. Her pads were blown. She kept howling, as if threatening the bear that she would gain her strength back and then she'd really give it to him.

When Robert saw the state of the dog, he knew he wasn't just being a wimp. He begged Curtis to stop for some sleep but Curtis insisted they must make it back to the truck at least. It got to the point that all the other dogs quit the track. Only Grit could be heard continuing the track and eventually, his voice faded out of hearing. The men decided to return the way they had come, but they did not know where they were in relation to the truck.

Curtis pulled a tube of super glue and a pair of woman's nylons out of a bag he carried into the woods.

Robert knew what it was for but teased Curt anyway. "Are you planning on dolling up? Cause it won't make me hot for you, if that's what you're thinking."

Curtis gave an honest laugh, then went to tending Prissy. "Come here girl. You need some help, if you're gonna be walking out of here on your own." Curtis held Prissy in his lap and gave her some affection before beginning the doctoring. He rubbed her ribs and scratched the top of her head. He looked her over for any wounds. There were none. She had escaped without any major attack from the bear. Even small bears are much bigger than a hound and can do serious injury to any dog.

The hound-bitch was familiar with being doctored. Curtis cut the nylons into circle shaped pieces to cover the bitch's feet with. He cut enough for three layers, then glued her pads. "I know girl. I know it stings. I'm sorry. You're such a good girl. I'll be done soon." Curtis layered the nylon onto her feet as if to make new skin for her. He did this on each foot to keep her tender feet protected on the walk to the truck. Once the hound was home, she'd be able to rest until she was fully healed.

∘ ∘ ∘

All the hounds had fallen behind Grit. He didn't wait for them. Catching his game was the only thing on his mind. He was worn out and tracking very slowly at this point but kept barking every thirty seconds or so to let the men and hounds know that he was still on the trail. On other hunts, fresh dogs would be dropped to take the track faster and he'd be rewarded in the end for his perseverance. He trotted slowly through the mountains for hours without sign of any man or hound coming to his aid.

The scent was dying, letting him know that the bear had gained considerable ground on him.

∘ ∘ ∘

Robert and Curtis stuck to the ridges to find their way out of the woods. They decided to sidestep along a ridge, assuming that it would wrap around to the ridge on which the truck was parked. With this in mind, they walked for at least an hour. They finally heard their beacon, Crotch.

"Oh, Hallelujah!" exclaimed Robert. "Crotch is just across to the other ridge. That means we're near where the dogs first treed that blasted bear."

Hearing the dog tied to the truck gave them new strength and they plodded on toward the howling.

"Man. The mountains make following that dog's howling almost impossible," Robert said.

"I know, right?" Curtis said. "It's like we keep getting further away and then closer again. But whatever the case, we will eventually get there, if we keep moving toward the noise."

The two began to ascend the final mountain. They made it about half way when they met Crotch, nowhere near the truck.

"You've got to be kidding me!" Curtis yelled.

Robert just sat down on a log and laughed, "The eagle never wasted so much time as when he listened to the advice of the crow. It is a beautiful thing, men listening to dogs."

"We might be lost," Curtis joked.

"You don't say. . . I don't know about you, but I am ready to crash under a log for the night. It's got to be near 4 a.m. by now."

"Nah. I don't want to sleep in the woods tonight. We've got to be close to the truck, if El Crotcho is here."

"Not necessarily. The dog could have been following the other dogs for who knows how long."

Curtis wasn't convinced to sleep in the woods. "Let's walk down a ways to the clear cut we passed. There has to be a road, for there to be a clear cut. Otherwise, they'd never be able to get the logs out of the woods."

"We're never going to get the *dogs* out of these woods." Robert rhymed.

The clear cut was a large swath of obstacles, branches and rotting stumps at every step. Wood-rats scampered everywhere along the dead white and grey wood. Many times Robert asked Curtis to stop for a sleep. But Curtis wouldn't hear of it. He didn't want to sleep in the open. Since he wouldn't separate from Curt, Robert chose to ignore the burning in his long-used legs. Crotch followed along happily, now that he had found his master. The long hike to the top of the ridge was exhausting but there was an old road there. Many trees were growing in the road and had already grown above the height of the men, indicating how long it had been since the road was in use. A mile or two down the out-of-use dirt road, they arrived at gravel.

"Ah. This is relieving. We've found a road. But what road?" asked Robert.

"That is the question. Look for the road number."

It was daylight by the time they found the gravel road. They had been hiking for the greater part of the night. They had no clue what road they had arrived on, despite having the numbers.

"I'd say now is as good a time as ever to catch some shuteye," Curtis said.

"It's about damn time! Now that I'm soaked with sweat and we're in the coldest part of the morning!"

They found a ditch to lay in and dug their way into the bank to try to avoid wind. They laid with backs to each other to stay as warm as possible. It was cold enough to give a person hypothermia. They slept uncomfortably for a couple hours before hearing a truck drive by, which woke them. Robert jumped out of the hole and flagged the truck down. There were dogs standing unchained on top of a dog-box in the back of the truck. Luckily, it was a houndsman that both Robert and Curt knew.

"What the hell-fire are you two doing out here?" The stout and strong Ron asked. He was the father to Curt and Robert's close friend Jon.

"Picking up chicks," Robert said. "What do you think we are doing?"

Jon laughed. "I should have known you two numb-nuts would be up here hunting. These are your stomping grounds."

"We're thankful you didn't think of us," Curtis said. "We don't know where the heck we are. Had you thought of us, we'd not be speaking to you now."

"Good thing I have no problem helping two should-be-convicts," Ron said.

"It takes one to know one, old man," Curtis replied.

"You're cutting into my hound hunting time, so you'll owe me one," Ron teased. "Where do y'all need to be?"

Ron took them in his truck and brought them to where Robert had parked. It was at least a 30 minute drive. Ron showed them on a map where they had hiked. As the crow flies they had ended up three miles from the truck, over ridges and through valley-bottoms. Three miles through that terrain was more taxing on the body than any road. And they had not gone as the crow flies.

○ ○ ○

The sun was high over the trees by noon. What little smell that Grit could find on the dewy ground under the bracken and silal had dried up. The bear had gained too much distance. Grit found a stream and laid himself in it to cool off. He took a deep drink and slept until nightfall.

○ ○ ○

The men spent that day searching for lost dogs. One of the hounds was at the truck when they arrived. But Grit and another hound were still out in the woods by the end of the day.

"I'm not too worried," Robert said. "Grit and that dog have been lost for several days before. They always return to where they last saw me. I'll come back tomorrow and find them."

○ ○ ○

Grit awoke to the young hound that had not found its way back to Curtis. The dog had stuck to Grit's trail, once the bear's scent was not to be smelled. Huddled together, licking their wounds, they remained the rest of the night and the next day beside the small stream.

∘ ∘ ∘

Night and day came and went but the dogs did not. Everyday Robert went back to that part of the woods. He asked every camper and every hunter if they had seen two dogs.

"No, but you say they're terriers?" asked a lumberman.

"Yes. A hound and a hunting terrier. A little red, hairy dog. And a big, long eared, black and white dog," Robert told him.

"No problem. Yorkshire terriers. I'll tell the guys to look for them."

"Not Yorkshire terriers!" said Robert, *you idiot*, he thought. "A hound and hunting terrier."

"Yorkshires. Yeah, I heard you."

Robert decided the guy was probably not going to understand him anyway, though they were speaking English. "Thank you," said Robert and he drove away.

∘ ∘ ∘

On the third night, Grit and the hound, named Two, found their way into a logging camp. The heavy equipment was parked on a large gravel landing every night. There were trailers and pickups parked around the equipment. Grit was leery of any people other than his own master, so he lingered on the outskirts. But Two had no problem running in to see the people drinking around a fire next to their trailers. He lumbered up friendily and crouched his way into the huddled group of men and women.

"Who's dog is this?" asked one of the women.

The men all looked at each other. "None of ours," one spoke up.

Two was friendly and nuzzled all the people with his nose and searched out a head scratch wherever he could get it. Someone finally looked at his collar. Curtis had put one of Robert's onto the hound.

"Says here that he belongs to a Robert Good-fellow," said the man. He was the watchman. "There was a fella looking for a couple dogs up here a few days ago. But them was yorkshire terriers or summit like that."

"If he's looking for terriers and nobody comes for this dog, we should keep him," piped up a young girl who had fallen in love with the goofy young hound as soon as she saw it.

"He's a nice hound," answered the watchmen, the young girl's father. "If he's still here in the morning, we'll keep him."

The people went into their trailers before the fire died. Two laid on the warm ground outside the fire ring. Grit had stayed quietly hidden under a bulldozer. Grease and tar coated the bottom of the machinery. The nasty black goo had covered Grit's coat while he was laying under the giant dozer. He crawled out from where he was hiding and cautiously walked across the open space toward the fire, where Two was laying comfortably. Then, he heard a chain rattle and feet thunder toward him quickly. Before he could react, a bull dog had seized hold of his head. He yelped and shook himself loose. Two was quick to his feet. As lazy as hounds look, they are surprisingly fast. He tore into the fight, grabbing the bulldog by the armpit and shaking his teeth deep into the tender meat there. The bulldog lost interest in Grit and spent his energy trying to get the hound off of him. Two was a goofy young hound but big and burly, nearly sixty pounds. The thirty pound bulldog had a hand full. Grit grabbed hold of the bull-dog by the balls and jerked to pull them off.

"What the hell'n'tarnation!" yelled a man's voice. Grit had been punished by Robert many times for dog fighting. He didn't want a whooping, so he ran back under the equipment and hid. But young Two just kept on fighting with that bulldog. The lumber-man came and kicked both dogs hard in the chests, knocking the wind out of them. The hound let go and became submissive, but the bulldog kept biting. The lumber-jack choked the bulldog until it let go of the hound.

"Damn hound! You don't know what's good for you." He grabbed Two by the collar and dragged him back near the trailer, away from the bull dogs chain-space. All of the other people camped there had woken and watched from their trailer doors. The little girl peaked around her mom's legs. When the man finished tying Two up, he went back into the trailer. His little daughter looked up at him.

"We won't be keeping that dog. Sorry girly."

His daughter went to bed crying. The next morning, the lumberjack did the decent thing and drove with his family and Two to find the address on the hound's collar.

o o o

On the fourth day a woodsman, along with his sister (or was it brother?), wife and daughter, arrived at Robert's home with Two but not Grit. Robert gave the people twenty dollars for their efforts. Curtis was glad to have his dog back. Robert, however, began to feel very down. By one week of searching everyday for his dog, he began to feel he may not wish to hunt anymore. He was heartsick for his dog. He was at a turning point in his life, ready to begin a family. He wondered if it was an omen, designed to inform him it was time to turn his efforts elsewhere. But he did not give up. He continued back into the woods everyday in search of his dog. He would bring books or his girlfriend, Hero, with him.

He would leave articles of his clothing in the woods for Grit to smell. He hoped this would give Grit a sign post telling him where to stay in order to be reunited with Robert. When Robert needed to relieve himself in the woods, he would pee in a stop and go fashion, sidestepping along the side of the road. Leaving urine in as wide an area as possible. Curtis laughed at him for this. He thought Robert was ridiculous. But

Robert was desperate to be reunited with his favorite dog.

o o o

Grit never crossed paths with Robert's scent posts and pee strings. He was many miles from where Robert looked every day. Grit was growing lean from lack of food. The mono-cultured forest was not hospitable to animals. The clearcuts held enough rodents and rabbits for Grit to catch a few now and then. But they might take as much energy as they gave. He grew very hungry out in the woods. The infection on his head from the dog bite was taking its toll on him as well. It throbbed and made busting through heavy brush after rats painful. But he lived day by day hunting up what food he could.

o o o

On the seventeenth day of searching for Grit, Robert had brought *The Three Musketeers* by Alexandre Dumas. He sat at the top of a wide clear-cut, in order to give him vision of more area. He called and honked the truck's horn but heard not a howl nor a yowl from Grit. He relaxed on a stump and read the afternoon away.

Of a sudden, a car came zooming up the gravel road, horns a-blairing. A stout woman (Robert wondered for days, whether it was a man or a woman), skidded her car to a halt and rolled the window down. It was one of the people who had brought Curtis' hound weeks before.

"I just saw your dog!" she yelled.

Robert jumped from his seat and asked her to lead the way. She turned her car around and Robert followed in his truck. It was a surprisingly long way from anywhere Robert would have expected, many miles from where he had first let the dogs loose.

She pulled off the road where the mountains met a meadow farmstead.

"He was here, before I went to find you," The woman said, looking flustered. Robert had given her brother a hefty reward for having returned his friend's hound to him. She was a kind woman but poor. Robert was sure she was a little upset that she may not reap the same reward, because the dog had disappeared again.

Robert walked to the woods and whistled. Coming from 100 yards away, breaking brush could be heard. Even knowing that it was his whistle that was being responded to, Robert's heart was in his throat, wondering if maybe another dog was on that mountain. He wondered if, perhaps, it would not be Grit greeting him.

Grit came out onto the road some way from Robert. The woman stood between Grit and his master. Grit shied away from her but she lunged at him, to grab him. He gave her a quick bite on the hand. It was the only time Robert had seen Grit bite at a person.

What a dope! Robert thought, *Why would she lunge at a dog that doesn't know her?*

Grit came right to Robert and sat submissively at his feet. The dog stunk to high heaven of fishy infection. There were large gashes, down to the bone on top of Grit's head. He had obviously tumbled with something very tough, *Likely a bobcat or a coyote*, thought Robert, *A bear would have crushed his head with a single bite*. He picked up the tattered dog and put him tenderly into his coat.

"You had me sick enough with worry to quit the dogs altogether, you stinky little mongrel."

Robert paid the woman a small reward and went home with jubilation in his heart.

° ° °

As soon as Robert got him home, he set to mending Grit. The dog was covered in tar from having slept under heavy logging equipment in the forest. His head was covered in gaping gashes and he had lost considerable weight, having lived off of nothing but scrounged up rodents. Robert first removed the tar from Grit, using olive oil to separate the sticky tar from Grit's hairs. He then filled a rubber-tub with warm water and washed Grit from head to toe. The gashes needed special care. He cleaned the dirt, pus and old blood out of them. The wounds stank terribly. Once the gaping holes were filled with ointment, Robert stapled them shut. He left enough of an opening in each wound to allow drainage. It was necessary that the wounds healed inside-outward.

Grit was two weeks in recovery. He gained his weight back quickly. Luckily, the infection was conquered with ease. After 17 days of not having his most valued dog, Robert decided he was done hunting Grit with the hounds. The dog had proven his worth as a tracker. Robert needed no more proof. Grit would be worked along the rivers from that time forward.

21. Bites and Pieces

Grit lost none of his skill as a hunter while he had been lost in the woods. If anything, he had improved as a dog. Robert hunted him endlessly along the river bottoms. For more than a year's span Robert took Grit hunting several times a week and never did Grit fail to catch game.

Grit was always a good looking terrier until this period in his life. Bite by bite, Grit lost pieces of his face, until finally, he was more battle scarred than an old tom lion. Not only flesh but teeth also were lost during this period. Grit worked alone. Robert needed no other dogs to help Grit. If Grit did ever work with other dogs, it was to train puppies in tracking and treeing.

Raccoons were the number one enemy on Grit's list. At times, Robert couldn't get Grit to hunt anything else. In the summer time, when water mammals were the target-game, Grit would still seek and find raccoons. But one day, Grit could not find himself a coon, and what he found instead, cost him dearly and limited his ability for the rest of his life.

Every dog has it's day, says the old cliché. Every fighter needs to know when he is outmatched. But with terriers, they do not have that option. Terriers are driven to work, no matter the size nor the strength of their enemy. He had gotten as good as a coon dog or terrier could get. There was no better dog. But everyone knows that where one thing is stronger than another, there will always be a stronger yet. Grit had his day late August of his seventh year.

Robert and Curtis took Grit to a forested creek to hunt nutria or whatever they might stir up. The water was low and animals were hiding in the thick brush from the sun. Robert hunted the terriers on water game specifically at this time of year, because the holes of animals were exposed above the water's edge. Tangled roots were always a refuge for water dwellers like beaver, nutria and otter. In the dry weather, the terriers could finally reach the game hidden beneath the trees.

The stream met the river with a wide, rocky mouth. Entering the woods, the banks turned to pebbles and sand. Most of the stream's banks had given way to floods and stood barren of all but stringy roots holding the sand up. The banks were twelve feet tall in many places. During the winter, the water rushed through its channels, cutting it's path ever wider each year. But in the summertime, the water was low and lazy with a few deep pools. Robert and Curt could walk easily on the sandy bed, next to the trickle of water.

The first den to be checked was on a high bank with the roots of large pines holding the weakening bank together. Underneath the thick roots of a pine was a well used beaver den. This den was dug in such a way that it had several stories. There was nothing in the holes. Grit had once fought with a large beaver there and taken some deep bites to his back. Luckily, the bites followed the skin and did not find their way into his organs, or he would have died of his wounds.

During the winter months, when hunted where there was much brush, Grit would be difficult for Robert to keep nearby. Grit would go off hunting, not to be seen until game was caught. On this August day, Grit trotted close to Curtis and Robert. There was not much brush on the banks of this creek and the heat had burned all tracks that had been laid the night before.

With a point of his finger, Robert would send Grit to check every jumble of roots, every hole dug into the banks, every beaver's dam. But it seemed Grit would be foiled for the first hunt in many hunts. The hunters came to a pile of drift wood that dammed the creek much of the year. The water was so low that the pile of wood was almost completely on land. Only a little trickle of water flowed beneath it. The aged white wood was stacked ten feet high. Grit came to life.

The woodpile was full of entrances that led deep to its heart. Grit ran around the pile with head cocked for scent until he located the precise hole he knew held his game. His tail went rigid and stuck straight in the air as he approached the entrance where fishy smell streamed out. Cautiously but courageously, Grit entered the dam.

Curt was soon on his knees to hear the goings on inside the pile. Cool, sandy smelling air hit his face.

Curtis looked up at Robert, "All I hear is breathing," he said.

"Grit has grown wise," Rob said. "When he's hunting alone, he's learned that he can get a jump on the game by sneaking up on it. He doesn't bark on scent much anymore, once he's close to what he wants to catch."

As they were talking, a commotion started in the center of the pile. A furious barking was emitting from the logs. Nails on wood could be heard. The game was on the move and just out of Grit's reach. Sand could be heard, kicked against the logs. Grit was digging his way under a log to reach his game. The men ran around the pile, looking for a gap to see the action.

"Can you get any vantage?" Robert asked Curtis, who had climbed on top of the pile.

"No. But they're right beneath me."

Grit met his game. What a rumbling came from the bowels of the dam! Grit and his game were rolling each other to death.

"No sound of coon. No moaning of a nutria," Curt said. "That leaves beaver or otter. And judging by all the crawdad filled crap up here, I'm going with an otter."

"Whooo hoo hooo! That ain't gonna be easy on Grit!"

Yelps yelled out to the listening men.

"Don't get too excited yet. That thing might kill Grit, from the sounds of it."

What Curtis said should have sobered Robert some. But Robert had full faith in Grit.

"That dog is invincible. Hell nor high water can conquer that dog and his determination to survive."

"Maybe so." Curtis laughed, knowing what travails Grit had been through and survived in the past. "Nothing has killed him so far. Defies all reason, really."

The raucous hadn't quieted in the log-jam. Hissing and snorting and the wailing of Grit could be heard.

"He may be invincible," Robert said, "but it sounds like he's getting a whooping."

"Hey! Come up here. I see them!"

Robert was up there in a few bounds. Curtis had crawled his way into the pile. He crawled out to give Robert a view. Curtis handed him a light and Robert squeezed into the logs. *Just the way to die*, Robert thought to himself, *squished between logs on a hunt, just like a terrier. God, keep these logs from moving.* The coolness in the dark was refreshing. He set himself steady and leaned his head under a log. The heavy breathing of dog and quarry could be heard more clearly. Shining his light through openings in the pile, Rob could see Grit holding his game. The dog was panting heavily, his legs underneath him, he was laying on the ground, exhausted but in grips. Robert moved some to get a view of the game. His light hit eyes. They shined hazy blue back at him. An otter's head looked straight at him.

"Otter!" he was able to tell Curtis.

The light and man startled the otter and it went into flight and fight mode, all at once. The otter ferociously shook itself and set to tearing itself free from Grit. Robert could see blood glistening in the light's beam. Grit's face was wet with red.

The otter bolted at top speed from the logs. Curtis jumped down to the sand and pebbles and ran after the otter, trying to tail it. He lunged with his long legs to pin its tail down with his foot. But without dogs to hinder it's speed, Curtis was too slow to grab it's tail. The otter struck, quick as a serpent at Curt's legs. Curt leaped back out of the way and the otter made it to water. But, it being summer, the otter was visible for a long way down stream.

Robert disentangled from inside the log-jam. Slithering, dragging his body up and out of the logs. As soon as Robert was out, he went sprinting down the creek bed after Curt, who was hallowing and hollering after the otter. He had picked up a long stick and was poking at the water, trying to get the otter to beach. But the otter was not having anything to do with land. It slithered through the water like an eel. In short time, it made it to a deep dark pool near the beaver holes under the pine trees. There was no seeing it in the darkness beneath the trees.

Robert made it to Curtis, who was jabbing under roots in the bank and wading through the pool searching for holes on the waterline.

"That thing is gone like yesterday, man," said Curtis.

"He didn't swim on past this pool?"

"No, I waited there where the stream narrows. It never passed by."

"And it didn't make it into the beaver's den under the pine?"

"Nope. Look yourself. There's no water on the bank. He didn't pass that way."

"That means there must be a hole still under the water, just under these trees I'm standing by." said Robert.

"Yessir, that'd seem the only place it could go."

While Curtis and Robert stood dumbfounded, staring into the dark water, Grit limped on three legs along the stream bed toward Robert. Blood was streaming down Grit's face and dripping from his chin into the sand.

"Holy Hell!" Robert said.

Curt's eyes widened and he waded back to shore to meet Grit.

Robert knelt and lifted Grit's head by the chin to look at him. Grit's nose had been bitten clean off. There wasn't anything but two little straws of cartilage sticking out where Grit's soft nose should have been. Chunks of lip were dangling from Grit's face and Grit was favoring his right foreleg.

"That son of a bitch did nearly kill you, Grit! Let's look at that leg."

He reached for Grit's leg. Grit tried to get the leg back from Robert but was reprimanded, "No," Robert commanded, "hold still." He examined the leg and saw that it had been bitten badly. In the creek he rinsed the blood from Grit and cleaned the sand out of his wounds. He then wrapped him in a shirt and carried him to the truck as quickly as possible.

Robert looked down on his shivering little dog and it brought an old song to mind,

"He'll yield not one inch though they maul him,
he'll fight to the death on his own.
So always remember your terriers,
protect them from wet and from cold."

262

Grit, try as he may, could never be the same hunter he had been after that day. Without a nose, he'd simply not be capable of the feats he once accomplished. But to Robert his worth was greater than that of gold.

22. Skinner and Nig

P oor Ol' Grit, his nose took two months to heal. Even then, it was forever pinkish and gurgled when he breathed. Robert assumed that the bite on Grit's leg had splintered bone. Grit didn't walk on it for many weeks and treated it tenderly for months. For his size, Grit was a strong terrier but he wasn't big enough for otters. So rarely could an otter be trapped in such a way, that Robert never worried much about his smaller terriers encountering them.

Autumn was falling when Robert next took Grit out to hunt. Jon called to inform Robert that he, Curtis and another fellow were going to be hunting with the pups that night. Robert had sworn off hunting Grit with hounds but he decided to take him along, because they were training pups and not hunting where there would be larger game, like bear, that could get Grit lost in the woods.

Robert and Curtis drove together to the appointed place of meeting, at around 11:00 pm. Jon and his friend were already there, kicking stones down a hill. Curtis and Robert got out of the truck. They joked with Jon a bit.

"Are you trying to scare up a bandersnatch?" Robert teased.

"Nah. You know me, I'm always on the look out for the snappenhauser," Jon replied.

Jon's friend stood quietly, not saying anything before being introduced. Jon did the honors, "Fella's, this is Skinner. Skinner, this is Robert and Curtis."

Skinner shook hands with the others. He was shorter than the others who all stood at six foot or taller. His hair was dark and buzzed close to his head. Jon and Skinner had taken on the appearance of the local working class, short hair, clothes made of canvas and leather. This was in contrast to Curtis and Robert, who kept their hair long and wore the clothing of farmers, denim and wool. Jon now chewed, as did his friend Skinner. Each was chewing their cud, as Robert called it.

Grit had been bred to a bitch, while he was not in Robert's possession. That bitch had pups and now, years later, those pups had had pups. Skinner and Jon presented them to Robert, who had yet to see them. There was a red hairy one that looked a lot like Grit but higher on the leg and more hair. Jon owned the red. Skinner had a big black terrier, also high on the leg. Robert liked both of them. They were a year old now. It was just time to start working them.

"What do you call this one, Skinner?" Rob asked.

"I call him Nig."

Robert snorted, "I can guess what that's short for."

"Yep, he's a regular jig-a-boo," Skinner joked.

Jon jumped in, "Looks like an oreo to me. That feist is black on the outside but a white curdog on the inside."

Robert looked Nig over. The dog was obviously built for work. Scanning the dog over, he noticed that the dog was cut.

"Oh man, Why'd you neuter this dog?" Robert hated to see a dog neutered. He was of the opinion that if a dog wasn't worth breeding, it wasn't worth feeding.

He'd cull a dog before he'd neuter it. He felt it stole the dog's will.

"I didn't want him pissing all over the house," Skinner said.

"Well, a hunting dog isn't meant to be in a house," Curtis told him.

"Did it help? Did the dog stop pissin'?" Robert asked.

"Nope. Pisses as much as ever." Skinner answered.

Robert was later to find that Skinner was not one to take ridicule lightly. It is surprising that he kept talking to Curt and Robert.

"If you intend to keep hunting with us, you'll come to a day that you rue cutting that dog," Robert foretold.

"Ain't nothing I can do about it now. What's done is done," Skinner replied and that was the end of it.

"Well, you two ready to see some real hunting dogs?" Curtis said.

"What? One of you finally bought one off somebody else? Cause, I know you didn't have anything but shit the last time I saw y'all," Jon mocked.

Curtis was up for the game. He opened up his box and let Crotch and Grit loose.

"Oh Jesus that dog is ugly," Jon said looking at Crotch, "I guess you know he's gotta be good, cause he woulda been shot for having a wompy face otherwise."

Crotch was a hound dog under a year old. Thick boned, probably had a bit of bloodhound in him. His ears and jowls hung low.

"Those lips are liable to act as a parachute, if that dog runs himself off a cliff tonight," Jon continued to rag on Curt's hound.

"That's his super power," Curt returned, "he can fly up a tree to catch his game, just by flapping his ears."

Grit had wandered around the front of the pickup to piss. Jon called to him with a whistle. Grit came trotting to Jon, his friend of old.

"God damn shame," Jon said, looking down on Grit's face. "Look here at this dog, Skinner."

"I don't want to get anywhere near that dog!" he said in a serious voice. The other men laughed at him.

"You might want to get used to these little monsters now that you own one. They don't stay pretty forever," Robert said. "Come on and pet him. He won't hurt you."

Skinner wasn't having any of that. "No thanks," He said.

"This once was the best nosed little dog you'd ever see," Jon told Skinner. "Not better than a good hound, but for some reason, he could track better than most. It's a shame about that nose."

After they had finished looking the dogs over. The men chained their dogs up on top of the dog-boxes to "box" a while. Boxing is what hound hunters call it when they put their dogs on top of the dog box and drive along country roads. The hounds can smell game from atop the box and will strike scent from there. They drove for miles around farm roads. There didn't seem to be a track to be had. Crotch struck a few trash tracks. Grit would hunker down and tuck his tail when he was put on bad tracks. This would allow the men to correct the young dogs for opening on game they should not.

Eventually, Crotch lit up on a scent that Grit did not hunker down on. But Grit didn't pull hard on the chain either.

"Maybe he just can't smell it," Posited Jon.

"Maybe so," Robert shrugged. "Who can say. Why don't we let that Crotch dog go and see what he does with it."

Curt let Crotch go. He ran up the hill into the thick brush like a mad dog.

"He wants it, whatever it is," said Curtis.

"It could be any number of things. Though it doesn't seem to be deer. I don't see any tracks," Jon said.

Skinner was keeping quiet. He was the type to learn through observance. Never one to boast of his knowledge, he stood quietly listening and soaking in what the others were saying.

Shortly, Crotch could be heard locking down on a tree. His bark changed from a long bawl to a short "chop-chop".

Jon turned to Skinner, "That's our signal."

The men walked in. They left the young terriers chained to the truck. They didn't want them running off on unknown game. Grit was let to run loose. There wasn't anything that would be a risk to him, already being broken off of trash (game the dogs were not supposed to run). The hike was steep. The men were all fit and made it to the tree in a short time. Crotch was treed up on a thick fir tree. The men shone their lights all over, to no avail.

"I don't see squat up that tree," said Robert.

Curtis was reserving judgment. He didn't want to jump to conclusions about his dog false treeing. He stayed quiet, looking up the tree with a furrowed brow.

Jon was willing to judge the situation, "Looks like Ol' Crotcho is treed on a slick tree to me, Curt."

"I don't know," answered Curtis. "That's a lot of branches to see through. I'm gonna climb the tree."

"I thought you said that dog of yours could fly," Jon quipped. "Why don't you send him up?"

Curtis chuckled, along with the others, and set himself to climbing the tree. He was a big man, and the tree, though 30 feet tall, was little more than a thin sapling at its top. Curtis climbed ever higher, shining his light down every branch. As he got near the top, the tree started bending, leaning Curtis toward the ground.

"No sense in going further Curt!" Robert yelled up to him. "There isn't anything up there worth falling and breaking your back for."

"I can see a thick shadow up here," Curt said. "It's just a bit above me. Could be a coon or something."

He climbed up to within good sight of the silhouette. He could see what it was.

"Did I tell you that hound doubles as a bird dog?" Curtis yelled down.

"How can he double as anything, if he isn't good at the one job he has as a hound," Jon teased.

"It's a bird's nest!" Curtis said.

"A bird's nest?" Robert said. "It would be Crotch who trees on a bird." He laughed. "Throw it like a frisbee and see if Crotch'll fly after it with those ears."

Curtis could hear the peeps of the tiny chicks in the nest. He left them alone and began his descent of shame down the tree. The guys hackled Curtis about Crotch treeing on a bird's nest for years after that. It seemed like Crotch couldn't tree without somebody bringing up a bird from then on.

° ° °

From that day on, Skinner and Robert started going hunting together. At first just a weekend here and there to run fox tracks down in the willow thickets along creeks. Skinner would call and tell Robert what his dogs caught. Both of them hunted more than any other two hunters could. Their lives both became dog obsessed. In time, they were hunting together three times a week. On the other days of the week they'd hunt alone and tell each other about it later.

Skinner's Nig was as good a dog as Robert had ever seen. Robert kept promising that Nig would outdo

Grit with a few years under his belt. Skinner would never admit it, but it struck up a friendly competition between the two men, to see whose dog could catch the most coons each hunt. Nig in his first year couldn't get close to the number of coon that Grit was catching but that didn't keep the men from recognizing Nig's potential.

Skinner, shortly after meeting Robert, bought a half brother to Grit from Robert. That was another great dog. That little black dog was an underground maniac. . . would fight to the death anything he found to ground.

For a year, Grit, Nig and Grit's brother were clearing the local farms of any coon they could find. It was the best team of coon dogs around and far and above the best terriers around. Skinner had trained his dogs exceptionally well.

"But Grit is King!" Skinner would always say, whenever Robert would compliment Skinner on his dogs. "It's cheating to bring that dog hunting," Skinner said. "It's cruel and unsportsmanlike to drop that dog on coons." Though, even with a missing nose, for Grit, it was almost too easy to find coons.

A year and part of another passed with Skinner and Robert catching uncountable numbers of game animals with their team of dogs. By Nig's second season, he was catching up with Grit's numbers each hunt. To the point that on one particular weekend, Nig was only one coon behind Grit.

One morning, in the middle of the flood season, Robert got a knock on his door from Curtis. Robert came to the door, not yet dressed for the day. Curtis and Skinner had been out hunting before the sun rose.

"What's going on?" Robert asked.

Curtis had a melancholy look, "We need your canoe," he said, "Can you come and help us."

"Sure, but what for?"

"Crotch and Nig treed a small coon on a tree overhanging the river. . . ." Curtis began. Robert already knew the end of the story. His heart dropped. Curt continued, "Ol' Nig climbed out after it and the coon bailed. Nig followed. The river is high, swollen and freezing, but we saw Nig was swimming strong. We saw him make it to the coon, then he floated to where we couldn't see him around all the brush. So we ran to the boat ramp to catch sight of them as they passed by. We hoped we could call Nig in from there. We beat them to the boat ramp and waited. The coon floated past, but Nig never made it."

"Damn," was all Robert could say. "Damn. Damn. Damn."

Robert threw his clothes on and loaded the canoe onto Curt's truck. Skinner was waiting a mile from Robert's home, leaning against his truck with his head down, staring at the mud. Robert hopped out and went to untying the canoe immediately. Every second was precious. There was little hope that Nig survived the swim but there was hope.

"I could cry, Robert. I've never been so heart-broken. I'm just trying to keep it together," Skinner told Robert.

"I hear you, man. I'll do my best to find him."

"If anything, bring his body back to me. I hate to think of him as a dead body for possums to eat."

Ron arrived on the scene. He was there as a to-ken of friendship. He and Skinner were very close. Curt and Rob had the canoe in the water by the time Ron showed up.

"I'd go with you to find him, Robert, but I can't manage that canoe like you and Curt," Skinner said.

"No, it wouldn't be safe for you to go," Curt said. "You don't worry. Robert and I know this river better than anybody. If Nig can be saved, we're the men for it."

Curt and Rob rowed hard upstream. At each opening in the brush, they'd see Ron and Skinner waiting with expectant grief. The men looked into every beaver's hole, every overhanging clump of brush that could have snagged Nig, every bank for dog tracks. The water was chocolate, thick with silt. There was no sight nor sign of Nig. Robert and Curtis reluctantly returned to the boat ramp, empty handed.

"I appreciate the effort," said Skinner. "There's nothing more that you could do. I know that."

"I've never seen anyone speed a canoe like the two of you," said Ron, trying to lighten the mood.

They loaded the canoe back onto the truck, then stood staring at the ground for a while. All remembering good dogs lost to death. Lee, Burdog, Jackson P. Coltrane and now, Nig.

"It was such a little coon," Skinner finally spoke. "I would have thought Nig could have retrieved that puny son of a bitch."

"It doesn't take much in this cold water to exhaust a dog," Robert suggested.

"I can't imagine it was the cold," Ron said. "Dogs can take some very cold water, without so much as a flinch. But even a little coon on top of a dog's head can put the dog under. And all it takes is one breath of water and the dog is dead."

"We can guess all day," Skinner said, "Fact of the matter is, my buddy is gone forever. No amount of guessing will bring my dog back."

o o o

Two weeks later, Skinner called Robert again, with bad news about Blacky, the dog Skinner had bought from Robert.

"Blacky is dead," Skinner told Robert.

"You're kidding me. Please tell me you're kidding me."

"I am not. I wouldn't joke about something like this."

"Geez!" Robert exclaimed, "How'd it happen?"

"Blacky found a coon in the ground near a stream. Normally the stream is small, but because of the floods, it was raging at about six feet deep. I didn't worry about it, because I was right there to help as soon as the game was out of the hole. I couldn't dig it because of a tree being right over the hole. I knew Blacky could handle this coon. I heard him really giving it a beating and figured he'd draw it out. He fought it for over an hour underground before he finally got it to the

277

entrance of the hole. When I grabbed for it, I slipped in the mud and slid down the hill. The dog and coon couldn't stand on the steep bank either and fell with me. We were all in the drink. I tried to grab Blacky, but my boots filled with water and I nearly drowned. I sank in over my head fast! It was all I could do to save myself. When I got out of the water, I saw Blacky snagged on a limb in the current. His head was under water and he was limp. I was able to pull the limb in and get Blacky, but he was dead. I saw the coon tangled in brush down the stream a ways, dead too."

"Unbelievable!" Robert shouted.

"If it weren't happening to me, I wouldn't believe anybody had such shit for luck," Skinner said. "It's all I can do to not cry all day."

∘ ∘ ∘

Robert decided after that to retire Ol' Grit from the working life. Grit had done his fair share and it was time to get some pups off of him. He was still in prime health, athletic and cocksure, just as Robert felt a good stud should be at the age of eight. The dog had proven himself in every way.

Skinner got himself some more dogs after a short time, damned fine dogs. But he and Robert no longer hunted together after Grit was retired and Nig and Blacky drowned. Skinner would come to visit several nights a week and chat dogs and talk about the hunts both had throughout the week. The men would sit by the fire in the winter time, Skinner chewing his cud and Robert oiling leather, sharpening tools, or just drinking tea. It seemed without those three dogs together, the excitement of hunting together was lost for Skinner. He hunted alone from that point on. He loved the dogs, but kept to himself in the field.

23. A Time of Rest and Repose

So much is lost with the death of an excellent animal. But with terriers, there is no hope of saving them from violence. As the Good Book says, "He who lives by the sword, dies by the sword." So it is with terriers. Violently they live and violently they die. There is sorrow for the loss of a friend with the passing of each good dog, but one must not let grief steal from the dogs what they are in their deepest natures. Blacky and Nig died as warriors do, fighting.

Some who do not understand the nature of things, would have dogs be sheep and cocks be canaries. But dogs are happiest to be dogs, with flesh in their mouths and blood on their teeth.

The deaths of several great dogs in such a short amount of time caused Robert to be thankful he had stopped hunting Grit. An excellent working dog is hard to come by and Robert wished to have Grit for a good number of years more to breed. For the next year, whenever Robert went hunting, he left Grit home. Grit had reached the ripe old age of eight, which is ancient for a terrier that is worked hard. Robert told himself that Grit had reached the age of rest. "And in the seventh year, Dog rested." he joked.

Grit was given reign over Robert's property. He was not chained or kenneled. Robert knew that Grit would get into trouble now and then, being free like that, but he felt Grit would need that trouble to maintain sanity. Grit could not be kept from hunting by any means but locking him up. The area surrounding Robert's home was deplete of most game for several miles. Robert, Curtis and Jon made sure of that when they were teenagers who killed far more than they should have. After depleting their home-turf of game, they quickly learned the concept of catch and release. As a man, catch and release was all Robert did, unless it was a pest animal killing poultry or eating produce. All nutria went unspared. Robert had no place in his heart for invasive rodents. They all died. So it was that Grit could wander around hunting at his leisure but rarely found more than possums or the odd wandering raccoon. Grit was content with this, as long as he wasn't forced to remain stuck on a chain.

Grit lost much of his training with total freedom. Because there were not many raccoon in the area, he learned to hunt what he had not been allowed when he was hunting with Robert. But it was a blessing to Robert none the less. Grit chased deer every night. Robert did not stop him from doing this. The deer couldn't eat his garden, if they were being chased every night. Grit had a strong drive to kill. Because Robert never hunted skunks with his dogs, there was an abundance of them around his home. Without competition from raccoons and such, the skunks flourished. They were slaying pigeons and chickens by the coop-full around Robert's neighborhood. With Grit on the lookout, however, the skunks were not so lucky. He would patrol the barns and coops, killing anything that came near the birds. Rats, possums and many skunks were crushed in Grit's ever lusting jaws.

When Grit wasn't roaming off and about, he laid on Robert's back porch, on the cool cement. Most of his time was spent there, waiting for Robert to arrive home. With Robert, he would meander through the gardens. Robert would sometimes command him to dig gophers, which he would do gladly. Grit never lost his puppyhood interest in digging for small rodents. Grit was incredibly valuable to the farm in that time of resting from hard work.

Robert bred Grit to every bitch he could. Grit was fertile and always seemed to hit the mark. In a short time, there were many pups from Grit running around. But many were too shy and scared to ever make great hunting dogs. They might have become like Sandy, Grit's brother, but never would they equal Grit. One by one Robert weeded through them, until two years passed and he only had three pups left from Grit's litters. He stopped breeding Grit when he realized that Grit could not reproduce dogs of his own caliber. It was a great disappointment to Robert. The truth of breeding is such that the best dogs may not be valuable as breeders. Grit was such a dog. He was by far the best hunting dog around but he was no good as a breeder. After his two year hiatus, Grit was put back to work, much to his pleasure. No need to hold him back for breeding.

∘ ∘ ∘

It was at this time of Grit's rest that Robert finally asked Hero to marry him. They had grown together like oak and mistletoe. She of course accepted him as her husband and they were married in the springtime.

The wedding was great fun. It was a merry time for everyone. Jon and Thomas started off the dancing with linked arms and a mockery of country swing dancing. The two tall, bearded, balding men looked hysterical, slapping their legs, dose-doing and swinging each other around.

Robert's nights of being lost in the woods and week long wild forays were cut short with married life. He always tried to hunt in the early mornings rather than the evenings and be home at night for his wife. Life was different as a married man.

24. An Invitation

It was Christmas time. Robert returned from hunting in the woods with Curtis and greeted his wife, Hero.

"Micah called for you today," Hero told Robert. "He is always such a gentlemen. So gracious."

"Micah, huh?" Robert took off his wet wool clothes and entered the kitchen. "I wonder what he wants."

Micah was a doctor in town who also happened to breed game bulldogs (called American pit bull terriers by many). He bred a good number of champion game dogs in his day. Whenever he came to visit, he was always quick with manners, helping Robert's wife set the table, helping clean up, always bringing gifts for the young couple. But without women around, he was as rowdy as any other man and readily quick with inappropriate quips. He was a big man with dark black hair and well kept goatee. He had been an excellent athlete as a young man. In his forties, he was still in formidable form.

After Robert settled into comfort, he called Micah.

"Hello," came Micah's voice.

"Hey bud, what's happening?" Robert asked.

"Hey there Robert, glad to get your call. I've got a proposition for you."

"Oh yeah? What is that?"

"I met a doctor from Ireland at a recent convention. The man has invited me to go out there with him and experience the hunting there firsthand!"

"That is awesome. When are you going?"

"I am going as soon as I can. I want you to come with me. It'd be great! Imagine it man, hunting the traditional way! Seeing how they do it in the old world! It is a life experience you won't ever forget!"

"That sounds amazing, but I'm broke as a bad joke."

"Stop being such a sissy! You're a clever man. Round up the cash for a flight two months from now."

"It's not just money Micah. My wife is pregnant. She really needs my help."

"Jesus man! I thought you were a go getter. Get off your ass. Work double time. And get your butt on the plane with me. Your wife is pregnant! So what? I'll tell you what. That means this is your last chance to do something like this. After the kids come. . . . You think you're poor now? Ho ho ho, You don't know what broke is yet."

"I'll think about it. That's a lot of money."

"Damn you! I'll pay half the flight, if you get the money together to leave in February. Merry Christmas you damned penny pinching scrooge."

"Alright. Alright. I'll start saving for it. Thanks for the gift," Robert said, not knowing how on earth he'd get the money to go.

○ ○ ○

The time came to fly to Ireland. Robert hadn't earned adequate money for the trip, so he sold an old pickup truck he had sitting on his property. The truck sold just in time and at the exact price of a plane ticket. He scrounged together the cost of a pet passport for Ol' Grit. Robert's wife gave him no grief about leaving. She had family to help her, if there were any emergencies. He was going to Ireland.

Ironically, Micah could not make the trip. He had some seminars he was required to attend. One night while visiting, he informed Robert that he would not be going on the trip. He made sure to inform Robert of the news before Robert purchased any plane tickets.

"I can't make it," Micah said, "but don't let me keep you from going. I've talked to the Doc and he says the invitation stands for you, as well as me."

"I said I was going, so I'm going, hell or high water," Robert said back. "I've put my heart on running with the foxhounds there. I'd be going, even if I had no friend to stay with."

"It's time you had a vacation, Rob. You've put yourself on a leash. When you get to Ireland make sure to hit a seedy pub and some grungy Irish brothels. Find the nastiest place you can and just live it up. You aren't flying halfway across the world from your wife to be a goody-two-shoes. This'll be your first taste of freedom since you've been married."

Robert looked nervous. "You go ahead to the seedy bars and nasty whore houses when you go there yourself, Micah." Robert stood to guide Micah to the door. "Now, I've got to get some sleep. I work in the morning."

Micah slapped his hand onto Robert's shoulder. "You do-gooder. You don't like grunge. I should have thought as much. Only English ladies for Robert. Find an upstanding joint then. You tell me what it cost you and I'll foot the bill. You could use an unwinding." Micah was grinning from ear to ear.

"I don't need to pay for love, thanks."

Micah laughed loudly. "You're too damn serious Robert! You know I am kidding, don't you?"

"I can never tell with you," Robert answered. Micah laughed all the harder.

"You're going to have a good time there. It's your type of place. You'll fit right in with the Irish peasantry."

Robert laughed and pushed Micah out the door. "Hurry on your way now, before my wife hears your talk of brothels and calling the natives of her ancestral home peasants."

∘ ∘ ∘

The doctor met Robert at the airport. Introductions were made, the doctor was named Eoin Murphy. He was a man nearly of equal proportions to Robert. He was stronger, being the senior of the two. He had the bearing of an athlete. Lean but built for speed.

289

"This is your little dog I've heard of, then?" Asked Eoin. His Irish accent was exactly as Robert had heard little children play at. It was a playful, excited sound.

"Yeah. This is Grit."

"He'll do good, by d' looks of 'im. He's seen plenty o' work like has 'e? "

"More than most," answered Robert. "I am excited to see what he does with Brock."

"Oh, He'll get da chance. But ee'd be more of a fox sized dog."

"Really? Your terriers are bigger than this?"

"Yeah, definitely," Eoin said. "He's what we'd consider a nice fox dog. Our badger dogs are moch bigger like. Some, very high at d'shoulder. Enormous chests on some of 'em."

"That's a surprise, I thought it was one size fits all."

"Don't mistake me, Robert, a small dog can do a bang up job on any quarry, if it 'as 'e brains and heart for it. But we tend to keep two types for the different work."

They loaded the dog and baggage, hopped into Eoin's jeep and headed for his home.

"I hope yer fit fer some runnin'," Eoin said. "We'll be followin' the hounds tomorra on foot."

"I'm no Olympian but I can hold my own in a footrace. Let's hope that'll do."

During the ride, Eoin and Robert asked all the basic introductory questions to do with family, profession, etc. They arrived at Eoin's family home. His old-man was in the living room by the fireplace. He was kind faced with keen icy-blue eyes and light brown hair. He was in extraordinary shape for a man in his late 60s. A Staffordshire bullterrier was lying next to him. Introductions were made. Neil was his name.

The talk from there on until they were settled into bed was of dogs and hunting. Eoin was excited to introduce Robert to some great terriermen of the area; men who were the terriermen for otterhound packs, men who could tell a tale that would make you laugh until ribs ached. The trip was going to be an extraordinary one.

25. Robert's First Irish Morning

Everyone in the house went to bed by 11:00 pm but Robert could not rest. He hadn't slept on the 22 hour plane ride, either. He read until the sun came up, then he prepared for the hours he was supposed to be awake by exercising. He jumped up and down, did push ups and crunches, stretched. He tried to make his body as alert as possible. When finally he heard someone moving around in the kitchen, he went out.

Neil, was in the kitchen. He was getting dressed into gardening garb.

"Mornin', Robert," he said. "Would ye like some breakfast?"

"Yes, please."

"Eggs wit' rashers 'n' chips sound good to ya?"

"That sounds great."

"Have at it then." Neil said, "The potatas are in the pantry. Here 'r th' eggs and the rashers. I'm goin' inta dh' garden."

Robert was a bit taken aback. The manners were obviously different in Ireland than America. He didn't know where the pots and pans were kept, so he bashfully searched the cabinets. He found them, and started his breakfast. He cooked enough for Eoin as well.

Eoin, entered the kitchen while Robert was cooking.

"Ye get any sleep?" he asked

"No. Maybe an hour of light sleep," Robert answered.

"Tonight, ye'll be sleepin' like a baby den."

They ate their breakfast, then got dressed for the day's hunting. Eoin brought Robert out to the yard and showed him the dogs. Grit was tied to an apple tree not far from the rest and already chewing on some leg of mutton. There were a few white dogs, for which southern Ireland was renowned. These were beautifully built dogs, though ugly by a showman's tastes.

"Ye'll be seein' more o' these white dogs while yer here. These dogs ha' been around these parts for generations like. Ya won't find better white dogs anywhere."

Robert could hardly wait to see the terriers work. But this day was reserved for the foxhounds.

Eoin unlocked a small shed, in which gardening tools were kept. There were a couple of bicycles. "Ye'll be riding my father's."

Robert put Grit in the basket on the rear of the bicycle and the two men went on their way.

The ride was a windy few miles. Stone walls lined the roads and trees overshadowed the way. Now and then Eoin would point at a home of a friend, "That's where So and So lives." Each of the homes Eoin pointed out were inhabited by someone well renowned in the hunting culture of southern Ireland. "Mind ye, these men'r only famous in these parts. Ya go twenty, t'irty miles farther down the road, nobody'll know who yer on about."

The ride took three quarters of an hour or so. They parked the bicycles in a dairy lot and walked into a small pub. Robert tied Grit to a gutter on the corner of the building. The huntsmen and all the followers were in the pub drinking warm liquors.

A man came up to Eoin and spoke heatedly, yet quietly, with him for a while. Robert caught portions of the conversation. But the man did not acknowledge Robert one bit. He was discussing the hare coursing that had gone on days before, letting Eoin know which handlers' dogs fared well and which did not.

"Why the whispering?" Robert asked when the man left.

"It's the state of things now. We're on edge like. City fools and anti-hont coonts are fightin' ta end our way of life. Secrecy is becomin' the norm, but this shit will pass. Fieldsports are Ireland's heritage, you can't outlaw that."

A huntsmen for another pack came to speak with Eoin. This was a big, tall, lean fellow with brown hair and hard features, though a kind look always on his face. This man Eoin introduced to Robert.

"This is me best mate, Darren," said Eoin. "We've known each other since we were small fellas."

Darren was very friendly and shook Robert's hand with a fervor. "What's the story, fella?"

"What's that?" Robert asked.

"Just a greeting. Yer all the way from America, then?" Darren asked.

"That's right."

"Whereabouts?"

Robert told him whereabouts he lived. They chatted about the dogs and hunting and how the culture of hound hunting is so different in America and Ireland. Darren couldn't believe that every hunter kept his own hounds and only three or four, at that. The packs in Ireland and England were very large, and packed together on scent like a flock of birds in flight. Some Americans would even only keep one hound. In Ireland, the faster and slower hounds were moved to packs that were either faster or slower. Each hound in a pack was meant to be about the same in skill and manner of hunting as the rest. In America, men wanted the best hounds and did not stop to consider the pack so much as each individual. Though a pack might be made up of dogs with different complimentary skills.

Darren bought Robert an apple cider drink to give him some energy for the day's running.

"Keep an eye out for me," he said to Eoin and Robert. "I'll be mounted today."

"Christ!" said Eoin, "Ye come into money den, have ya?"

"Nah, just one o' the many benefits a bein' a Hontsman." Darren winked at Robert. The job of Huntsman was done for the love of hunting and naught else. There was no money nor benefits to being a Huntsman except for the freedom to be with the hounds and horses.

"We'll be walkin'. We're no rich men, Darren," Eoin said. "We'll keep an eye out for ya though. What'll ya be ridin'?"

"I'll be on a grey cob gelding. 'E's a pain in the arse, that focker. 'S likely, they're tryin'a break the green horse t' hontin' 'nd I'm the mog that'll do it."

Robert listened with deep concentration to pick up on the thick accent.

"No doubt. No doubts 'ere. We'll 'ave some comedy, then." Eoin laughed. "Let's get out 'n' have a scance aboot, Robert. There'll be a terrierman just 'ere."

"Has he got good dogs?" Robert asked Eoin.

"Nah, they're utter shite. But th' man's from England. Ever'body t'inks bein' from somewhere else bestows a person wit' special knowledge. The bloke don't know shite about terriers.."

Darren broke from Eoin and Robert and went his way to the stables. Robert untied Grit from the gutter and led the way to where the hunt would begin. As they walked they passed the terrierman. The terrierman had three short, hairy, gray and white terriers on leads. The heads on the dogs were short and round. They looked nothing like jack russells. The man wore a flatcap.

Eoin couldn't help but mock him for his hat. "Will ye be sweepin' chimneys today or diggin' terriers?"

The man was caught off guard. "What?"

Eoin mocked again, "Will ye be sellin' us papers?"

The terrierman didn't answer but looked at Eoin quizzicaly and somewhat perturbed as Robert and Eoin passed him. They went to untie Grit before walking to the hunt.

"Did ya see that hat 'e wore, Robert?"

"Yes, my wife tried to pack one for me. I told her to put it away. I'd feel pretentious wearing one."

"T'ank God ya didn't wear one a those hats, Robert. I'd a hated ya immediately like. We native Irish see it as affectatious t' wear a cap like dat. I wouldn't come t' America and wear a cowboy hat. Fer Christ's sake! Now would I?"

"Were those the white terriers you were telling me about last night?"

"They aren't. Fock. That man wouldn't know what to do wit' a fine terrier, if he had one. Those are English dogs 'e brought from home."

Robert was taken aback by that talk. He had anticipated that the terrier tradition would be more open in Ireland and England and that camaraderie of the hunt would unite the men of different nations. Truly, the isles are the homelands of the best working terriers. The Irish and the English really just couldn't be expected to get along, no matter the hunting.

The two men walked together for a half mile or so. There were trucks, cars and vans parked all the way to the location where the hunt was planned to begin. Grit showed no nervousness. He was a dog with one thing on his mind, hunting. The smells of the countryside filled his nostrils. With brush, hounds and horses on the wind, the little terrier didn't think a thing about all the people and traffic. Old folk and children who could not keep up with the hounds nor ride a horse, found it more convenient to listen to the hunt from the comforts of their vehicles. The Huntsman's trumpet told the learned person's ear all it needed to know. Different blasts indicated whether a fox was spotted or caught or pushed to ground.

Eoin and Robert passed a woman walking with two children. Eoin knew her and stopped to chat.

"Hello Roisin. Not stayin' for th' hont this mornin'?" Eoin asked.

"No," she answered, "The little fellas are a handful like and I've work t' do today."

299

Robert noticed that the bigger of the two young boys had tears running down his face. Eoin noticed as well.

"What's the matter, Thomas? Ye don't like the hounds?" Eoin asked the little boy.

"I do! I do like hounds! I love 'em!" little Thomas yelled.

"It doesn't look like it, Thomas." Eoin was chuckling. He knew it tortured the boy to be taken away from the excitement.

"I love hontin'!" he yelled. The tears started flowing stronger. "I love hounds! I love hontin'!"

Eoin laughed out loud and nudged Robert. He pointed at the boy, proud at the scene he had created.

"And how are ya, little Donald?" Eoin asked the littler of the two boys.

"I'm fine Eoin, t'ank you." Donald was in good spirits and cordial.

"Fine t'ing for you to rile Thomas up, Eoin. You don't have t' walk home wit'im," their mother said.

"It's always a pleasure causin' ya trouble, Roisin." Eoin grinned.

Horses and hounds began to trot by at that time. Robert and Eoin left Roisin and the boys to their walk.

The hounds were not like most hounds in America that Robert was used to. These hounds were thick in bone, flat backed and short eared. Hounds in America had much longer ears, were leggier and usually had bony, triangular backs. There were over twenty of the tri-colored hounds. Black and white, brown and white, dog after dog moseyed past. Grit stood tall, his tail rigid. The hounds up close made him curious and ready to trot off in search of a fox.

The horses were gorgeous. Many had their bodies shaved to disperse heat and keep them cool during the long day's running. Some had designs such as arrows and geometric patterns shaved into their hair and along their rumps. The Huntsman rode past first, wearing his red jacket to set him apart from among the crowd. His head was helmeted with a fashionable cap, as were all the riders'. The Whip followed close behind the hounds, which followed the Huntsman. The Whip was there to keep the hounds from rioting (chase trash, livestock, or otherwise messing about). He kept them mindful of their purpose to catch a fox.

Robert and Eoin came to an opening in the road where the path broadened. The Hunt was gathered there. Horses, hounds, cars and people were all crowded together. A broad expanse of fields lay just beyond the rock walls bordering the road.

"Do ya see the horses witta red ribbons?" Eoin asked Robert.

Robert looked and noticed several horses with red ribbons tied to their tails. Most of the horses with ribbons were beautifully groomed with plaited manes and bound tails. Young women were atop these horses.

"Yes," Robert answered.

"Stay away from those. That means 'ey'll kick. They may overrun ya as well. Best be wide of 'em."

"Thanks."

An older man in a van pulled up behind Eoin. Rolling down his window, he signaled with a finger to his lips for Robert to keep silent. The old man pulled out a riding crop and lightly slapped the side of Eoin's face. Eoin turned with a look of agitation, then a smile spread across his face.

"Seamus, ya old bastard! What're you doin' here?" He clasped the terrierman's hand firmly in both of his.

"D' Hontsman knows dat English twat's dogs can't do a proper job o' dis. I brought my dogs. I'll follow d' hunt in me van today. T'ought I'd give a hand." His accent was thicker than Eoin's.

Eoin laughed. "Can't blame the Hontsman fer wontin' a proper dog on the job. And it'll be nice t' have a terrier here too."

"Har Har Eoin. I'm not de only son of a bitch 'ere." Seamus squinted at Eoin, "Ye helpin' wit' d' dig today?"

"Sure will, Seamus. But I've got a favor t' ask of ya."

"What's 'at you'll be needin', Eoin?"

"My friend's 'ere all the way from America like. He's got a crackin' dog. Ya mind if we dig it today?"

Seamus lifted the cap off his head, the same kind that Eoin had insulted the Englishman for, and scratched his head. "Eeeh, ya sure d' dog'll stay til' dhe job's done?"

Eoin looked at Robert for the answer.

"He won't do you wrong. He's as steady as a stone once he's found his game."

"I hope yer right, man. I've looked forward to makin' a fool a dat Englishman all week," he said with a grin.

"Don't you worry yourself," said Robert.

"Yer dog it is, dhen. But put 'im here in me cab til' we're needin' 'im. Don't wear 'im out chasin' hounds. Yer like t' wear yerself out draggin' 'im t'rough d' brush."

Robert was confused by the accent. Eoin tilted his head toward the rear of the van signaling Robert to do as Seamus said. When Grit was put in a box, Seamus was ready to go.

"Till dh' fox goes to ground lads." He tipped his hat and drove slowly through the hounds and horses. He was headed for a hill top where he could get a better listen.

Just then Darren came riding in on the cob. It was a beast of stunning power. It was enormous. Darren was wearing the green colored jacket of his own hunt. He was the master of a beagle pack.

"Don't fall," Robert warned Darren, "or you're like to be following the tale of Humpty-Dumpty."

"I may be a bad egg," Darren quipped, "bot I'm a tough nut t' crack."

His horse lunged and pranced around the open area on the road.

Eoin asked Darren, "D'ya have the slightest control o' that beast?"

"Not a bit," Darren answered. "I'm along for th' ride. Keep an eye out fer this big grey and my green coat and you'll be sure t' have a show."

At that, he rode off to meet with the rest of the hunt. Eoin and Robert waited for the horses to leave the area. The hunt had begun.

26. Chasing the Mounted Hunt

R obert had read in books about the roar and thundering of the horses' hooves when going to battle. The sound was just as a heavy storm. The horses' hooves rained down on the stony roads; hundreds of shod feet, like steel water on rock. The noise died away for many minutes then rose again. The hunt could be seen on a road above where Eoin and Robert stood. The two men watched as the hounds poured through a hole in the stone walls surrounding a field. In a straight line they went, quietly, noses to the ground, dozens of hounds.

The Whip guided the hounds to cover. Brambles and briars ran along a small creeklet, just as they did in Robert's home territory. Blackthorn and white-thorn hedges lined the waterway, with blackberries interspersed. The horses were ridden behind the hounds, led by the Huntsman in all his livery. The sight was majestic and reminded Robert of ancient times, when kings rode out with their court, or knights on some mission of valor. Hunting in this manner linked Robert to the lives of many who had lived before him, hundreds and perhaps thousands of years were bridged with the scene of horses and hounds.

Eoin led Robert on. Showing him the places to get through or over the rock walls and hedges. The horses set the pace, a jog for the men, for two miles. The hunt went right by homes and farms. The farm folk would come out their doors to view the hunt as it passed. It was within view of a farmer's front door that the scent of fox was struck.

A broad swath of thorny trees and tall grass housed a fox, no doubt resting for the morning. A thick boned hound led the pack, striking the scent first. It threw its head back to announce the discovery of a fox before crouching its black and white body to enter the thick brush. The hounds poured into the thick mess of trees. They bawled through the dense foliage for no more than five minutes, before leaving, one by one, into the field on the same side from which they entered.

People who had not yet come out to see the hunt were exiting their houses and standing in the front yards. Some people shewed their dogs into kennels or indoors. The race was on and the hounds were in full cry. The horses crowded into the narrow street. The rock walls kept them closed in. The Huntsman stopped the riders from proceeding further down the road. The hounds seemed to be pushing the fox to a gated opening in the rocks. The fox was spotted shooting under the gate, the hounds closing in on it. The Huntsman blew notes on his horn, indicating the fox was seen. He then commanded the riders to move back and unclog the road. Automobiles had pressed in behind the mounted hunt. Confusion ensued when the riders all tried to move back the way they had come. Robert and Eoin leaped out of the way of the frenzied mess. They climbed up a rocky wall and dropped on the other side into the field the fox had just ran from.

"Let's get past those horses and into the real action," Eoin said to Robert.

The hounds were nearly out of hearing. The day had started with calm weather but the wind was picking up into a breeze, carrying the cry of the hounds away from Robert's ears. He pulled his hat down snug to keep the wind out.

They ran to the gate where the chase had passed. They hopped it and crossed the road into another field. This field was lumpy and had lain fallow for sometime.

Briars and teasel grew amongst the dead grey grass. Eoin and Robert bounded and leapt through the tall wet grass, attempting to keep their pants dry. They could not see the hounds, but they saw two men ahead, who appeared to have a good vantage. They went down into a creek bed and crossed the stream, stepping on some old farm equipment that was buried from years of silt. The teasel was growing thick on the other side. Robert was careful of his movements. He did not care for the scratching of the prickly plants. The field they entered was full of round smooth rocks. Piles of rubble, stone and dirt were scattered across the field. Fox and rabbit holes riddled these mounds. Eoin and Robert joined the two men they had seen ahead of them. There was a stout bald man, very strong. Robert thought he looked a bit shady even. The other was a thin wiry man, wearing rubber boots and leaning on a walking stick. Both were young, less than 35 years old. From the tallest mound they could see the hounds following the creek.

"Seen anyt'ing?" Eoin asked the men.

"Na," answered the skinny one. "Haven't seen a t'ing since 'e made fo' d' creek."

Robert couldn't comprehend the men's words over the wind that was blowing, so he focused on what he could understand, the hounds. At that point they looked to be piddling around, totally at a loss for where the scent led. The wind was whicking it off the ground as soon as it was laid. There were hounds scattered from one end of the field to the other for half a mile. But the lead hound eventually caught wind of the quarry and led the hounds into a tilled field, half a mile wide and longer still than that.

"Bugger," the bald man said. "Dhere's little chance a dhem catchin' good scent t'rough dat field."

Robert looked and saw that the hounds were blowing out across the field like the wind. The line bowed in the middle, where the scent drifted and caught in pockets of tilled ground.

"They aren't on the exact line," Eoin said. "They're prob'ly just catchin' the scent on the air. It's blowin' from further down the field, maybe even outta the brush. Bot that's where the hounds can smell it. Let's catch up."

Robert and Eoin ran the half mile to where the hounds were funneling out onto another road. The Huntsman and a few of the hunt had made it there. The Huntsman was calling it quits on that particular fox.

"We're outside our hont boundaries now," he said. "Let's find anodher fox. Dis un's been a poor race from dhe start." Most of the hunt had not caught up. The Huntsman blew the notes on his trumpet.

Eoin whispered to Robert, "That signals the fox went t' ground. But we know 'e didn't. That's a way for the Hontsman t' save face wit'he hont. See?"

Robert did not wish to give up on the fox. But sportsmanship among the different clubs required it. Good relations were important among the different hunts. The hounds were led to the same thicket in which they had started the first fox. The thought was that the cover was too good to house only one fox. The notion was correct. They were soon on another. This one tore out of the dense swampy area it was resting and shot into a thicket of hawthornes. There was a worn path through the thicket, wide enough for a horse to pass.

"C'mere t'me!" Eoin coaxed Robert, yelling to be heard over the din of hounds and horses' hooves on the road. Eoin pointed to a gate of barbed wire that was covering the trail. They began to move it, but some of the riders' horses got over anxious and kicked the fencing out of the way and into the ground. "Forget about it," Eoin said. "If the fools can't manage 'eir horses, it's best we stay outta the way."

There was a rubble of mossy rocks piled in the trail. The horses had to jump this to get into the hawthorne thickets. Several made it clear. Then up came Darren. His horse was unwieldy and competitive to take the lead. It leaped the rocks without taking account of its rider. Darren hit his head on an overhanging branch. The hard knock peeled the top of Darren's helmet off. Darren crumpled under the branch, like an accordion. But he stayed mounted. Robert was worried for him, but saw that Darren reached up, felt his helmet and kept riding on.

"Now's our chance," Eoin said. He darted into the thicket after the lead horses.

Is he mad? Robert thought to himself. *We're likely to get trampled by the rest of the horses driving through.* Yet, he followed. Congestion caused by the barbed wire gate allowed the men some time to get through the thicket but not quite enough.

The mud was thick and gloppy through the thicket. It was swampy turf. Robert stepped high to get from grassy clump to grassy clump. It was little help. His feet were sinking in the mire. The horses came thundering behind him.

"Be wide, Robert," Eoin said. "Horses' shoes sometimes fly off in this stuff. Keep an eye out."

Robert was pressed by the horses and so pushed his way into the hawthornes where horses could not navigate. Many rode by, the horses churning the soil into slop. Robert watched for a moment. The sight made his breath catch. It was frightening to be near so much out of control power.

Eoin was not waiting for Robert. Robert had to move extra quickly to catch up. When they reached an open field, they ran down hill into a gully. The bald man and the thin man with his walking stick were already ahead of them. They had followed the creek rather than the hunt. Wisely so. They were well energized. Robert was nearly out of breath. Eoin kept a brisk pace.

The fox ran down into a gully where three hills met, shot down a stream bank and crossed the creek on a branch that a monkey shouldn't have been able to balance on. The horsed riders had to find a place to cross the creek. Eoin bailed into the creek and splashed across. It was two feet at it's deepest. Robert crossed carefully balancing on the same branch the fox crossed on and using a branch above his head to hold steady.

"Just jump in like," Eoin said. "The hounds are gaining on us every second." He ran through the field and onto a mud road bordering the forest. He was out of sight before Robert had set foot on the opposite bank.

You'd be careful too, if you only had one pair of boots, Robert thought. He hopped onto the opposite bank, dry as a cricket by the fire. But his hat had snagged on some branches overhanging the creek. It drifted with the water. Robert grabbed hold of a sapling on the bank and reached out, grabbing his cap. *I hate this hat*, thought Robert. It was a ridiculous wool beanie with a second hat sewn on top of the first. It was bulky and silly, always falling off or falling over Robert's eyes. He had to pick up pace to catch up to Eoin. He came to the mud road. It was churned by many hooves. He couldn't tell which way the hunt had gone, nor Eoin. Robert stood still and listened for hounds. The forest and the gathering storm blunted all sounds other than blowing trees. Eoin appeared up the hill from around a bend in the muddy road.

"Come on," He yelled. Robert picked up his exhausted feet and jogged up the hill. Eoin was already on the trot again. "If all else fails," Eoin spoke to Robert, "follow the horse tracks."

The fox led them up and down hills, through the woods, back up hills, again through the woods, a dairy yard, and back across the creek. Miles they ran.

Eoin and Robert halted back on the mud road near the creek crossing. All the horses were lined on the road. All the riders were watching and listening to the hounds working out the scented puzzle on the creek. Darren separated from everyone else and walked his horse to Eoin and Robert. He was soaked from head to toe.

Eoin nudged Robert, "State a him, laa."

Darren put his arms up, as if to say, "What can ya do?"

"Howza horse treatin' ya, Darren?" Eoin eyed Darren up and down. He knew what had happened to him.

"The horse is fine. I decided t' go fer a swim."

Robert and Eoin laughed. "Jus' cleanin' the mod off yer cloes 'en?" Eoin said.

"Tha's right," answered Darren.

The fellows chatted for a bit before the hunter blew his horn. The fox had been spotted in the field opposite to them. Off the horses went, tearing the grassy fields to pieces. Eoin was not one to take rest. He and Robert shot after the horses. They'd been running with few breaks in between. Robert crossed the creek in the same manner as before. This time Eoin waited on the other bank.

"'E shouldn' be long before goin' ta ground somewhere," Eoin conjectured. "This un's run fer a long time. 'E seems t' be tryin' ta head back inta familiar ground."

Robert was much quicker crossing the creek the second time. They climbed out of the brush lining the creek and ran up a hill to get a view of where things had progressed. Robert wondered how Eoin kept from collapsing. The run had exhausted Robert's energy. They got to the top of the hill and looked down on the valleys below. The horses were soon seen crossing an open flat field below. The Huntsman came to a rock wall with his horse but didn't slow a bit. The horse cleared it with ease. The horses spread out, each finding a spot to jump. Some jumped the ditches lower down the field. Robert kept his eye out for the big grey cob. It was in the very back. Darren had waited for the rest of the hunt to get moving. He planned to make a big jump over the rock wall. He urged his horse into a canter and charged at the wall. The horse leaped the wall. Darren made it over as well, however, he was no longer on his horse. He flew off his horse through the air and rolled into the wet grass on the opposite side of the wall. Tumbling a few times, he got to his feet. The cob was already on its way to meet the rest of the horses. Darren ran with his long legs to catch the horse, halfway across the field from him.

Robert and Eoin were laughing their heads off from their perfect vantage point. "We can laugh at Darren all we want," said Eoin, "but I'll give it to 'im, that he 'as some o' the biggest balls around. 'E can't ride a horse fer shite, but he'll risk life and limb t' take the biggest jomps."

Most of the riders who went to the hunts were there for the riding. Nothing gave one better opportunity to jump a horse and ride in new, challenging terrain than a fox hunt.

Eoin led the way again. Down the hill they went. Robert's feet were blistered in several spots and his legs felt like they were moving through water but he kept after his friend. The fox had entered a new valley. It was no longer going up any hills. It was taking the path of least resistance. It had become as exhausted as Robert.

The two men rounded the bottom of a hill and saw the hounds clumped together, bawling like mad. The Whip was there pushing them back. The Huntsman blew three long notes on his horn, "to ground, to ground, to ground," then swung down from his horse.

Eoin urged Robert to speed up. "Here daa, the fox is to ground."

Many of the horses had not yet made it to the scene.

27. To Ground, To Ground

Robert and Eoin arrived and were given freedom to look at the earth. It was a rocky sette, on a slope, with small boulders between 20 and 50 pounds in weight.

"This looks like a pain to dig," Robert said.

Eoin nodded his head. " Ya very well might be right. This fox's given a good run. The Hontsman may decide ta let it go. It's earned it."

The Huntsman blew "to ground" on his horn again. . . . About five minutes passed before Robert saw Seamus trudging through the field with Grit and a little red bitch in tow. Every few steps he'd start skipping forward to quicken his pace, then slow again, as if he were an excited boy who was too shy to show to the other boys how badly he wanted to get to the fox.

"Hurry, ya fat arse!" Eoin yelled.

Seamus arrived, puffing for breath. Grit and the little red bitch were straining on the lead. Grit was screaming to get in on the hounds' action.

Seamus squinted at Eoin, "Take a shovel ye twig piece a shite and make yerself useful when dhe time comes." Then he turned to Robert, "Do dhe honors, man."

The Whip pushed all the hounds away from the earth. They needed silence, if the fox was to be bolted.

Robert walked with Grit straining on the lead. Grit was pulling so hard on the lead that his front feet didn't touch the ground. He plowed with his hind legs right up to the entrance of the den. When Robert unclipped the lead Grit calmed. He went to ground with the patience and calm of a weathered veteran.

"I brought dhis littl'un along, just in case," said Seamus. "Notin' against ya, Robert. Simply dhet I need t' ensure da job is done. Not dat yer dog will fail. Always good like t' have an ol' faithful, so ta speak. Dhis'n here, she'll get a bolt or she'll be dhere 'til we dig 'er out. Dhere's not an ounce of quit in 'er."

Eoin put his finger to his mouth to signal silence to Seamus. Seamus looked at the Huntsman, who understood. The Huntsman kept the riders and viewers away from the earth. The Whip held the hounds back the best he could. For the most part he did very well. But there was one hound that kept pushing past. It was a giant among the rest of the hounds, big and covered in thick red fur, with only a little white here and there.

"Keep dhat brute away from the sette!" Seamus yelled at the Whip.

Eoin leaned in to whisper to Robert, "That hound's notorious fer bein' overzealous. Doesn't matter how hard the Whip tries, that hound'll break from the pack."

"Will he kill a terrier?" Robert asked.

"He won't. I've never seen that happen in all my life," Eoin answered.

"Really?"

"Really. Even witta little red hairy bitch like the one Seamus's got. The hounds know in an instant like whether it's a fox 'r not. Though I've heard of terriers bein' torn by a pack, I've never seen it and I don' t'ink I ever will. The hounds know what's what."

They were silent for a number of minutes before they heard baying. Seamus stood back from the holes with Eoin and Robert. Everyone was as silent as possible, standing back from the sette. In order to bolt, the fox would need to feel it was safer outside the den than in it. It took a good terrier to work the fox properly.

Too much stick and the fox wouldn't be able to bolt. Not enough and the fox wouldn't want to.

The Huntsman came to Seamus. "How long?"

"Dhere's never a set time fer dhes'ings."

"Give it a bit longer, den get ta diggin'," the Huntsman commanded, then walked away.

Seamus nodded his head but once the Huntsman was out of hearing he leaned in to Robert and Eoin. "Have ya ever heard dhe like?" Seamus whispered. "Dha man tellin' os how t' work our terrier? No wonder 'e's got a messer fer a terrierman." The three looked over at the Englishman, now standing with his three terriers on leads next to the Huntsman. Those two were huddled, just as Seamus, Robert and Eoin were. "I'd not dig fer dhis fella t'ree days a week. Not for dhe wages of a paid terrierman."

They listened for the dog a bit longer, then Seamus spoke up again. "Dhere could still be a bolt but I'll do as'e man says and start dhe dig."

"Once Grit hears the shovels hit the earth, he'll set that fox in it's place and there's little chance of a bolt then," Robert told Seamus.

Seamus shrugged his shoulders, then listened intently with his ear to the ground, until he found the spot that the sound traveled the clearest. To Robert, it seemed an impossible task. He could hear the baying coming out of the open holes. The wind whistling didn't help matters. He didn't know how Seamus drowned out that noise to hear the dog where it actually was. Seamus, after deciding where the dog was, took a steel bar and wiggled it through the ground. It came to a hollow spot in the earth and sank through. Barking could be heard through the hole made by the bar.

"Looks ta be a t'ree footer. We'll be t'rough in no time," Seamus said to Robert and Eoin.

The men set to digging. The Englishman entered the dig to help out. That made two shovels for the work. The four men worked fast, each switching with another, whenever one got tired. The Englishman kept quiet through most of the dig but dug his fair share. There were some big rocks in the dig, digging around those made the work slow.

When they got close to breaking through, the Englishman kept digging. He wanted the glory of breaking through to the quarry and tossing it to the hounds. Dirt crumbled away, while he dug, showing the men the tube in which the dog worked.

"What's'e idea?" Eoin said to the Englishman. "Ya never seen a fox before?"

Over hasty people at the dig were often mocked. It was impolite for anyone but the owner of a dog to pull it from the earth. Tossing the fox was also the job of the man who's dog kept it bayed.

"Robert, ya want t' toss de tod t' dh' hounds?"

"Honestly Seamus, I haven't grabbed many fox from the earth. I'll let you do it this time."

Seamus pushed the Englishman away from the hole. "T'anks for dhe help mate. I can take it from 'ere. Ya can unhand me mate's dog." The Englishman had already taken hold on Grit. "Now get on outta dhe dig. I know da job well enough."

The English terrierman went his way to the Huntsman. Seamus pulled the dog out of the hole. He handed him to Robert. Seamus then looked up from the hole and spoke to Robert. "Ye may see people usin' tongs while ye here, Robert. But a good terrierman should never need tongs for a fox. 'E should've dug close enough to de fox dhat it's wit'in reach. Dhen, if 'e knows his work at all, 'e knows 'ow to handle the quarry wit' 'is hands." Seamus moved his hand slowly toward the fox then shot it like lightening for the fox. He had a hold of it by the scruff before it could strike him.

"Now move back lads. I'm about to show dat English mog det de Irish can work dha hounds 'n' terriers 's well as any."

He climbed out of the dig with the fox scruffed in his hand, like a cat carries its kitten. He faced the pack of hounds. Holding the fox by the scruff and the rump, he got ready to toss the fox headlong into the pack. One aiming swing for good measure. . . And he let the fox fly.

Only, the fox didn't fly. The hunt erupted into laughter and applause. Seamus looked at his hands dumbfounded. The fox seemed to have disappeared. He then scanned the ground quickly with his eyes and turned himself around. He saw the fox twisting along the ground into the hedge, with one big red hound on its trail. The rest of the hounds followed shortly.

The hunt ended there for Robert, Eoin and Seamus but the mounted hunt carried on for a few more hours. The three terriermen walked across the fields to where Seamus's van was parked. Seamus was feeling a bit foolish.

"I looked down 'n' dha fox 'ad simply disappeared," Seamus said.

Eoin couldn't stop laughing about the incident. "That big red hound snuck up behindja like and grabbed the fox by the white of 'is tail, jus' as you were tossin' him. He pulled it right outta yer hands. The look on your face was beauuutiful, Seamus. Magnificent!"

Robert and Eoin laughed and re-enacted Seamus looking dumbfounded, searching their hands and the ground for an invisible fox.

"Dhat's enough ya damned fockers. I've had enough already. Dha hont's taken dha mickey outta me."

28. Leisure at the Pub

The wind that had been building all day had turned into a torrent of rainfall. The men had to park far from the pub. The streets were jammed with cars from the hunt. It went from a white sky to nearly black in no time. The raindrops were as large as pennies and drenching the men. The three ran to get out of the weather. Robert was thankful to be wearing wool but he reminded himself to wear a slicker from then on. The wind had the rain pelting them sideways. The pub was a welcome sight.

When they got into the pub there were some American riders who had made it in before the terriermen. They had made time on horseback. The American group was made up of a man and a few women. They spoke loudly above everybody else. Eoin looked annoyedly at them. He wasn't a fan of noisy folk. Noisy

American folk, that is. They made their way over to Robert, Seamus and Eoin.

Eoin laughed, " Lamp. Dey're comin' for ya Seamus. Yer famous."

"Shut up, ye ass," Seamus told him. When the Americans got to the bar where the three men were sitting, Seamus just kept his head down.

"That was some toss," the noisiest American woman said to Seamus, who ignored her.

"It was. He's a grade A tosser. Thaat's fer sure," Eoin said. Grinning, he patted Seamus on the back.

The American's didn't catch the slant on Seamus. They stayed and talked with Robert and Eoin for a half hour or so before Darren arrived. Seamus kept his head down and his hand on a pint. The visitors were horse breeders from the southern states. They bred thoroughbreds of the highest quality and were in Ireland for a hunting festival that would go on all week in the Northern parts of Ireland. The best packs around the country would be hunting each day during the festival. Though the folk were loud, Robert enjoyed them. Eoin may have even enjoyed them a bit as well, though he wouldn't have acknowledged it.

Darren showed up to the pub covered in mud. The top of his helmet flapped like a puppet's mouth.

"How'd you like riding like the rich folk today, Darren?" Robert asked.

"Oh, it was fine. A fine day's ridin'. I loved it."

Two of the American women gasped and giggled at the state Darren was in. But the oldest of the women and the American man came to talk to Darren. The American man was putting on airs of Victorian Aristocracy or some such thing. All of his movements were slow and effeminate. He had a glass of wine which he held daintily, wrist limp. His small pencil mustache, among his jowls and coupled with his weak persona, was not much for bespeaking manliness. It was obvious, though he was present in the countryside, he was no native to it.

The woman touched Darren's elbow. He was so tall, that was all she could comfortably reach. "Are you alright, Sir?" she asked. "By the state of your clothes and helmet, I'd say you took a few more hard knocks."

"Hard knocks? Nah," Darren said, reaching up for his helmet and removing it. When he looked at it's top, he was astonished. "I s'pose I did take a hard knock or two."

Darren looked at Robert, who raised his eyebrows and nodded his head, to share in Darren's surprise, though Robert had seen the knock.

"This is the man who escorted me all through the day, dear," said the American woman to her drowsy feminine man.

"Ah," he said, with a slightly croaking voice, "Dear me. All that muck couldn't have come from your little swim my wife was telling me you took."

The woman laughed and looked to Robert and Eoin. "Oh yes. Your friend here took a headlong fall right into the creek. He went right over the horse's neck." She laughed and rested her hand back on Darren's arm.

Robert and Eoin laughed out loud. They had a good image of Darren's tall form bouncing from the horse's back as if spring loaded and crumpling face first into the creek.

Robert looked at the American man. He was dressed in what looked like a silk turtle-neck sweater. "You didn't ride with the hunt today?" Robert inquired.

"Oh no," he said, still holding his wine glass high, "I never ride."

"I heard your wife and her friends talking about breeding thoroughbreds. All that fine horse flesh and you don't ride?"

"No. It is not my passion. I love to travel, so I go with my wife wherever the horses take her."

Darren interjected, "Let me getya a drink Robert."

"I'm not a drinking man, but thank you Darren."

"Not a drinking man? No problem. I'll getya dat apple drink. That's the job, i'n't it?"

Robert sipped on his drink until the majority of the hunt arrived. Soup and sandwiches were served to all, free of charge. Robert ate his fill of ham sandwiches and soup. The hunt, after eating a late lunch, dispersed to their homes and dwellings. Though, some of the people remained out. The two men with whom Robert and Eoin stood watching the hunt were still out, as well as the Huntsman. The terrierman had not returned either. Robert and Eoin hitched a ride with Seamus and returned to Eoin's father's and cleaned up, changed clothes, cleaned up Grit and checked his wounds, then went to visit Darren. A storm was raging by then, thunder and lightening. Seamus went straight home from Eoin's father's. He had been embarrassed too badly to show his face that night.

After cake and tea at Darren's with his wife and children, Eoin, Robert and Darren left again for the pub. They got to the pub and it was roaring inside. Everyone's voices were raised as loud as any American's, despite Eoin's insistence that the Irish were quieter. The Huntsman and his fellows had returned and were already sloshed with the drink. Darren found seats quickly for he, Robert and Eoin. They sat with the greyhound man who had chatted with them that morning. His friends were there too and lively. In the morning they had ignored Robert but in the evening, they treated him as kith and kin. They leaned in close and taught him many secrets and ways to cheat in the hare coursing.

"Why would you cheat?" Robert asked, "Doesn't that just lessen the quality of dogs being bred?"

"It doesn't," said the oldest man. "Everyone cheats like. If ya aren't cheatin', yer not competin'. Bot sometimes it backfires. Ye give a dog a booster shot fer energy like, and ye have a small window of opportunity t' get d' best outta yer dog. Once 'e energy's spent, dere'r no reserves. If yer dog's race is postponed, yer fokked."

Eoin leaned in so Robert could hear him, "It's a pity ya missed the coursin'. The last big meet was the day before ye arrived. That's why they're all still stoked up about it like. But more on the subject. . . Ye can catch cheating sometimes. When the man who slips the hounds releases 'em t' course, ye may see 'is knee knock inta one a the dogs like, faulting the dog's start. Little t'ings like that can't be proven. See?"

They went on for an hour or so chatting about the running dogs. In the middle of the conversation, the Huntsman and the bald, hardened fellow that Rob and Eoin had met earlier entered the group.

"How was the rest a the hont?" Eoin asked the Huntsman.

Darren's interest perked up, "Yeah, didja ever recover that fox after Seamus fombled it?"

"No, no, we never again caught dat fox. 'E outwitted us. 'E gave a good run furdher but 'e line was lost witta wind and d' storm. I t'ought I might be shot off me horse by a bolt o' lightening."

"Aye, the wind nearly knocked me off the cob on my way t' the stables," Darren agreed.

"It was a good fox," Robert said, though truly, he had not much experience.

"Dhat it was," the Huntsman nodded. "Dhat it was. It'll be a pleasure 'avin' dat one around for later. Doze are d' foxes ya wish ta hont every day."

"No' li'e da' one las' week." The man who had been in rubber boots, carrying a walking stick was now in the conversation.

Robert leaned in to Eoin, "Is he speaking Gaelic?"

"He isn't. He's jus' langers." Robert didn't understand. "He's drunk, Robert." Robert understood that.

The man in the boots was still talking. " 'E' wenta gron' in five minus in a fairy fort. Da bogger."

"Fairy fart?" Robert looked puzzled.

"Fairy fort!" Eoin laughed. Slapping Robert on the back. "Ancient buildin' sites. I'll show ye some while ye' here."

Robert was excited to see that. He had heard of fairy rings and fairy trees but not forts.

"There's superstition that tamperin' wit 'em is bad lock," Darren told Robert. "Farmers, nor no one'll toach 'em. Ye shouldn't even set foot in one."

Robert went back to Eoin's that night and slept well. The storm raged out the window. Robert dreamed of faeries and ancient sites of ritual. Ireland was a place of wonder for him.

29. Bright Eyed and Bushy Tailed

The morning came quickly for Robert. It was dark when Eoin shook him awake.

"Get up Robert. Ya've got a great day ahead of ya."

"The great day couldn't wait for. . . day?"

"Nope. Get up. I'll be in the kitchen."

Robert got out of the warm bed. He had quilts as thick as mattresses to keep the heat in. Stepping out into the naked air gave him goose bumps tough enough to sand metal. Even through his wool under garments he was chilled. He threw a warm cotton sweat suit on and headed to the kitchen. Neil was already up drinking tea and reading the paper. It was still raining and blow-ing outside. Eoin didn't seem to care. He was going to ride his bicycle where he liked that morning. Seamus had been courteous enough to load the bicycles in his jeep the night before when they three left the pub to-gether.

"I'm goin' fer a ride," Eoin said, "then I'll take ya ta hont wit' Mick 'n' Craig. Then ye'll see some good white dogs work."

"Are these the white dogs this town is famous for?" Robert asked.

"Yes, one'n the same. Ya don't know how lucky ye are. These blokes won't even let me hont wit'em. Noobody honts wit'ese fellas. But I told 'em ye'd be sworn ta secrecy like if they took ya ta their diggin' spots."

"Man, that's great. I'm stoked."

"Good. This is a rare privilege. Make the best of it."

"I will. Thanks for setting it up, Eoin."

"No problem, Robert. Ye'll enjoy yerself, I'm sure. Now, Craig is a close mate o' mine. 'Is diggin' partner is Mick, 'e's a different sort. You'll see. But y'll like 'im."

While he waited, Robert made himself breakfast, read and listened to a philosopher who was on the radio that morning. Neil went with Eoin into the stormy weather of the dark morning. Neil paced Eoin with a motorcycle to make sure he kept good pace. When they returned, Robert was plenty awake and the two Irishmen were spattered and muddy. The morning had been a hard one by the looks of them. But the weather was calm as a white cloud by the time Eoin and Robert left for Craig's place. Robert put on his slicker and the hated double topped beanie, in case the weather turned bad. Eoin had already loaded Grit into the Jeep.

Robert recognized Craig from the pub the night before. He had been introduced briefly. He was a young man in his thirties, tall and dark haired. He looked tired.

"Jesus, Eoin. Ye couldn't wait 'til humans were movin' like before startin' yer day?"

"Yer gettin' old, Craig," Eoin answered. "Smell the fresh wetted soil. Hear the birds. The mornin's where life happens."

"Whatever you say. . ." Craig walked over to Robert, who was unloading Grit. "Story, Robert? Gettin' on well wit' dis git?"

"Doing well, Craig."

Eoin was already leaning on his back foot. "I'll be off then. Take care a me friend, Craig. 'E's a bit green when it comes ta real diggin'. Don' make 'im do all the work."

Eoin hopped in his jeep and drove away. He made faces at Craig as he drove past. Craig just shook his head, trying to stop a grin from spreading across his normally stoic face. Then he looked down at Grit.

"Dhat's a fine little dog," said Craig.

"Eoin said the same thing. Said he's little."

"Little fer Brock maybe, but it's not de size a dhe dog, as 'ey say. . .Tie yer dog ta dha hitch 'ere." He pointed at his vehicle. "It's early yet fer Mick. Let me show you me stuff, den we'll head t' Mick's place."

"Sounds good," agreed Robert.

Craig took him to his kennels. They were very well made, with cement dividers higher than the dogs' heads. He had a couple grey hounds and four or five terriers. The white dogs were much bigger than Robert had imagined.

"Dhese aren't fox dogs, Robert," Craig said, when Robert looked at the giant terriers with wide eyes. "Dis stuff was bred for d' otters. But it's not time fer otters, so we'll be out fo' dhe grey lads today."

The white dogs were easily 17 inches at the shoulder, built lean and tall with heads like bulldogs and hair like a wheaten. Robert liked them, despite how ugly they were.

"Hideous, I know. Mick's are prettier. I hate da coats on some a deeze. Dhey could stand some improvin'. All well. Ya saw Darren's bitch las' night?"

"Yeah," Robert answered, "I liked her a lot."

"If ever dhere was a good bitch, daat's 'e best of 'em, she's some pure good stuff." Craig said, "but damned if she 'asn't dh' bitchiest head of bitchy heads."

"I thought she looked great." Robert said.

"Oh no. Look again. Her head is terrible. But 'at bitch'll work all day ever' day. She's pure hard like but keeps herself well in a fight. Never takes long t' heal. She never really gets too badly mauled."

"It's the work that matters over all else in the end."

"Aye. Dat's d' trut'. She wouldn't have a place in dha show ring like. Nor would any o' mine. But 'ey're fine workin' animals."

Craig then showed Robert the recovery room for the dogs. There were cabinets and a refrigerator full of medical supplies, suturing kits and antibiotics. Beds were made up high for the dogs, off the ground. The room was heated with lamps. There was an old dog lying on one of the beds. It was evident the dog had seen many a day's digging. But today it was merely taking rest in the warmth.

"Old Betty comes and goes from here as she wishes," said Craig. "She's retired now. Da best terrier I've owned, dog or bitch. I love 'er like a like a little one." He went to her and scratched her old head. Where once there were red spots on her head, there now was grey. She was ancient.

"How old is she?" Robert asked.

"Ya won't believe me if I tell ya, but she's 19 years old."

"19 years old?! That's fantastic."

" 'Tis. Sometimes workers don' make it t'rough dh' firs' season. Odhers live two lives' wort'."

"Ain't that the truth," said Robert, shaking his head and staring at the old bitch in disbelief.

"Well Robert, it's aboot time we head t' meet Mick."

"Alright. Let's get going then."

Mick was a five mile trip. He was in the drive when Robert and Craig arrived. Introductions were made. Mick seemed normal enough to Robert. He was a short old man, very friendly, probably 60 years old. He was dressed all in green and black rain gear. Dull colors. What was odd, is he had a double stuffed cap on his head, just like Robert's. He stared at the cap, while shaking hands with Robert.

"Dhat's an odd cap ta have," he said. "I made dis meself. Alway's t'ought it was a bit unlocky meself. I hate it."

"It's the same for me," said Robert. "I hate mine."

Mick led the other two back to his kennels where he kept a few young pups and a couple workers. Craig hadn't been lying, Mick's dogs were better looking. His pups had thick full coats. They were healthy, stocky pups. He nabbed a thick boned, heavy white dog from the kennels beside the puppy pens.

"He's big, mind you," said Mick, "but dat's never stopped 'is dog from gettin' where he wants t' go. Ye'd be surprised, dhe kind a settes dhis dog can get t'rough."

They packed up the dogs and drove off to a farm where the lads knew of a few good earths. This farm was a hilly place. The sheep would have liked to have one side's legs shorter than the other's to navigate the steep slopes. Craig leashed his big strong white dog, Robert leashed Grit and they set off down a hill. The soil was wet, heavy and full of shale. Mick knew where he was going and led them straight to a sette that went under a rock wall. The wall was no more than two or three feet high. The walk was down hill and back up again.

Robert's legs were sore from the running of the day before but he managed.

"Dhis is a badger sette," Mick said, "but it wreaks of fox." He looked at Robert, "Can ye smell it?"

Robert was just about to say no, when a strong scent filled his mouth and nose. It was thick, at first sweet but turned bitter to him.

"What say we try Robert's dog in 'ere?" Craig offered.

"I won't argue witcha," Mick said. "Hold my dog for a bit, wontcha, Craig." He handed Craig the leash and hopped over the rock wall to investigate the points of entry. "Alright. Alright. Dis is well used." He peeked his head back over the rocks. He was on his knees. "Hand me dhat little dog a yers, Robert. Dhen climb over 'ere and see what I'm lookin' at."

Robert lifted Grit over the rocks then hopped the wall himself. He looked down to the wide hole where Mick was kneeling and peering into. The earth was well packed all around it and a muddy rut ran along the wall where game moved every night.

"Look how deep da track is." Mick pointed to the muddy rut. "Dhis is well used like. Well used."

He took all the collars off of the dog and it slipped effortlessly into the earth. "No fear o' d'dark in him, is 'ere."

Robert winked at Mick. "Now all we need to do is wait."

There was silence for a long time. The men kept listening for something, but there was silence.

"Dhis dog is 'e right size for dh' job," Craig said. "How's 'e do on fox?"

"I've only caught a couple with him. Usually, if he can reach them, he'll try to kill them."

"Dhis'll be a trick dhen. Fox don't make a peep." Craig said.

"Really? Fox won't make a sound?" Robert asked.

Mick answered, "Dey don't. Dhey're stone quiet. But sometimes, if a dog is strong enough, a badger'll make noise. But a dog's got ta be a tough one ta do. . ." Mick perked up. "Didja hear dhat?"

The other two looked at each other. Neither had heard anything.

"Right 'ere," said Mick, "A t'ud." Mick laid down in the wet grass and stuck his ear to the ground. "Just 'ere," he said. Whining could be heard through the soil. "Dhe dog's made it dis far at least. Now, where's dat yoke?" Craig handed him a bar. Mick pushed and swiggled the bar through the slate filled soil until he broke through near the dog. The dog was about three feet deep under the mens' feet. Mick got on his knees and put his ear back to the ground. "Yep. I was dead on. E's right 'ere. But no game. He's diggin' on like." He lifted back up to look at Robert and Craig. "We'll jus' continue our chat, den."

Mick and Craig bombarded Robert with all sorts of questions about hunting in America.

"Dhose raccoons'r nasty animals!" exclaimed Mick. "I always t'ought badger were bad like, but Christ! Dhose raccoons sound god awful."

"Nah, by the looks of your dogs and their size, I'd say badger are the stronger opponent. But coon ain't no joke," Robert told them. "Fox bite deeper than the coons but coons seem to have a crushing bite. The dogs just hate getting bit by them. Nutria slice the dogs up. But coon are our best test on a consistent basis. Otter are the toughest by far though. But they usually just bolt."

"Dhey're d' same here. Ye don't want a dog wit' an otter long. Dhey have dh' strengt' of a badger and dh' speed of a fox. Dey'll tear a dog ta pieces. Ya want de otter t' bolt to dhe hounds as fast as possible," Craig said.

"So you don't dig many otter either?" Robert asked.

"No. Dha hunt wants 'em bolted. Terrier work isn't 'e goal of otter hunting. Listenin' to da hounds is all da fun."

"Ah."

"Otter hontin' is not like d' fox hontin'. Wit' otter hontin', ever't'in' is slow paced. Everyone is on foot. Da hounds are slow 'n' loud 'nd swim most a d' time like. People can take 'eir time walkin' on dh' bank, chattin', havin' dha craic. Ye never heard anyt'ing like de hounds in a canyon, voices boomin' off dha wolls like. T'irty hounds all in unison. It's beautiful."

"I can only imagine," said Robert. He had heard up to ten hounds in the mountains at one time, but he hadn't heard thirty or more with their voices bouncing off walls of stone.

"Want a cuppa?" Mick asked, pulling a flask from his pack.

Robert's hands were cold. A warm drink would be just the thing for it. "Yeah. Might as well. There's digging ahead, I could use the boost."

Mick looked at Craig, who nodded. So Mick poured his two friends a cup of tea. He always had an extra cup on hand but was short one for himself. "Don't let me keep you from your own tea," Robert said to him.

"Oh no." Mick held up his hand to ward off the cup Robert was offering back to him. "Ya need it. I plan on havin' you dig. You're a young feen and I'm old. I have whatchu need and you have what I need. It's a fair trade like, across dhe board."

Robert was thankful for the warm tea. The weather never reached freezing but there was always a biting wet wind. Robert thought he had known the bite of cold from his travels in the Rocky Mountains, but this was worse. Though the temperature would read warmer on a thermometer.

Mick walked back near to where the dog had last been. On his hands and knees, ear to the hole he had drilled into the ground with his T-bar, he listened.

"The dog has moved on," he stated. He crawled forward a few yards and waited quietly. Robert was so intent on listening, he had to remind himself to breath from time to time. After minutes of waiting, a muffled thud vibrated through the soil. All three of the men felt it. When they listened closely, they could hear the dog's high-pitched whine.

"Ah." Mick crawled a few feet over to where the thud had come from. He sat back onto his knees. "Yeah. I feel 'em right 'ere." The vibrations of a commotion were buzzing up through Mick's bones. "Hand me dh' bar again."

Robert quickly got the bar and handed it to Mick. The ritual began again. Mick drilled through the slate filled soil. He wiggled the bar to widen the hole as he went.

"Notice how I work in dh' bar, steady like?" he spoke to Robert. "Dis is important. Some lads'll jam da bar down like. Tryin' ta punch a hole t'rough d' eart'. Dhat's no way t' do it." He was swirling the bar round and round, "Nah. Ye got to take it easy. Ol' Seamus, who ya met yesterday, he had a dog stabbed right t'rough wit' a bar on a hont. Seamus's been leery a de bars ever since. Doesn't let anybody but his close diggin' mates use 'em, while 'is dogs are in dh' ground. See, 'twas a young cocky fella dhat stabbed 'is dog. Rammin' the bar down like a fool chimp." At two and a half feet, the bar broke into the tube. "And. . . Dhere we are." His head went down for a listen. "Yeah. Dhere it is. He's found 'is game. Dat's a fox I'd say. Dhe dog would be havin' more trouble witta grey lad. Have a listen."

Robert knelt down to the small hole drilled in the ground. Mostly, all he could hear was heavy breathing. He could hear the dog tug a bit, here and there. Robert sat up. Craig was there with a shovel. "Have a turn at it, Robert. It'll be good fer ya."

Robert got up, grabbed the shovel and started the dig. He felt self-conscious while he dug. He had seen how quickly the men in Ireland dug to the fox the night before. He was nervous to have his terrier in the ground in the isles where terriers originated. But he knew Grit would never fail at his task. His hat kept falling down over his eyes, slowing him down. Finally, he took the hat off and threw it on the ground. "Damned hat!" Hitting rocks every shovel-full, he was not making time like he and the fellows did the night before. The digging was slow but he broke through in not too long a space. Mick spoke up then.

"Careful now, Robert. Dis is where t'ings can go bad. Don't tug on dh' dog." The ruddy fur of the dog could be seen through the small hole Robert had opened. Mick stepped in to widen the dig past the dog's tail-end. Then opened up around the top of the dog's head, toward the fox. "I've anodher lesson for ya Robert. Do ye mind if I pull dh' dog for ya?"

Robert nodded consent.

"Come close," Mick said. Robert drew near. "Look at d' situation." He made sure Robert was looking, before he continued. "I wouldn't tell ya dis, except 'et ye haven't dug t' many fox. Some messers'll ruin a dog's face in dis situation. Lots a dogs've lost their palate t' dis exact situation. Yer dog has his palate, so I know you've never had dis problem, but dhe advice will help ye none d' less. Many t'ink da fox 'as done a great amount o' damage t' dh' dog, because at 'e end a dh' dig, dh' dog's nose and mout' are torn t' shreds. But a fox doesn't shred dh' dog. It'sta people dhet cause 'e dog ta get shredded. Now look 'ere."

The dog and the fox had each other by the mouths. The fox's bottom jaw was in the dog's mouth. The fox was biting down on the top of the dog's snout. Grit wasn't making a peep.

"See 'ow dhe fox 'as 'e dog. De fox's canines're deep in dh' dog's snout. Ya never pull on dh' dog in dis situation or you'll strip d' dog's palate 'n' shred 'is muzzle. Especially a dog dhat is hard on 'is foxes like dis. Dig around 'e fox and 'e dog. Give yerself some room t' work." This had already been done by Mick, before the lesson. "Dhen, getcherself a stick t' pry d' jaws apart. . . Craig, help me."

Craig was already prepared. He laid down and reached into the hole. With a stick, he pried Grit's jaws apart. The fox snapped his teeth down a quick few times into the dog's snout before letting go and trying to get back from the dog. But Craig already had the fox by the scruff of the neck. Mick handed Grit to Robert, who pulled him away from the hole. Grit was screaming for the fox now. Robert patted him and encouraged him. Craig let Mick pull the fox the rest of the way out of the hole. He looked the fox over. It was a vixen, bright eyed and bushy tailed.

"She'll be havin' kits in a few mont's," Mick said. He saw that she was undamaged and healthy, so he let her go. She shot along close to the ground and ran down hill away from the men and the dog. "Don't tell dhe farmer I let 'er go," said Mick. "'E doesn't want t' have t' worry about lambs bein' worried."

The rest of the day was spent in like manner, digging, swapping tales and anecdotes. Robert learned a great deal from old Mick. They accounted for a couple more fox that day. They planned the next day to take Robert where they knew Brock was home. Robert slept well again that night and woke in the morning with excitement and joy for life.

30. Brock

The next morning found Robert and Eoin at Craig's again. Robert brought Grit, a little sore but still strong. Craig grabbed a stout young white dog. And Eoin had taken along a tiny black and tan bitch that was new to work. They hopped in Eoin's jeep and drove to meet with Mick.

Eoin let his bitch off lead to find her own settes. The little black and tan shot to ground in a fox den in a hedgerow. The dig was easy and they opened up to her and an impressive todd fox.

Grit was up next. They drove to another farm for more settes. They arrived and helped the farmers sort some cattle in the barn, then walked across the muck of the barnyard and into the fields. Two fields they walked, hopping the rock walls as they went. In the third field they saw a fox run down a hill and into the gorse and rock hedge that divided the field from a gorse patch. They moseyed their way up the hill.

When they reached the top of the hill and surveyed the 'scape, Eoin spoke up,"I t'ink that fox went inta the nearest sette on the other side a this hedge. Let's skip over that and move on t' the next sette. I t'ink we'll find Brock there."

All agreed and moved on. There was another rocky hedgerow just 50 yards from the other. Gorse was growing through large white stones. Giant boulders littered the area where gorse had been allowed to take over the field. There was a single, horizontally oval hole dug right under the rocks of the wall. The Irish men noticed that the sod was torn up all around the den.

Craig sat on his haunches and picked up some of the torn sod. "See here Robert. Look a' dis." Robert came to look. "Dhis," said Craig, "is badger sign. Dey tear up da ground lookin' for worms and grubs 'n' such." Robert hadn't noticed it but now it was obvious that the earth had been torn up by something. "Dhis is quite a bit more torn up den mos' places, 'ough. It's quare dhet 'ere's only one hole 'ere. It looks as if many more badger are in dhe area."

Robert led Grit to the entrance. His heart was in his throat. He didn't know if Grit was up for the chal-

lenge of a badger. He'd heard so many tales of the ferocity of badgers. *Does Grit have will enough to stay until
dug to?* Robert wondered.

Grit tried to push down the hole. His tail went
straight, like a pointer's and twitched in anticipation.

"It's your time to shine, boy. Get in there and
do what you were bred to do." He unleashed the dog
and he shot to ground without hesitation. In under a
minute he could be heard baying.

"From what I saw of yer dog dhe odher day, I
don't t'ink he's quite up t' 'is game, yet," Mick said.
"His first few digs he went in like a steam roller on dh'
game."

"But this probably isn't a fox," said Robert. "I
don't know what he'll do with a badger. He's never seen
one."

Mick was the correct of the two. They listened
for a while to Grit baying and whining. Scratching
could be heard through the wall. Stones let the sound
through very well.

"D' tunnel is right into dh' wall, I'd say," Craig
suggested. Mick and Eoin nodded but didn't look up or
speak. They were listening intently. Both were squint-
ing, as if that helped them hear better. Robert didn't

know a badger would pull stones out of a wall and make his cavity in there.

Grit made contact. There was hardly a huff out of the badger. But the dog could be heard growling. The sound was so clear through the stone wall that each foot step and claw drag could be heard. Grit charged valiantly. But the badger outweighed him. It pushed back with a fury. It crumpled Grit back up the pipe like a bottle brush. He could be heard trying to push back with all his might.

"This is where size can play a part," Eoin said, nodding to Robert.

Ol' Brock pushed Grit right back to where he had been forced to dig around stones to enter the bad-ger's lair. But his body was too big to be pushed back over the stones in that fashion. Brock couldn't pass him, nor push him further. Grit used the tight space to his advantage. Pressing against the rocks at his rear, he ex-tended, bossing the badger back. He would sometimes let out a bark, but for the most part muffled biting, scratching on the stones and snorted breath was all that could be heard. Grit pushed back with his might and the badger eventually retreated. He pushed Brock right back to it's stop end in the wall. He lit up there and bayed with a fury. He was right in the badger's face. Another huff and the badger charged again. Grit didn't let it get away with pushing him again. He pushed back with what weight he had. They came to a stand still between the stop-end and the tight spot where rocks blocked the tunnel. It was back and forth from there on. Grit wasn't letting go of his opponent. It attempted to draw itself back to the stop-end but Grit wouldn't have it. The badger tried to push past Grit but he maintained a strong hold. He wore his opponent out.

"Let's get to it lads," Mick said. He had hopped the rock wall and was at work in no time, pulling stones from the wall. What could not be seen by Robert before they started moving stones, is that the rock wall went deep into the ground. It was not merely a surface structure. It must have been there for hundreds of years, slowly being buried by ever growing and dying grass. Robert imagined hundreds of years worth of earthworms filling the cracks of the stone with mud. He was there with Mick on his hands and knees, taking the rocks that Mick moved and getting them out of the way. Eventually, Mick got to earth.

"Shovel," Mick said. Robert supplied him with the tool. Mick dug from his knees. It was only a foot and a half through stone and earth to get to the dog. He held tight to that badger. Mick had to take care to clear the stones properly, or the wall could collapse in on the animals. "Tongs." Robert supplied him the tongs. The badger would bite at Grit's shoulder every now and then. But mostly, the badger just wanted to get out of sight. The dog had the badger by the side of the neck, right above the shoulder. Mick gripped the badger's thick hide near its neck with the tongs. The animals were right at ground level with the terriermen.

"Move in 'ere Robert. When I get 'ese two outta d' ground, grab Grit as fast as ye can. Don't let him maul da badger or get close t' it again." Robert positioned himself for the job. Mick pulled the badger out away from Robert. Robert grabbed hold of Grit around the chest. The terrier released and tried to go for a better hold. Robert pulled him away from the badger in that moment and didn't let him near it again.

Mick got a hold of the badger's tail and stood up to inspect it.

"Looks like a boar," said Craig.

Robert looked from his vantage point. The badger was very thick and lowly slung. It's arms were as thick as Robert's forearms. This animal was built for subterranean life. It was a stout beast, fat and fluffy but obviously powerful.

"Looks healt'y to me," said Mick. He released it to live another day. Only sickly animals were killed by this group of terriermen. The badger was sluggish from his quarrel with Grit. Mick poked Brock in the rear with a boot. That got him moving for a bit. He tried to clamber up the rock wall to the other side but was too exhausted. With a shovel, Mick helped him over. The badger went right back down its hole.

"He looked pretty groggy," Robert said. "You sure that badger's alright to go?"

The Irish men chuckled. "You don't worry about 'at badger or any badger, Robert," Mick said. "No terrier can kill a badger in d' ground. Not a healt'y adult badger, anyway. Dhat badger is hardly bruised, jus' winded. But damned fine dog work!"

"Grit put up one hell of a fight. I'll give 'm dat," said Craig. "It's a rare dog dhat'll wear one out like dat. And t' hold one mid-tube is no easy task. He did very well. But 'e wasn't hurtin' dhat badger by any means. Dhose are d' toughest animals alive, pound fer pound."

"Let's fill in this hole. Then we can chit chat on the move lads. Let's get on down t' the settes back across the gorse where that fox went."

Robert inspected Grit. He had a bit of his lip pulled back down the chin, like a peeled banana. But

358

nothing too bad. They cleaned Grit's eyes and wounds with water from a bottle.

"That'll be fine. I'll show ye how t' doctor that tonight," Eoin told Robert.

The dog being in order, they picked up the tools and moved across the field. As they went, they saw that the sod was torn like a miniature plow had been raked across the ground. Dirt and grass clods were strewn across the hill. "I never seen d' like in my life!" said Craig, "Mick, Eoin, are ya seein' dhis?"

"Aye," they both answered.

"Never seen d' like," answered Mick.

Eoin spoke to Robert, "This is very unusual indeed, Robert. This looks like an army a badger been t'rough. This is'n extreme amount a diggin' gone on here. Very unusual like. You'll never see it again, I promise ya."

They came to a sette with trails heavily used. It was dug right in amongst boulders, blackberry vines, hawthorn and gorse. It was not a comfortable place for man. But for badger or fox, it was a cozy, fortified home. There were holes all through the boulders, buried deep under soil, grass and moss growing atop many of the stones.

Craig's white dog was brought to inspect. The other's were staked in the ground some 10 yards from the sette.

"This dog's wort' it's weight in gold," Eoin told Robert. "There's not much better in Ireland. If there's somet'in home, which'ere is here or I'll quit callin' meself a terrierman, he'll find it 'n' graft."

The dog didn't hesitate. Once he was let loose, he pushed his way into the rocky earth. Within minutes he could be heard baying.

"Dhis isn't normal fer him," said Craig. "He's a more hands on type, ye could say. Him bayin' dhis much wit'out any scuffle says 'et he can't reach 'is game." They waited twenty minutes but the baying didn't make any progress. "Damn dha big brute!" Craig cursed. "We'll have t' dig 'im out lads."

Robert was handed a shovel and he went to work. He chopped what brambles he could away from his digging area. A hawthorne above his head caught his cap and let his long hair fall about. "I swear, I am burning this hat after this trip!" he shouted.

Mick put his head down, closed his eyes and shook his head, "Bad luck, dhat cap. Jus' like mine."

Robert was two feet down when he started hitting rocks. He got out of the dig and Craig got in. He used the bar to pry rocks out of the hole. Robert was there to collect what he pulled out and move it aside. By three and a half feet, Craig hit a stone that filled most of the bottom of the hole. He dug around the edges of the rock. Mick and Eoin took a turn at digging, making room for lifting the large stone out of the dig. When room was made, Craig switched spots with Mick. The stone took two to lift. As soon as it was budged, the white dog made his charge. The stone had blocked him from his goal. Eoin and Craig rolled the rock onto the dirt pile. Then, Eoin jumped out of the hole to let Craig handle his dog and its quarry.

The dog had it's opponent by the side of the face. Tongs were handed to Craig. He subdued the badger and broke the dog off. Luckily, the dog hadn't taken much damage in his short scuffle, just a scratch on the chin. Robert had a stake ready to tie the dog to, as soon as it was out. Then he went to look at the badger. It was a big hefty brock. Robert wondered how it squeezed back past the rock where the white dog could not fit.

"Looks like dis fella's ready ta head back inta dhe eart'," said Craig. He let the badger go and it shot down the tunnel opposite the one from which he was pulled. "Hand me dat yoke," Craig said to Mick. Mick handed him a light. When Craig peered in, he saw another striped face. "Oh. Dhere's a second one in 'ere. Most be dha boar's sow."

Craig climbed out of the hole to give the game some space. The men watched quietly from their vantages around the hole. The badger stuck its head out of the tunnel cautiously then it made a dash across the dig and down the other tube. Right behind it, another head showed itself. The men all looked at each other in quiet, wide-eyed surprise. The third squat critter shot across the opening and down into the dark ground again. And a fourth and a fifth shot across the opening.

"I can't believe my eyes!" yelled Mick, once the badgers stopped flowing through the tunnel. "Like t'ree I've seen. But five?! Unbelievable. Ye brought us pure good luck, Robert. It's 'e American luck. Aah, I felt 'ere was luck in dhe air dhis morning! I should've known ya'd bring us a good day." He slapped his knees with his cap and clapped his hands with excitement. "T'ree or four. But FIVE! For Christ's sake. Dhat's amazin'." The other men were all laughing at Mick's show of excitement. He then went to Robert. "Let me get some a dhat luck off of ya before ya go anywhere." He rubbed Robert's head through the soggy wet cap. Robert chuckled. "It's 'e hat, I t'ink," said Mick. "I should like a hat like dhat. Full a luck! Dhat's why it's so lompy."

"Dhat really was somet'in'," said Craig. "I never seen dhe like myself. I've 'eard of people diggin' to a full burrow but five is somet'in' else. 'At's a new one ta me."

"I tell ya, I'd like t' 'ave meself a hat like dhat," said Mick, "I'd wear it every mornin' fer luck."

"Then it's yours, Mick." Robert handed the hat to him. Mick exchanged his own hat for Robert's. He looked as ridiculous in Robert's as he did his own, which was nearly the same hat.

"Ah, I like de feel a dat. Dhat's a hat of a terri-erman." He put his hands on his hips, held his head high and stared at the other men and winked.

The men went home and agreed to meet at the pub that night for some merry making. There was sport to be had at the pub that night, besides story telling.

31. Games Afoot

All the men went to their separate homes, cleaned up and doctored the dogs that were worked, cleaned themselves, ate and got rest. At the appointed hour, Eoin led the way with Robert to the pub. This pub had a sign with a large blue rooster painted on a white background. Inside was noisy and hazy. The men were singing songs, a few women were laughing. Robert could barely hear Eoin speaking right next to him.

Mick and Craig yelled and holloa'd Robert and Eoin over. Robert noticed Seamus, the failed fox-tosser, was at the bar. He came back with hands full of drinks. Passing them out, he was in a cheery mood.

"Aye lads, I'm gonna bate dhe trousers off a ya's tonight. Dhe drinks are on me, because my chicken is gonna cause ya a lot a heartache tonight," taunted Seamus.

"It'll be you, det needs dhe drinks to refresh yer supply of tears, after our chicken beats dha piss outta yers," Mick came back.

"Big words from a little man, Mick."

"All men are small in comparison wit' yer belly! Ye damned wormy pup!"

At that, they slapped each other's backs and set to drinking and laughing. Robert listened to the chatter intently. He did not know there would be a cock fight in the middle of the week.

Seamus stood on a chair. It seemed he was already a little tipsy. "Hear! Hear! Lads, in honor of our friend visitin' from a far away land like across dh' big pond, Mick 'nd I have brought a couple chickens tonight fer entertainment!" The crowd cheered.

"This is no derby, Robert," Eoin informed him, "jus' on weekdays, mates get together 'ere and spar a chicken now and then. No blades or any a that. Just 'e roosters and 'eir spurs. It's a tradition at 'is pub. Not Ireland wide or anyt'ing like that. Usually, the handlers don' let the fight last to it's end."

"Ya ever seen a cock fight, Robert?" Seamus asked.

"No. Can't say that I have. Though it is very popular where I live and my dad breeds some fine roosters. I just didn't make the time."

"Dhat's no problem. I'll tell ya. Dhere was days when cock fights were a shady sport like. Men poisonin' roosters and such."

"There was days?" Craig laughed. "Yer tellin' stories 'bout yerself from last week, are ye Seamus?"

"Shutcher hole, Craig." He shewed him off with his hand. "I'm givin' Robert a history lesson. As I was tellin' ya. Times was when people poisoned cocks like. Dhey'd put a bit on dh' tip a dh' rooster's beak, so when dhe roosters got a peck at each odher before da match, one'd go drowsy and get killed."

"See how much he knows about 'is, Robert. Da cheatin' win'bag," Mick jabbed at Seamus.

"You shutcher mout' or I'll shut it for you, ya ghoulbag. Anyhow's Robert, if these cheeky coonts will let me finish my story. . ." He paused and eyed all of the men round the table. "T'ank you. So, dhey'd have a midget or a cripple or some such person; a societal reject, you could say, would suck dhe cock t' see if it was poisoned."

"Jeeezus Christ!" exclaimed Eoin. "Yer one twisted man Seamus, you know dhat."

"God's honest trut', Eoin! I wouldn't lie to ya."

"First yer tale of an affair witta Queen a England 'n' now midget cock suckin'. What kind of journals are ya subscribin' to?"

Seamus looked solemn. "Hand to heart," Seamus put his left hand on his chest (his right was holding a drink) "God's trut'. Dhey'd have a midget suck dh' cocks. Mindja, it would only make dha midget sleepy but it'd kill a bird."

An hour's drinking and all the pub started funneling through a rear door. There was a pit in the back, with room for spectators around the sides. The walls of the pit were two feet high and made of wood. There were trophies, taxidermed otters and badgers, antlers and Robert recognized. . . A lumpy wool beanie-cap nailed to the wall. Hanging below it was a little plaque that had quickly been fashioned by Mick. It read, "Touch For Luck".

Seamus and Mick each had a lovely red rooster of their own, kept in wooden barred cages. The men continued to taunt each other the entire time the pit was in preparation.

"You can put dhat pheasant hen away, Mick. It won't have dhe speed nor dha heart to put one o' mine down."

"Ye've been bushin' again, Seamus. Dhis'll give ye a taste a what t' expect next derby. Better t' go home now and tell dha Missus you'll be losin' 'er money again. Ye lazy fat arse!"

First, Mick touched the hat on the wall. "Powerful magic 'ere lads!" Then, he reached into his cage and pulled out his bird.

Seamus, showing off, opened his cage and the rooster walked out onto his hand like a tamed parrot. "Dhis is how ya spot a good handler boys. Observe and learn," Seamus taunted.

Mick was ready with a retort, "My birds'd do dhat too, if I were hirin' midgets to suck dheir wee cocks!"

The room was in an uproar. They'd all heard Seamus tell his story a time or two. Mick, imitated a tipsy midget and stumbled about.

Seamus was no the less ready. "I'd be more bashful 'an you, Wee-man, seein' as yer dhe man hired fer dh' job!"

Mick glared. The crowd was laughing, many slapping their knees.

"Let's get these games afoot lads!" yelled the owner of the pub, a short fat man with sparse brown hair on his balding head.

Mick and Seamus walked up to each other. Both were caressing their chickens from nape to the end of tail. These men cared for each individual chicken. Everyday, they rationed their chickens' feed, handled the birds, ensured they were in perfect health. Kneeling in the center of the ring, they let the cocks each get a peck at the other. Seamus's was the more aggressive acting of the two. He tugged at his rooster's neck feathers. The birds went into an offensive stance, lowered heads, spreading their brightly colored feathers like head-dresses. The men pulled them briefly apart, then let them at each other. The roosters leaped at each other with full speed. Though the birds were of almost exactly the same weight, Seamus's aggressive rooster took an immediate upperhand. Its legs met the chest of the other rooster, flattening the opposing cock onto its back. Seamus's rooster ran right over the top of Mick's rooster, slashing with its spurs as it went. Everyone could see Mick was not feeling so confident anymore.

Intermittently, they would stop the fight for the birds to have a period of rest. The men would talk about how the fight was moving forward. As it turned out, both Seamus and Mick weren't abashed to suck their own cocks. They sucked on the beaks to get blood and fluid out of the birds' throats.

As the fight wore on, it seemed Seamus's bird could not maintain the pace it had set for itself. Though the other bird was not as quickly enraged, and not as ferocious at the start, it had been conditioned more thoroughly and kept a steady pace. It had a poor start but truly was game to the end. By the time Seamus's bird was exhausted, Mick's still had plenty of wind. It began to kick the daylights out of the other bird. Red and black feathers flashed around the ring. Blood was dripping from the roosters' wet heads. In the end, Mick's bird was triumphant.

Seamus handled the defeat well, though abashedly. He shook his friend Mick's hand and spoke to the fact that Mick's bird was the better conditioned, "Dhe race belongs not to dhe swift, nor dha battle to dh' strong," he said.

Mick grabbed the hat off the wall and proclaimed loudly, "Ay, findin' dhis hat was like findin' de end a dh' rainbow." He walked around the room and gathered his gambled winnings. Each loser put a sum into the hat. Mick spoke to each one. "Dhat's a good lad. Don't be too hard on yerself.", "No problem losin'. Jus' don't tell dhe missus." and so on. Finally he got back to Seamus. "One good turn deserves anodher, Seamus. Let's get pissed!"

Mick bought every man a round of Guinness, spending all his winnings. He pinned the hat back to the wall. Then both the men who had roosters to care for went home to heal the injured birds. Robert, Craig, Eoin and the rest of the spectators remained behind to celebrate the excitement and to jeer each other for the money lost and won that night. Mick and Seamus were constant rivals, each having the best chickens in the area.

The Pub owner was set for another round of fun, this time between human combatants. "Who's man enough fer enterin' dhe ring dhemselves?"

Darren had arrived at this time and walked through the door to hear the challenge. "I'll step in!" yelled Darren above the crowd. He was fully a head taller than everyone else. Once everyone had returned to the back room, he stepped over the wall easily with his long runner's legs.

Eoin nudged Robert, "Give it a whirl, Robert."

"With that giant? I'll hold myself back, thanks."

"He won't kill ya. He's strong as an ox but hasn't any trainin'."

"Neither do I," said Robert. But he walked toward the pit anyway.

So, Eoin talked Robert into the ring. The Pub owner acted as a referee of sorts. Darren was all smiles. He gave heart to Robert, who was also laughing. Sawdust had soaked up the roosters' blood and the blood dust had been scouped out. It was clean for man's use.

Eoin strapped a pair of boxing gloves onto Robert's hands. There were always a few hanging on the walls in the back room of the pub. Craig helped Darren in the other corner. When Robert and Darren approached each other in the ring the pub-owner spoke.

"Nothin' too serious, lads. Just a bit of a show fer dhe fellows standin' about."

Darren was a colossus compared to Robert. Fully 50 to 60 pounds the larger, with a much longer reach. Robert knew his only chance was to get in close and rapid fire on Darren's body.

The two men touched gloves and the match was on. The men around the ring were all cheering, egging the fighters on. Robert dodged a few jabs by Darren and got in close. He riddled Darren's torso from the side and front with swift punch after punch. But he did not guard his face. Darren stepped aside quickly away from Robert and punched a single swift blow into the side of Robert's face.

All went black, then stars appeared in Robert's vision. After a moment, he could see again. He wasn't even facing his opponent. Though Darren, a sportsman ever, was smiling and giving Robert a bit to catch himself. Darren waited near his corner, bouncing lightly on his feet.

Robert went back in for another set of blows to Darren's stomach. He was leery this time, but knew no other stratagem for such a large fit man. He could not wear him down through exhaustion, as Darren was the fitter of the two from running with the hounds all week, every week. Robert shot in under the long reach of Darren. He threw his hands again and again into Darren's stomach. This time he was watching for Darren's side step. The side step happened and Robert leaped away as quickly as he could. But he still got caught by the blow in the front of the face. Again, he saw dots, but did not see black this time.

Robert made another attempt to get into and under Darren's guard. Darren quickly hit Robert fully in the front of the face. A fourth attempt for Robert to reach Darren only succeeded in getting another strong blow to Robert's face. His ears were ringing now and Darren was fine as could be.

Eoin called an end to it. "Wo Wo. That's enough fer poor Robert. Gimme a chance in the ring wit'is animal." Robert sat on the ringside to regain his senses. Eoin untied his gloves for him. "Ya did well Robert."

"I barely touched the man. I did well, only as a moth batters a light-bulb with its wings."

"No. You could not see as I saw. Ya were doin' good damage to 'im when ya got inside t' 'is body."

"That is heartening. But I've learned my lesson. I won't be fighting a man of his size anytime soon."

Eoin looked Darren in the eye, "I claim ya, you big brute." He got in the ring. He was a trained boxer and a good one. Darren couldn't touch him. Eoin slid around Darren's punches like water and returned each throw of the arm for another. Darren was getting battered quickly.

"I'm done, I'm done," said Darren, backing away from Eoin. "I'm too tired to carry on chasin' 'is gnat around'e room."

Eoin beat a few more fellows into submission, then summoned Robert into the ring. "Have another go wit' someone 'ere more equal t' yerself." Eoin handed his gloves to Robert.

A thick built athletic man got into the ring. Robert and he were the same height but Robert was the smaller of the two. In age, they were equals and in learning. They touched gloves then came together for a bout. Robert struck the man in the face, quickly starting the blows. The man looked stunned, then came back at Robert. Neither were angry, but being equally matched, the fight heated quickly. Robert was landing more blows but not letting the pace escalate out of his comfort zone. Then the man shot a straight jab at Robert's nose. Blood began to spill out. Robert's eyes began to water, blurring his vision.

The Pub owner asked if Robert wanted to stop fighting but he insisted on continuing the bout. Robert had kept his pace slow up 'til then. Now, he went in for a faster pace. He dodged the man's next few shots then flew through the man's guard and began knocking him senseless. Punch after punch to the man's face had him stumbling backward. His head was like a jack-in-the-box, bobbing this way and that from the punches. Robert saw that one more punch would have the man falling out of the ring, so he stopped throwing his fists. He wanted to know the man was alright. He did not wish to knock him out senseless. Another few hits and the man may have become so. But he was still in operating order when Robert stopped beating him back.

The man took the pause to come at Robert full force. Robert, put his fists up to protect his face but the hits were still coming in. All he could think to do was hit back. It became a bloody mess of a fight. Blood covered both mens' faces and dripped onto the floor. Eoin, Darren and the pub owner jumped in to break the men up.

"Christ, lads! Are you two mad?" the pub owner asked.

Both Robert and his opponent were breathing hard and covered in blood but were all smiles and laughing.

"Great match!" said the bloody man to Robert. His teeth were red with blood and his lips split.

"Same to you," Robert said. He felt exhilarated. It was as if he couldn't feel the blows that had rained down on his face and body.

Eoin spoke to Robert, "Are ya feelin' alright? Yer nose looks broken."

"Nah," Robert answered, "my nose can't be broken. It hurts. But not so bad."

Many men were huddled around to see. They all were agreeing with Eoin. "Yeah, it's broken," said one. "Definitely," said another. A couple women came into the room and saw the bloody faces. They screamed in momentary shock. Then they saw that the bloody men were smiling and laughing with each other.

"How're you two laughin'?" one asked. Both women looked completely petrified.

Eoin decided it was best to get Robert to the house to be cleaned up. His face was caked with blood. The other man went home too. When they got to the house Darren rang on the phone, asking for Robert.

"Are ya alright, Robert? Ye took quite a wallopin' and gave one too, I might add."

"My ears are ringing and my jaw hurts something terrible, but I'll be fine."

"Well, 'at's good then. I wanted ta make sure ya weren't havin' a poundin' headache. A head can only take so much. Yers took its fair share tonight."

"That it did. Best I clean myself up now. We just got in."

"Right, Robert. Take care."

After the blood was washed off, it was plain to anyone that Robert's nose had at least been severely bruised. It was swollen to twice it's normal width.

Eoin was there to inspect. "I shoulda toldja t' stop when I saw yer nose gush like that. But ye weren't actin' worse fer the wear. Ya weren't bad tonight. A bit o' trainin', ya wouldn't be bad at all."

32. Welcome Home

Ireland was the first place Robert had ever been, other than home, that he did not want to leave. The culture and sport there was warm to him, though the weather was cold. Eoin went to the airport to see him off. The men shook hands and promised to see each other again. Then Robert took the long trip across the world. He thought it amazing that a place so distant held so much he loved. Grit was cozy, curled up in a kennel beneath Robert's seat. Robert had gained a new respect for Grit. He knew now that he truly had made Grit the best dog his father had ever seen.

He loved Ireland but home he loved more. His wife awaited him at the airport to take him home to his own hearth. Her belly was large. Soon, Robert would be a father. For the first time in his life, he truly feared that his dog days might be over. He feared the terriers were too gruesome a lot to have around small children. But there laid Grit, next to the fire. Gruesome, yes, Grit was that, but ever kind to children. Robert ate warm soup, drank hot tea and told his wife of his adventures in Ireland. She laughed at what was funny and winced to see his broken nose. A blessed life Robert had been given. He hadn't a wish in the world but that life could remain so fine.

Grit spent the winter indoors with Robert and Hero. Soon, little Heidi was born and Robert's entire family rejoiced together. The day Heidi was born, Robert couldn't stop laughing. His happiness was un-controllable. With the baby in the house, Grit was con-fined to the kitchen. That was fine by him. He was old and merely wished to bask in the warmth of the fire-place. Robert only took him hunting three times that winter. Though Grit could have went much more often, Robert was busy with other affairs. Grit was happy to be welcome in his master's home.

33. Farewell

Spring came and with it warmth. Curtis invited Robert out to fish. Grit came along and Robert let him run the banks, while Curtis and he floated down the river with their lines in the water. Grit hunted energetically, as if he were not the aged dog that he was. But the shores were rocky and without game. Some otter were playing, always hundreds of yards ahead of the men and Grit. Grit would catch wind of them and seek them, but they were too elusive. When finally there was a place with briars and brambles, Grit entered and would not return out again. He stayed and stayed. For hours, he roamed inside the brush. He had not caught anything in months and was determined to find something. Robert and Curtis just fished, waiting for old Grit to return.

Finally, they cut their way into Grit. The dog would not come by command. He wished to hunt forever.

That sunny day was Grit's last day out. Three days later, he no longer could stand on his own. He was well fed and without injury. Never had he been sick in that way before. He would not eat, nor drink. Seeing him in such a way was difficult for Robert, who sat and watched him every extra minute. Feeding him broth and egg with a syringe, he seemed to cope well for several weeks. Robert hoped to see him recover.

While Grit was so sickly, Robert received a call from his old friend the Goatherd, Joseph.

"Hi Robert," came Joseph's ever raspy voice. He talked to Robert of all their enjoyments, pigeons, sheep, goats and of course, dogs. Joseph was very saddened to hear of Grit's condition. "It never gets easy to lose a good one Robert. You will always love them. You'd be heartless if you didn't. But it is on just such sad news that I have called you."

"I have heard you had to give up your dogs, Joseph. I am sorry to hear that," said Robert.

"I am very sad to say that is true. But it is me I am calling about now, Robert. I am dying, shortly."

Robert could not believe his ears. Robert knew that Joseph had been ailing but Joseph never acknowledged it as serious. "Don't you worry about me," Joseph would always say. Now his ailments had caught up with him, though as tough as any old dog could be, no man's mortal life lasts forever.

Robert packed a bag that night. He was going to say farewell to his friend. Robert told his wife that he must leave and that she would be caring for Grit until he returned. For Hero, this was a responsibility that she did not wish to bear.

"What if he dies while you are gone? You love Grit more than anything in the world. What if he dies because I don't know how to care for him?" Hero began to cry.

"Besides my family, I do love Grit more than anything in the world. No man could offer me anything that could replace him. But I will love you, whether he lives or dies. Keep him to the best of your ability."

Robert kissed his wife and daughter goodbye and left that night. He drove until morning, until he reached the hospital at which Joseph was being kept. He napped until visiting hours began, then went in to see his old friend The Goatherd.

"Thank God you're here Robert. The nurses have been molesting me all morning. I'm old and dying and the women still can't keep their hands off me."

"Sounds enjoyable to me. What's the matter? You didn't like the catheter?"

Joseph laughed and shook Robert's hand heartily. His eyes always had a twinkle of mischief.

"65 years old and the women still want a piece of this action. I promised one of the nurses, that if I get out of this, I'd take her on a cruise to Spain. She liked that. I've never been there, but I kinda like the music." He winked.

Robert grinned. "Hell, even a scruffy old billy goat like yourself could talk me into *that*."

Robert spent a few hours swapping tales with Joseph and laughing. Though, it became hard for Robert to choke back his tears, even through all the jesting. Robert took his leave in the afternoon, so that he did not keep Joseph from his family. He thanked Joseph for giving him the most valuable gift one man could give another, friendship. Robert kissed his old friend on the forehead and said farewell.

∘ ∘ ∘

Robert slept at a houndsman's home, where Joseph told him he'd find good company. In the early morning, he began the journey back home. He arrived home to see Grit able to walk around the house some. *There is some hope*, Robert thought. Grit even began to eat meat again. Hero was thankful she had cared for Grit properly and that he could stand now.

But the improvement was short lived. Though Grit walked, his urine was still very dark and he could not pass any food through. He'd eat, but it was as if he were blocked up. He was soon back to not being able to stand any longer. On Robert's third night back from visiting Joseph, Grit slowly let his breath out. Robert sat on the ground with Grit in his lap. Robert knew it was Grit's time. He didn't disrespect the dog with shaking him or trying to waken him. Grit had conquered all his enemies and was unconquerable save to only one thing. All must succumb to death. Grit never spent a moment of his life fearing death and Robert hoped, perhaps Grit welcomed it like a warm bed after a long fight.

Robert could not, however, keep from crying. His tears dripped down onto Grit's sandy-red coat. He continued to hold his old friend for some time. It was midnight when Robert finally stood to take his old dog to be buried. Hero and Heidi went with Robert to his father's house to bury Grit next to Lee under the black walnut tree. It was a warm raining night. Robert went out into the dark and dug a hole. Hero carried Grit out to Robert and brought Robert's Grandfather's hunting horn to him.

Grit was placed caringly into the ground. Until then, Robert's emotions had been trickling, but now he sobbed as he filled in the grave of his bravest friend. Each shovel of earth reminded Robert of Grit's virtue as a working terrier. Each shovel put Grit permanently out of Robert's reach. He tamped down the grave-earth. With wet, muddy fingers, Robert grasped the horn and blew "To Ground, To Ground, To Ground" the last time for Grit.

∘ ∘ ∘

The next morning Robert awoke to his phone ringing. It was Joseph's daughter.

"Robert,"

"Yes."

"This is Joseph's daughter, Mary. I know you loved my father and he loved you. He has passed away in the night. He wanted you to know he thought of you as a great man from the day he met you."

Robert thought to himself that Grit and Joseph were manifestations of a powerful spirit that lives in all terriermen. In some ways, all hunting dogs and dogmen were linked at the level of the soul. He hoped that there was a special place in the universe for all dogmen and their dogs. Perhaps, Joseph would keep watch of Grit, until Robert joined them in The Great Hunting Grounds.

Robert went out to his coops and opened a flight full of pure white tumblers, Joseph's favorite birds. He watched them fly and perform aerial feats. Now he understood, as did Joseph years before, the peace that birds brought the warlike Soul of the Terriermen.

Thank you for reading *Grit – The Tale of a Hunting Terrier*. I spent several years writing the book and many more years hunting, training dogs and having run-ins with genuine hill-billies to be able to tell the tale. I wanted to portray the many types of life a working terrier might experience. Some live the good life and others live a life that is not so good.

I hope you enjoyed the book. I also hope that you have been changed by reading it. I know I have changed while writing it. If you want to contact me or see what I am up to, check out my website or email me personally: info@adamhowardbooks.com

Adam Howard
March, 2016

About the Author

Adam Howard was born and raised in the garden valleys of the Umpqua. He spent his youth skipping school to hunt, fish and get into all sorts of trouble good for the development of a young man. He grew up reading books like Watership Down by Richard Adams, White Fang by Jack London and The Fox and the Hound by Dan Mannix. Books like these were not so much life-changing as life-affirming for the young Adam Howard. These classic authors wrote of a world Adam recognized and lived in. He now writes outdoor fiction and non-fiction in the hopes that his books will bring as much joy to others as the classics brought to him; that the traditions of outdoorsmen will never be lost, but always remembered fondly for what they are, a way of life.

Be sure to check AdamHowardBooks.com for new releases, outdoor articles and free ebooks.

Printed in Great Britain
by Amazon

71482176R00234